He knew they were giving up on apprehending him right now. But parting shots? They'd have some. He heard someone gun the engine of their panel truck.

Mason held tight to the iron fence, keeping himself flush. They could only do small things. Rupture his spleen. Break his backbone. Split his skull.

Shoot him as they departed.

FALSE FLAGS

Noel Hynd

BANTAM BOOKS
TORONTO · NEW YORK · LONDON

for Maryann
with appreciation
and love

*This low-priced Bantam Book
has been completely reset in a type face
designed for easy reading, and was printed
from new plates. It contains the complete
text of the original hard-cover edition.*
NOT ONE WORD HAS BEEN OMITTED.

FALSE FLAGS

*A Bantam Book / published by arrangement with
The Dial Press*

PRINTING HISTORY
*Dial edition published February 1979
2nd printing .... April 1979
Bantam edition / July 1980*

Published simultaneously in the United States and Canada

*Bantam Books are published by Bantam Books, Inc. Its trade-
mark, consisting of the words "Bantam Books" and the por-
trayal of a bantam, is Registered in U.S. Patent and Trademark
Office and in other countries. Marca Registrada. Bantam
Books, Inc., 666 Fifth Avenue, New York, New York 10019.*

PRINTED IN THE UNITED STATES OF AMERICA

1

Now, deep down, Robert Lassiter felt the Vassiliev case slipping away from him. The case had meandered for months and, for that matter, the damage was already done. Vassiliev had made his connection in Mexico, made it cleanly, and had returned to London after a stopover in Cuba. What Vassiliev had done in Havana was anyone's guess. Lassiter might never know. But London was something else again.

It didn't seem like London. Oh, Lassiter still felt, as always, that the cars were on the wrong side of the street. But the heat at night? Abnormal. Still in the high seventies. Lassiter couldn't sleep anyway. He'd finally passed along his recommendations to David Auerbach, the English liaison officer. Pick up Vassiliev. Pull down a bare light bulb, don't tell him his rights for a few months, and soak him for every bit of information to be had. Yank out his toenails, if need be.

Of course, it wouldn't be quite that easy or quite that much fun. Vassiliev was a member of the consular staff. Diplomatic immunity, naturally.

Lassiter was going slowly insane. He'd had his triumphs in his forty-seven years and he'd had his defeats as well. More of the former than the latter, thank you, though there had been that wretched affair in China in the late 1960s. Poor Bill Mason, he reflected. A lifelong friend like that tossed to the wolves. What a stinking world it was. Filled not only with serpents like Vassiliev but populated also with the invisible vermin who protected men like him.

The more Lassiter considered the Vassiliev case, the more he knew it had slipped through his fingers. How? Where? Who?

He walked on a quiet residential street in Bloomsbury, not far from the British Museum. He could hear his footsteps, and wondered who else could. Had there been enough light, a passerby might have seen the dark circles of sweat beneath his arms. His necktie was loose. He carried his jacket over his shoulder. With a mixture of anger and anxiety, he puffed a small cigar. Tobacco was his second addiction. Black intelligence, his first.

He glanced at his watch. Eleven fifteen P.M. Almost time. If anything was to happen, it would happen now. Lassiter was there as a precaution. He would wait and see.

He silently pulled a key from his pocket. He unlocked the Hillman Hunter which was parked by the curb beneath a thin tree. He sat on the left side of the front seat and he waited. Again he considered the small, barrel-chested Russian, a man whose activities had become Lassiter's obsession. Vassiliev, he'd long since concluded, was something of a serpent—in spirit if not in physique. Quiet. Deceitful. Endowed with a forked tongue, venomous, and able to strike lethally from a coiled position as well as slip away quietly. The type of reptile, or man, who'd steal eggs from an unguarded nest. Lassiter hated Vassiliev, though he'd never gone eyeball to eyeball with him. The Russian had been masquerading as a university professor, Lassiter recalled. The nerve.

Lassiter felt the perspiration between his leather watchband and his wrist. Heat, not nerves. He glanced at the luminous dial which shone clearly in the semidarkness.

Eleven twenty. It was time.

Vassiliev, detained for three hours, would now be allowed to telephone his embassy and inform them of his detention. Then Lassiter would see which flies flocked to the honey. If any. Why didn't anyone believe him, Lassiter wondered. Ivan was up to more than computer parts. Lassiter *knew* it. It was a feel, a taste. Did a man have to have proof to be right? Eight minutes passed. Damn that Russian, Lassiter cursed. This was either the end of something small or the beginning of something—

There were five of them. Security goons from the Soviet Embassy, an entire quintet of the thick-browed, baggy-suited musclemen who normally accompany Soviet trade delegations around the world. Better to keep the merry voyageurs untalkative and out of the whorehouses.

"Damn them," he thought. "Damn them to hell!" Lassiter sat still and watched. He fired the butt of the

2

cigar out of the car window and onto the otherwise clean sidewalk.

The five gorillas were intercepted at the front door of the apartment building by two uniformed Metropolitan London police officers, the only post-arrest assistance Lassiter had been granted. Lassiter couldn't hear it, of course, but a discussion ensued in mixed Russian and English, the constables telling the Russians that apartment 4-A had been sealed off by their government, and the Russians nodding abruptly and replying, *da, da,* that was fine. They understood. But they had their instructions.

Then the Russians belligerently threw aside the police guard. They stormed past, through the building's lobby and up the stairs. Whatever they had been sent to retrieve, they weren't planning to go home without it. The move brought Lassiter springing from his car to a pay telephone ten yards away.

He dialed, his eyes still on the Vassiliev residence, as the befuddled police followed their antagonists into the building.

Four, five, six times the telephone rang. Finally an answer.

"Now, listen Auerbach, God damn it," Lassiter intoned sharply. "Remember that apartment we said was clean? Well, Ivan Russkie's got five apes knocking over all humanity to get into it. I'd suggest some help. Unless you want to kiss off the whole operation."

He slammed down the telephone, cursed the British liaison officer aloud and stood a few feet from his car. His eyes were squinted in anguish at the building which he couldn't, under any circumstances, enter. Damned fool. Auerbach should have listened, he thought to himself. He wiped his face with his hand to mop the sweat. Even his short brown moustache was wet. He folded his thick arms and waited.

It didn't take long. It only seemed like it did. Within minutes a phalanx of police noisily arrived. Apartment lights illuminated the block and the silhouettes of heads appeared at windows.

On Vassiliev's very floor neighbors' eyes peered inquisitively from doorways as two dozen large-framed London police squared off rudely against a quintet of Mother Russia's most faithful servants.

Numerical superiority prevailed. Vassiliev's apartment

door remained sealed. A four-man armed guard was now posted. Whatever souvenir Vassiliev's cohorts had wanted, it would stay put. The Soviets had tried to play their hand quickly and grab the chips. They'd failed.

They were in a sound-proofed, white-walled room deep within the United States Embassy on Grosvenor Square. A cozy little threesome it was, Lassiter with Garcia and Sanchez.

Garcia and Sanchez—Pancho and Cisco to embassy staffers who knew them—were part of a roster of specialists kept on permanent call. By coincidence, both were Mexican-Americans, endowed with specialized skills and trusted, despite their background and outside activities, by the intelligence bureau within the embassy. They were listed on embassy ledgers as "housing specialists," which was a kind terminology for what they were vocationally —professional cat burglars.

Garcia was a graying, small man who appeared to be fifty going on forty, while Sanchez maintained a youthful face combined with a balding head and scarred cheek. He was twenty-nine going on forty, counting three years he'd spent in an Arizona prison. Something about the wrong signature on a series of checks. Nonetheless, Lassiter needed each this morning, and for just such exigencies they were tolerated. Each relished a good burglary. Garcia was retired. Sanchez, judging from the money he frequently tossed around the Dorchester bar, and the morally askew women he often had in tow, was perhaps not quite so retired. Each had disquieting habits. Sanchez would whistle softly while being spoken to. Garcia liked to chew cloves.

Lassiter, while not caring for them personally, accepted their presence—and backgrounds—routinely. The ordinary course of events: To kill a cobra, you needed a mongoose. Maybe two.

It was three twelve A.M. and Lassiter was concluding the story of the evening: A Soviet chemistry professor, on exchange at the University of Mexico, arrested for sedition. An escapade involving a Maryland computer-systems analyst. That was enough for Sanchez and Garcia. They needn't know more. The essential story was what had followed Vassiliev's arrest: immediate KGB interest in the accused's apartment. Despite the fact that the computer parts scheme was blown ozone high, there was still

4

something critical in the arrested man's possession. Something of major interest which transcended computer parts.

"So," concluded Lassiter, positioned behind a metal desk at the front of the small room, "you go in. Find what they—and we—want. And you bring it out."

Lassiter gazed at both men. Sanchez had a disconcerting occasional twitch to his left eye. The older Garcia had taken to stuffing three or four sticks of peppermint chewing gum into his mouth at once, pumping his jaw noisily for five minutes, then spitting what was left into anything that was convenient. In this case, a paper coffee cup.

Garcia spoke. "Do we have any idea where to look?"

"Wouldn't I have told you if we did?" countered Lassiter. Idiotic question was the implication. Lassiter continued. "No idea at all. And you're going to have to dig like hell. Scum like Ivan is too smart to leave something sitting on the kitchen counter."

"How do we know there's *anything* in there at all?" asked Sanchez with more than a trace of skepticism.

Lassiter looked imploringly to the two faces in front of him. He tried to convey a feeling, an emotion. "We *know*."

The room was quiet, thoughtful.

"We'll need luck," said Garcia, almost defensively. He started some more gum.

"Make some," answered Lassiter.

As the Russians were setting up their own guard around the building, studying everyone going in and out, looking for familiar American faces, two Mexican-born Americans were being dressed in delivery men's uniforms. As the KGB delegation waited helplessly outside during the next day, and as two London police stood by and did nothing, the two Americans broke into the apartment. After spending three hours on four locks, they went in and went to work.

They wore rubber gloves and carried every tool imaginable for a sophisticated bag job. They took the place apart.

Wall panels were opened, then closed again. Every book in the bookcases was opened, shaken thoroughly, and replaced. The furniture was stripped down and reassembled. The floorboards were examined for new nails or

5

loose planks—none of either—and the plumbing pipes were probed. Even the heels of Vassiliev's shoes were loosened, examined, then replaced.

"Nothing," they reported to Lassiter at the end of the day, the message coming by hand during a changing of the guard.

Lassiter was deeply annoyed. It couldn't be a false alarm; not with all those extra security apes still watching the building. Not with the hunch he'd had all along about Vassiliev. There had to be something.

The two Americans slept in the apartment.

"Nothing," they reported again at one P.M. the next day. Time was passing too quickly.

Lassiter ordered them to try again, starting from the beginning. This time he sent them an extra piece of equipment. A metal detector. "Go over *everything*," he commanded. "Something's there. God damn it. Find it."

They spent four more hours, examining the walls and the furniture, and checking every nail which made the detector tick. Then, exhausted, they went to the bookcase and started running the device over the books.

The needle went berserk.

In their enthusiasm they pulled the books out of the shelves, trying to get through to the wall.

The needle stopped.

Pancho and Cisco stood perplexed, trying to deduce what the metal detector was telling them. They looked at each other and both had the same enlightenment at once.

They said it aloud. "The books."

Not *the* books, but *one* book in particular. Sealed invisibly into its binding was something small and metallic. The two bagmen were elated. But they were disciplined enough not to tear the spine open, much as they would have liked to. Instead they sent it back to Lassiter and continued to see what else might be ferreted out with the metal detector.

Nothing was. But as they continued their search, the book binding was undergoing an operation. Dr. Timothy Artis, a trained American surgeon, cut open the stitching to the book's binding, using a small jeweler's scalpel which had been electronically honed for the occasion.

Then out of the loosened cloth rolled a small flat capsule no more than three centimeters in width and ten centimeters in length. Lassiter, standing over the surgeon,

6

frowned and looked quizzically at the capsule. He reached over and took it with both hands, then opened it. The contents spilled forth onto the sterile surface of the operating table.

Six small square chips. They slid out almost reluctantly. Each was a perfect square of no more than a sixteenth of an inch. They were about as thin as a dime.

Lassiter stared blankly at them. There was a morbid silence before Lassiter spoke.

"Fuck Ivan," he said.

Dr. Artis looked up, his own eyes bloodshot and tired. "What?"

"Fuck Ivan."

The doctor was pensive. "That's not even his real name, is it? Ivan, I mean. I thought it was *Dimitri* Vassiliev."

"They're all named Ivan," muttered Lassiter. "I don't learn Russian names. Other things to learn. Jesus, I hate these Russian bastards."

Artis drew a long breath and glanced again at the chips. "Nothing?"

Lassiter felt like grabbing the small square objects and flinging them violently against the wall. Electronic hardware so small, yet so monumentally important. After all these months, Ivan still had one up on them.

"Don't ask," Lassiter said sourly. "It's just several months of work screwed completely to hell. That's all." He was tired; his voice was barely audible.

"That's good, huh?" asked Dr. Artis dispassionately.

Lassiter stared blankly at the chips for several seconds, then shook his head slowly. "You couldn't imagine," he grumbled. "You simply couldn't imagine."

7

2

She sat at her dining room table and looked out. During the four days she'd been away, the autumn leaves had begun to fall. It was no longer hot in Maryland; the summer heat had given way to a milder temperature of early September. There were leaves on the grass and there'd be bushels more within another month. It was a nice piece of property, she consoled herself. Mortgaged, but nice. It was what she and Brian had always dreamed of. They were just beginning to make a go of it when . . . Sarah Woodson, at thirty-six, felt herself very alone.

Perhaps it was the house. She could sell it, *would* sell it, in fact, as soon as she could finance the repairs it so badly needed. Repairs? There was no money. Or very little, anyway, and the fuel bills alone would push her to a financial precipice during the next winter.

She stopped herself. She snuffed out the cigarette in the ashtray before her. Smoking too much. Must stop. *Must* stop, she thought. Brian had been after her for years to stop. And now. . . .

Again, Brian. It always got back to him. Every facet of her life now evolved from his death. She had spent many hours, days, and nights thinking about it. Was her obsession with his death due to her having allowed him to be the focal point of her life when he was alive?

Did it matter now? Did anything?

She again gazed out the window, far back beyond the back lawn and into the boundless trees. Three wooded acres. That's what she and her husband had had. Wooded land touching on a seventeen-acre wildlife preserve on the other side. Ideal. How many times had she strolled with him through the woods, his arm around her waist, hers around his, taking a different path each time, the forest never the same twice. Still had opossums and raccoons out there. On a good day, if you were quiet enough or clever

8

enough, you might be able to glimpse one scurrying evasively across brittle twigs and dead leaves.

Or maybe at night, when Brian and she were upstairs in a warm bed together on an autumn or winter night, they'd hear the rattling near the garbage cans off the driveway. The possums and the coons again, foraging for the scraps of food in the garbage pails. If you crept downstairs and threw on the kitchen light quickly, you could catch them racing into the darkness of the woods. Then if you shone a flashlight on the woods, you'd see the glimmering pairs of eyes looking back at you.

"Why not just put it in a dish for them?" she'd asked Brian. "Make it easy for them. They need the food and we don't want it."

"Well, we could," he'd said thoughtfully and analytically one night. "We could put it in a pie tin and leave it out." He'd wrinkled his nose and then added, "But you know, honey, they *can* carry rabies and with Priscilla playing out there sometimes after dark. . . ."

Enough said. No pie tins. In fact, Brian had added . . .

There she went again, back to Brian. His every word, every movement, every memory.

A small cloud of smoke was still rising from the ashtray. She snuffed the cigarette again, firmly this time, rose, and went to the antique mirror behind her. Standing close to it she examined the reflection of her thin face and looked critically at her dark hair. She searched it for the isolated gray strands she had been finding for the past two years, then stared hard at her features. She tried to envision how she had looked years earlier when she and Brian had been married. How many fewer lines had there been? How much firmer the skin? Funny, she said to herself, she didn't think she looked much older.

Yet she must, she told herself; the calendar told her so. She had aged. She'd never thought of it much while Brian was alive because, well, they were journeying together and if she aged, well, so did he. So what? But with his death came a realization, a definitive statement that she suddenly found herself perched between the certainty of their past together and the uncertainty of a too youthful widowhood. She recognized where she was: midway between her twenties and forties, mother of a twelve-year-old daughter, partial possessor—with the bank—of a comfortable, secluded home, and the owner of a beleaguered

9

savings account. No way around it: life would now be different.

She heard something.

She turned from the mirror and stopped. "Priscilla?" she called.

There was no response. She had thought it was her daughter returning early from a friend's house. But she was wrong, there had been nothing.

Nothing. The word keyed other memories. Her husband's life-insurance policy. The insurance company's outright refusal to pay.

"We're greatly sympathetic, of course, Mrs. Woodson," they had told her four days after her husband's interment. "But you must understand our position. Your husband's policy didn't cover—in fact, *no* life insurance policy covers—the way in which he departed."

Depart! He didn't depart, he *died,* she reminded herself bitterly.

The idea hung in her mind, played upon her soul, and permeated the atmosphere of the house where she and Priscilla continued to live.

A man like Brian. A man with so much to live for, as the cliché proclaimed. A man with a good home, a faithful wife, an adorable daughter, no ill health and no financial trouble. Over and over the question haunted her—all morning, all day, all night.

Suicide. *Why?*

Outside, the yellow sun was burning brilliantly in the center of an azure sky. Noon. The London temperature was in the eighties again. Inside the United States embassy the air conditioning was on full blast.

"Circuits," said Dr. Lucille Davis, an American physicist doing research at Oxford and a sometime consultant.

Lassiter frowned and looked at the tiny chips which were on a small white felt pad. Functioning on two hours' sleep, he could only utter one word: "What?"

"Circuits," said Dr. Davis, as if it were self-evident. "They contain electronic circuits. Rather complex ones, if I do say so." She frowned. "Should I ask where they came from?"

"No."

She grimaced. "As I suspected," she said. "Don't like to tell a soul anything, do you, Bob?" It was his turn to grimace but he remained silent. "How long have I worked for the embassy?" she asked. "How many times have you hauled me out of bed or away from a restaurant? And you still won't tell me a thing." Her voice was calm and measured and totally dispassionate. A scientist, she was reciting facts. "I could have been playing chess today," she said. "Not helping you. Bobby, you're *hopeless.*"

She was a bosomy, Teutonic-looking woman, despite her surname, and seemed like central casting's idea of Rosie the Riveter. She was just shy of six feet tall, and, many people insisted, an equal distance in circumference. Her hair was blond and short, her glasses were thick— *bulletproof,* some said—and her IQ defied measurement.

"Just an analysis, just an analysis," repeated Lassiter with fatigue. "Please, Lucy, if I could tell you, damn it, I—"

"—you would. Yes, I know the story." She was doodling now, drawing hourglass figures on a piece of scrap paper. Her puffy eyes were lowered. They rarely met anyone's. "Lord, lord," she declared. "You have problems."

"Go ahead." He spoke with a sigh. He felt a headache coming on. Damn Ivan, he thought.

"Circuits," she said, moving back to where she'd begun. "Electronic circuits. I can show you a microscopic blowup of what you have within these chips. Or I can tell you."

"Tell me now. Show me later."

"These chips are from an ultra-complex computer system, about as complex as any that exists. Each of those little silicon cells has an individual printed metal circuit within it. When I said microscopic, Bobby, I meant it. There are about three thousand wiring routes within each circuit. Printed by computer, you see. IC chips, they're called. Stands for integrated circuits."

Lassiter, though confounded by the complexities within each minuscule square, followed her explanation.

"I took the liberty of consulting with a computer specialist," she said. "I wanted to know what a circuit like this would be used for. I figured you'd ask. I mean, it's the logical question."

She finished one of the drawn figures on the paper. She laid down her pencil and raised her eyes to the electronic watch on his wrist, one which read out the time in pocket-calculator-style numerals.

"How's the watch I gave you?" she asked.

He was distracted, then realized what she was referring to.

"Perfect, perfect," he said hurriedly, not wanting a conversation. "Come on, Lucille, get to it. What about these IC chips?"

"You're involved with aeronautics," she said. "Things that fly. Projectiles. What you've got here is part of an aerospace guidance system. Circa maybe 1975 or so. Pretty recent stuff. Pretty new."

Lassiter pictured Vassiliev and he envisioned the five apes who'd headed for Vassiliev's apartment so soon after the arrest that they'd hardly had time to pull up their socks and tie their shoelaces.

"Aerospace guidance," he said, repeating her words. It was alien to him. The sky was filled with lots of hardware that Lassiter didn't have the training to understand. "Satellites? Airplanes?"

"Try missiles, Bob. I told you you had problems. You see, I'm guessing that you got these little devils from someone who wasn't supposed to be playing with them. Correct?"

"I'll give you that much," he said.

"You're giving me nothing. I knew that much before I got here. You're in counterintelligence, Bobby, and your usual beat is security leaks. By the way, do I look any thinner? I stopped eating. *Completely*. Lost fourteen pounds. Another ten and—"

Lassiter hadn't noticed. "What kind of missiles?"

"Missile missiles," she said. "I don't know what kind. Off hand, it's almost impossible to tell. I suppose if you get Defense in Washington they can wheel out the team of Krauts who build our ICBMs and maybe they can tell you which system it's from. I can't."

Lassiter looked at her coldly, his eyes met hers. "Wait a minute," he said. "Ours?"

She laughed. "Well, of course," she said. "Naturally, *ours*. I tested the metal in that circuit. Bethlehem's best. Made in the good old US of A. How's that? Bless you, Andrew Carnegie. It's a circuit from a US missile guidance system."

She watched him as he exhaled slowly and pensively, a man with new, unwelcome weight on his shoulders. Her mood became more sympathetic as she watched him.

12

"That means real trouble, doesn't it? I mean, what's this Russian doing with our circuits in his hot red hands? What's he want them for?" she asked rhetorically as Lassiter looked up at her. "Where'd he get them from? Where was he sending them?"

Lassiter spoke angrily: "How the hell did you—?"

"Know where *you* got them?" She laughed contemptuously. "Just put two and two together. You told me yesterday you were watching a Russian last night. Figured whatever you had, you must have taken it off him. So I'm right, am I? Well, don't feel bad about it." She scratched her left cheek absently. "Can you tell me anything more?" she asked sympathetically.

A long moment passed before he raised his eyes to hers and spoke in a disturbed voice. "Some sort of false-flag job," he said. "A good one."

She hesitated and frowned. "That's spook talk, Bobby. What's it mean? False what?"

"It means someone is made to look like he's working for one country when actually he's in the employ of another."

She shrugged. "Doesn't mean much to me," she said. "Sorry."

He seemed almost not to hear her. He was muttering softly. "They've got a chunk of our defense system, Lucy. I can't believe it. I *can't* believe it."

Dr. Davis pondered it. "Guess that means you'll be out of town for a while, doesn't it?" she concluded. She shook her head slowly and with resignation. "Well . . . what's a woman to do?"

3

Bill Mason, by the end of an uncomfortable August, was still letting the earth settle beneath his feet. Or if not the earth, at least the sand.

Delwood was one of a string of tacky South Jersey —never "southern New Jersey"—beach resorts. It was marked by a steel pier which jutted into the tepid Atlantic Ocean and which was said to be the second largest on the coast. Atlantic City, to the north, had the largest. No matter. Bill Mason toiled this summer as a lifeguard on the Delwood municipal beaches and, from the position he occupied in the tall white stands for seven hours of each day, six days a week, Mason could see the long pier extending into the water to his left.

Delwood itself wasn't much to speak of. A series of billboards and glowing signs for motels, gas stations, and fast-food emporiums blighted the highway leading in. One billboard promised an evening of fun and possible fortune at Atlantic City Raceway eleven miles to the north, while another assured a policy of PROGRAMS NOT PROMISES from a local incumbent embattled in a reelection campaign. A motel on the outskirts of town invited the traveler to HAVE YOUR NEXT AFFAIR WITH US, and still another curious reminder, the last before entering Delwood Center, proclaimed simply in white letters on a blue field, CHRIST DIED FOR THE UNGODLY.

Having endured such messages, a visitor to Delwood would then pass two supermarkets and enter the three main streets of the town, streets lined with candle shops, hot dog stands, modest fish restaurants, a Chinese restaurant, and a drugstore which had cornered the Solarcaine and Noxema supply. Farther on there were four newsstands which carried the Philadelphia, New York, and Trenton papers, and various smaller seasonal enterprises which

14

changed from one summer to the next, peddling anything from leather belts to live (or slowly dying) lobsters.

The sidewalks were cluttered during the summer by an army of youths who seemed uniformly clad in cut-off blue jeans, shaggy sun-streaked hair, and occasional footwear. They congregated on sidewalks, sipped beer from cans, littered, ate potato chips, and smoked twisted cigarettes of nontobacco content. They were harmless, docile, and lackadaisical, as if the relentless sun had baked out any intellectual ambitions they might ever have entertained. The boys could be told from the girls quite readily as the girls, generally, wore bra tops to their bathing suits. Although on Saturday night, when the sidewalks were packed sometimes shoulder to shoulder and fast encounters were the custom, even this one rule would go by the wayside.

To Bill Mason the job of lifeguard offered little challenge. Nor had he sought challenge when he accepted the post. It was both a mood of restlessness and a desire for quiet which had brought him to apply back in April.

Applications were filed with Jake Robertson, the paunchy head of the Delwood Recreation Department and the presiding Neptune of the local seaside. Robertson, gruff, graying, and in his fifties, had been a world-class ocean swimmer in earlier years. That was before the stomach muscles had drifted into disuse and melted, earning him the title Fat Old Robertson, which was what everyone called him. Yet he did capably run the town recreation department out of a beachside office which doubled as the lifeguards' headquarters in the summer months. It was Robertson's opinion that the town was already overflowing with "pansies," "beatniks," and "hippies," terms he used interchangeably, and they could just as soon have drowned for all he cared. Nonetheless, he was in charge of hiring people to pull the weirdos out of the water. And Jake Robertson liked to do an honest day's work.

Mason had filed an application in April, had handed it personally to Robertson, in fact. Bill took the written test, the difficulty of which sorted the chimpanzees from among the applicants, and then moved on to more serious matters.

"Can you swim?" asked Robertson, using a clipboard as his triton.

"Throw me in some water," retorted Mason. "You'll find out."

15

"Yes or no?"

"Like a fish."

"We'll see."

Bill passed the swimming test with astonishing ease. Fat Old Robertson was starting to like him. The Delwood Recreation Department had discovered, in fact, that Bill was one of the most powerful swimmers they'd ever seen. As for the lifesaving and first aid, Mason knew it all, apparently from practical experience, though he declined to give specific details.

Odd things did surface about him, however. He'd been to some of the best schools in the country, and had graduated from Yale in 1962. Yale? A lifeguard from Yale, Robertson had snickered suspiciously. But in checking with the university, he found that Bill had indeed graduated as he'd said. Majored in Southeast Asian Studies, and finished in the top quintile of his class.

Robertson did encounter difficulty checking Bill's past employment. And he couldn't quite figure why a man of Bill's age, background, and articulateness would be kicking around from job to job and settling for a lifeguard's pay in Delwood. But such doubts were quickly shelved. After all, the man was reliable, and who cared where he'd been or what his private life was, as long as he could fish drowning people out of the water faster and more efficiently than the next person?

Bill began his job in May, when the kids were in school and the beach was quiet. It was not till early June when he first pulled someone out of the ocean. Toward late June it became a regular event, particularly on fading Sunday afternoons when every moron who couldn't swim descended on Delwood, guzzled beer for four hours in the sun, then tossed himself into the undertow.

Between such rescues, there was time for idle chatter, particularly among the twelve men and eight women on the lifeguard staff. Each of the tall white lifeguard stands was manned by two persons at all times, an arrangement which led to various degrees of acquaintance over the summer.

Among the other guards, most of whom were no more than twenty-two, Bill Mason was known as the quiet, pensive senior citizen, a man who in his private hours read a lot. He spoke little of himself or his background and politely fended off all questions on such matters.

16

Julie Heasman, dark-haired, dark-eyed, and the second best swimmer on the staff, was working between graduation from Brown and graduate field work in archeology. She and Bill enjoyed their hours on duty together. In June, Julie, not a shy woman, took the initiative and invited Bill to her apartment for a steak dinner. Both curious and attracted to him, she let him drink three quarters of a bottle of wine to see if it would loosen his tongue. It didn't. In fact she discovered virtually nothing about him that night except that he hadn't accepted her invitation in order to seduce her. He didn't try, which led to other suspicions. But the fact remained, he behaved as a gentleman unwilling to give much of himself at all. The only new theory she came away with was that beneath Bill's gentility was a very firm layer of circumspection. Somehow she sensed that he distrusted everyone, particularly new people trying to befriend him.

Other dinners followed. Bill began to relax. So did Julie. In July, in the privacy of her apartment, she and Bill were naked together for the first time. After they had made love Bill lay on his stomach next to her; she lay face up, and ran her hand gently from his strong shoulders down his back toward his waist.

His eyes flashed open. Her hand stopped at the odd touch of his skin. He looked at her, she at him, and Julie discovered that the whole left side of his lower back was a sea of scars. They were scars from deep wounds, crisscrossing each other. She guessed that they'd been there for many years.

"Don't ask," he said with resignation, "and I won't tell you any lies."

"Sorry," she said. "I didn't mean to act shocked. I just hadn't noticed." She wondered why. Then it occurred to her. Mason, when on duty, always wore either a tank top or an orange nylon windbreaker.

"Had a car accident once," he said. "Not much to it beyond that."

Julie recognized it immediately as a lie. But she said nothing, not then or any time afterwards when making love with Bill. She was content to have him worry about the details of her own body, particularly those which were white and untanned.

The rest of July passed. As did most of August. They were happy weeks for both Julie and Bill. Bill privately

17

felt calmer with himself. Julie allowed herself to relax totally from the academic endeavors which would bracket her summer months.

Then in late August there occurred an incident so bizarre and unexplainable that it became the topic of perplexed whispers up and down the boardwalk. It began, of all places, in the local Chinese restaurant, The Szechuan Fire.

One of the Fire's specialties was the greasy, overcooked eggrolls which much of the Delwood population mistook for Chinese cuisine. Somehow Bill, Julie, and three other guards were lured into the Fire late one evening for beer and food. They were unaccountably confronted by a pair of particularly surly waiters.

The pair took turns waiting on their table and fell into the habit of mumbling in Chinese at Bill's party as orders were taken and as food was delivered. (Food was not *served* in The Szechuan Fire, it was delivered.)

The others at the table tended to shrug at the incomprehensible running dialogue and one younger lifeguard from Philadelphia suggested that neither waiter had his yin or yang together.

This brought gales of laughter from everyone except Bill and the two waiters in question. Thereafter Bill was icily silent, as if a fuse were burning somewhere. The two waiters took to addressing only the women at the table, particularly Julie, in stern, adamant Chinese, accompanied by gestures which could hardly have been interpreted as polite, gracious, or complimentary.

The desserts arrived. So did one scatological reference too many.

Slowly Bill got to his feet and excused himself from the table. He crossed the dining room to where the waiters were noisily stacking plates and trays.

He spoke to them for a moment in clear, concise English, though no one could hear exactly what he was saying. The waiters ignored him. Then, as Bill's expression changed slightly, the waiters froze. Perhaps it was *what* he said that shocked them. Or perhaps it was the fluency with which he said it. Though they could easily pretend to not understand English, Cantonese, their native dialect, was another matter altogether.

They stared at Mason with the hollow, stunned expression of men who have just witnessed a great disaster.

For a moment they were fearful, face to face with a man who'd understood everything they'd said all evening. Mason continued to speak. Graciously, they began to smile.

The incident had partially silenced the restaurant. Bill walked back to the table, seated himself with no explanation whatsoever, and resumed the table conversation where he'd left off. No one summoned the nerve to ask Bill anything. He volunteered nothing. But there was a change in the service.

The orders placed to the kitchen were ignored. Someone out there with the woks and the stoves had taken special note of their table as the normal Chinese-American fare was bypassed in favor of a more traditional Chinese banquet. No one had ever before seen such fare emanate from the Fire's kitchen. No one would again.

"See?" Mason finally said as their party paid and left, passing obsequiously bowing waiters and busboys. "I didn't say much at all. I simply changed the order."

No one believed him.

The group went their separate ways, Julie and Bill returning to her apartment. It was there that she inquired.

"Okay, Bill," she said, "I can't not ask. Where'd you learn?"

"Chinese?"

She said nothing, letting an obvious yes hang in the air. She looked at him from a seat on a couch.

"I used to send my shirts out a lot," he answered.

"Bill," she said firmly. She waited and he said nothing more. "We've been sleeping together for two months," she persisted with annoyance. "I don't want to know the innermost secrets of your life and I never ask you a damned thing about your past. But I did think that we trusted each other." He sat down across the sofa from her, sipped from a green botttle of imported beer, and crossed his legs in silence. "It's a simple question, really," she said. "I think I deserve an answer."

"Yale," he answered. "Then language school."

"*What* language school?" she snapped. "No one learns a language that well in a classroom."

"Navy language school," he said. "Intensive program. Very intensive, you could say. Several years."

She exhaled a long sigh and appraised him, as if to view him in a different, fresher light. "Bill," she retorted thoughtfully, "twice you told me that you were never in the military."

He seemed taken aback, somewhat like a witness trapped in a falsehood or a soldier who isn't quite sure from where the hostile fire is coming.

"Did I tell you that?" he answered. "I guess I'd forgotten. Or been mistaken. Sorry if I mislead you. It's really *not* important."

"Weak, Bill," she said, getting ready to let the matter pass. Okay, so what if he wanted to be secretive? He respected her privacy, so she'd respect his. "Very weak. All right. Don't tell me."

"Thanks," he said. But she had won a small, seemingly pointless skirmish. Again she'd trapped him in a lie.

Two days later was the Friday before Labor Day. Delwood was braced for a last big summer weekend. The entire recreation staff spoke of the Szechuan Fire Incident. The two waiters now rarely spoke to anyone and were quite polite in all languages when they did. Behind his back, Bill had acquired the nickname Confucius from the sophomoric, younger lifeguards. Bill knew of the name, was frequently pressed for the basis of his language skill, and now warded off all questions with a brief story about being born in Hong Kong and having a Chinese nurse until age ten. The story washed, except with Jake Robertson in the administration office who pulled out Bill's work application again and noted that Mason had been born in Medford, Massachusetts. And he had started school there at age four.

On the Saturday of Labor Day, Bill was on the number-three post from eleven to one, then left for lunch as Julie and a thin nineteen-year-old lifeguard named Kevin, a youth with a volcanic complexion, arrived to take over. When Mason returned to the central lifeguard station at ten of two, Robertson called to him.

"Hey, Mason! Where you been? We been looking all over for you."

"Why?"

"You had a guest."

"A what?" Bill was attentive.

"A visitor," Robertson affirmed. "A city type in a business suit," he said. "And a tie. Imagine. First necktie in Delwood all summer."

20

Mason's eyes tightened perceptibly. "What did he look like?"

"A bit shorter than you. Moustache. Short, dark hair. Looked like a God-damned ex-Marine or something."

Mason seemed thoughtful. "Did he say what he wanted?"

"Said he wanted to say hello. Said he knew you from Yale."

"Nobody from Yale knows I'm here," Mason snapped angrily, then was immediately sorry that he'd spoken. Robertson clearly observed Bill's annoyance.

"Gave a name," Robertson said. "Didn't get it clearly. Something like Brian Park."

Bill shook his head. His voice softened. "Name means nothing."

Robertson shrugged, not knowing what to add.

"Oh well," said Bill with studied casualness, "if it's important, he'll find me."

"That's what he said."

"*What?*"

"He said it was important. And that he'd find you."

Mason nodded and went ruminatively to his two-o'clock post.

Saturday turned to Sunday, Sunday to Monday. The summer officially wound down with close-out sales at virtually all the shops in Delwood. Great hordes of debris and beer cans were left all over the beach and main street from the final Sunday-night blast and a groggy Monday afternoon.

Bill was scheduled to take a shift on Tuesday since the lifeguards worked through mid-September. He never appeared that morning.

As Bill hadn't missed an hour of work all summer, his absence raised concern. Robertson telephoned him. No answer. Robertson figured there had to have been some misunderstanding over days off. Surely Bill would reappear on Wednesday.

He didn't. Thursday, too, no Bill Mason.

His vanishing only enhanced the subtle mysteries that had surrounded the man all summer, particularly when Julie could offer no special insight into the disappearance.

Then toward Friday the Recreation Committee had to know one way or another, was Bill gone for good or not? He hadn't even picked up his last check or remitted a forwarding address. Robertson and Julie Heasman went to the superintendent of his building. Bill's two-room apartment was opened.

The superintendent, white-haired Mr. Yankus, was perplexed. Fat Old Robertson and Julie were not. The rooms were empty, except for furniture. They were, in fact, pristine. All trace of Bill had been expunged; not even an old magazine, a scrap of paper, or smudge of dirt had been left behind.

In a way it was eerie, as if all summer everyone had seen some sort of spook. Mason had very carefully obliterated his path behind him. It was as if the man had never existed. It was as if he had never been there at all.

4

Hargrove had a certain facility at the wheel of a car, even now, in the rain. Some might have called it a talent. But by any name it was a liking for hanging unexpected U-turns in the middle of the block. The better to see who was following him. The better to see who would slam on the brakes and pursue. Suspicion went with Hargrove's terrain. Recently returned from Madrid, he was Robert Lassiter's immediate superior, a fact of daily life which pleased neither of them.

Hargrove was an Oklahoman for whom the frontier had never ended. Today, as on other days, in the car proceeding west on Oxford Street near Regent Street, he resented the fact that he had been born too late. A generation and a half sooner might have pleased him more. The opening of Oklahoma, the taming of the western United States. "And none of this fucking London traffic," he cursed to himself.

Among those who toiled in Western Europe for United States intelligence, Frank Hargrove was a walking, talking, cursing, abrasive legend. Based simultaneously in London and Madrid, Hargrove was a tall, lean man with sandy hair and graying temples. His eyes were too close to each other and his nose, from a World War II grenade, was slightly misshapen. He was not handsome, nor did he aspire to be. His height, six two, was a source of annoyance, as it not only hindered his pleasure in driving a Volkswagen, but it made him more conspicuous in crowds. Hargrove, like most professional espionage agents, liked to be a gray man without eminence, part of the woodwork. Frequently he wasn't.

His reputation, for example, tended to precede him. As everyone knew, he'd been in the employ of his government since 8 December 1941, the morning that he had gone out and enlisted in the Marine Corps at the adventuresome age of twenty. He'd wanted combat, and one way or another he'd been finding it ever since. Two years of the Philippine jungles—three months of which he'd spent behind Japanese lines—had made him even more nostalgic than ever for the Indian wars of the 1890s. It had also put the rest of his life in perspective. Peacetime intelligence was tame after the years in the jungle. But that didn't mean a man should ever lose his fighting edge. "Lean and mean" were the adjectives he smilingly liked to apply to himself; then each day he'd feel obliged to go out and prove it. And why not? It went without saying that a bureau chief in Western Europe was not expected to convey the outward mannerisms of a fairy.

He waited for a lull in the traffic. The steady drizzle and the streaking windshield wipers of the rented Volks-wagen didn't make his task any easier. When nothing was coming he jerked the car's steering wheel hard to the right and pulled into the next lane. Somewhere someone hit a horn and yelled. A taxi, probably, as if *they* had any-thing to be unnerved about. Hargrove arrived at the Dor-sett Arms Hotel within fifteen minutes.

The Dorsett Arms was one of those tasteless modern London hotels which cater to travelers who are euphe-mistically described as "budget conscious." It was a nine-story affair in white brick and glass, located on the far fringe of east Kensington, which was to say it was nowhere near anything that tourists wanted to see. It was, however, accessible by car from several different routes; and, almost more importantly, it featured an American-style bar which overlooked the rear parking lot. Hence Hargrove could, as he would wish to, drink a draft Schlitz beer which was on tap and watch his car at the same time. It wasn't so much that he feared anyone taking the car or any of its contents. It was the idea of people leaving things in it which grated upon him.

He parked his car and locked it. He entered the hotel through the back entrance and turned right through the lobby. As it happened, a tour bus of Iowans, freshly arrived from France via Calais and "motor coach," had just pulled in. While they were admiring the red, white, and blue London scenes on the lobby wallpaper as well as the Edwardian outfits of the bellboys, Hargrove strolled unnoticed to the bar.

He ordered his standard beer ("Cold, as cold as you

24

can get it!"), and went to an empty corner booth. Why, he wondered, couldn't they turn up the heat in this damnable hotel? Hargrove's body was still acclimated to Spain. Why was the beer warm and the room cold?

He glanced at his watch while he waited. Fifteen minutes.

A moustached man, younger than he but also American, entered the bar. Hargrove watched him, keeping an eye on his car at the same time. The man ordered a soft drink at the bar, puffed a cigar that was no longer than a cigarette, and turned toward Hargrove. The man wore a beige suit which had been soaked through with rain. He joined Hargrove in the corner booth.

There was no handshake, no sign of recognition or of friendship.

Hargrove put down his beer. "You're late, you know. Have trouble getting here?"

"Traffic," said Lassiter. He sipped his ginger ale. "Sorry."

"Always something, isn't there?"

Lassiter let the remark pass. Exchanging insults with a superior was unhealthy. Exchanging pleasantries with Hargrove was out of the question. Hargrove spoke again.

"I don't suppose you'd want to tell me where you've been for five days?"

"The States," he admitted after a pause.

"What for?"

An instant passed before Lassiter could answer. The admission would be painful. "My network's rotten. I'm blown."

Hargrove glared at him contemptuously. He sipped the beer and leaned back against the vinyl wall of the booth. "Jesus fucking Christ," he snarled. His eyes were riveted to Lassiter accusingly. "How do you know?"

"The Russian we had the locals arrest the other night," said Lassiter. "Somehow the Russians knew in advance." His eyes shifted. "That makes something very rotten. Somewhere someone's blown."

Hargrove had a troubled look in his eyes.

"Honest to God," Lassiter continued emotionally, "I've got five people in my network. Airtight people. People with credentials. People who've worked with the highest security clearance that exists. And I've got a leak, God damn it."

25

The waiter brought a menu. Hargrove dismissed him rudely. He was Pakistani and didn't completely understand at first, so Hargrove dismissed him a second time even more adamantly and with increased coarseness.

"Nobody knew what night Vassiliev was going to be pinched," Lassiter explained. "Not even me. I didn't decide until that same afternoon when one of our people learned that Vassiliev might be recalled to Moscow within the week. Well, hell. We couldn't take the chance of letting him catch a night flight to Sweden, then take off for Moscow International at his leisure. We figured with his American connection dead, we were on borrowed time anyway. Follow me so far?"

"Go ahead," muttered Hargrove.

"Try this," Lassiter suggested with bitterness. "For the hell of it, I staked out Ivan's apartment all evening. Wanted to see what would happen. We ordered the locals to grab him at nine fifty, no matter where he was. Then at eleven five they were to allow him to call his embassy. I was waiting. I wanted to see if they'd dispatch someone to collect Ivan's dirty laundry."

"And they did?"

"Sure," said Lassiter. There was a pause and he added, "They dispatched a whole squad of goons and they arrived at eleven thirty. Ready to roll over anything in their path to get into that apartment. Wanted the chips, we guess, though we can't be sure." Lassiter studied his superior. "Makes no sense."

"Makes sense to me."

"It won't. Vassiliev smelled our people following him and slipped the first surveillance crew at nine thirty. But I had a backup crew of two."

"Two? What two?" Hargrove was disturbed.

"Two extra legmen. From *outside* the network. The original five within didn't even know about them." Hargrove was silent and seemed to be smoldering. "Came in damned handy this time," Lassiter added defensively. "Ivan would have finished us if my two extras hadn't called in his location and let me put the original five back on his tail."

Hargrove was shaking his head. His eyes were furious. "Lassiter, you damned fool! *There's* your leak. You brought in two nobodies without any clearance or authorization. You—"

26

"I knew what I was doing, damn it! And you're leading away from the point!"

"Which is?" barked Hargrove heatedly.

"Ivan wasn't arrested until ten forty-two. He didn't arrive at the police station until eleven thirteen. He wasn't pushed in front of a telephone until eleven twenty-eight. The apes arrived at his apartment two minutes later, meaning they'd left the embassy at eleven five, when Ivan was *supposed to have called.* See? They knew the call was coming. They reacted to his arrest before they knew about it."

Hargrove's expression was one of exasperation. He snapped out each word as if his patience with a slow student were at an end. "What's the mystery? You blew your network. Again. Take your five originals, then take your two extras and skewer them all."

Lassiter's answer was long in coming. "No," he said, shaking his head. "I've checked them over and over. My network's well scrubbed *internally.* It's *externally* where—"

"Oh, for Christ's sake!" Hargrove snapped. He finished his beer.

Lassiter valiantly tried to present his best case. "The chips mean something important which hasn't yet been determined. Whatever it is—"

"How about that fat woman?"

Lassiter bristled. An ugly second passed. Lassiter replied without his teeth moving. "Doctor Davis has the highest possible clearance." He stressed her title. Doctor.

"I'm sure," Hargrove noted sourly.

"They've had an agent in place just waiting for us," said Lassiter. "That shows you how important the chips are. They had to play their trump card. They had to risk betraying the fact that they had someone in place in order to retrieve those chips."

"Know what I wish?" mused Hargrove, without waiting for a reply. "I wish I'd known you were sitting on a Russian. I would have given it to someone who could handle it."

"Like who? Yourself? You haven't been out from behind that desk in fifteen years."

Hargrove exhaled deeply, as if it were too much of an effort to become angry. "All this was when? Seven days ago now?"

"Eight."

"Where have you been for the last five? I've been trying—"

"I got help. From outside. If one thing's rotten here, chances are other things are too."

"Lassiter," said Hargrove hopelessly, "what in hell are you talking about?"

"I've brought in a specialist."

"Who?"

Lassiter was silent.

Hargrove inclined forward sharply as he spoke. "God damn it, Lassiter, hear me and hear me well. You may have been a good field officer a few years ago or when you were in Asia, but I haven't been able to trust you with a fucking thing since you transferred here. Now you're pulling in outsiders to do professional work. What the—"

"There's a leak on the inside of the London organization. Don't you understand what I'm—"

"All I understand is that you're staring suspension right in the eye."

"You *can't* suspend me. Oh, you can try, you son of a bitch. You've been trying for months, anyway. But the fact is, Hargrove,—"

The waiter reappeared. Lassiter, red in the face from anger, cut off his words in mid-sentence.

Hargrove was strangely without such decorum. "I'm sorry, Bob, really I am," he began. "But we're not in a business where we can afford to be sorry. You used to be good. But face it. You blew this one and you blew it good. Your work was sloppy again. You've got us holding a bag and we don't even know what's in it. *Chips!* What the rat-fuck do they mean?" He shook his head in frustration.

The waiter swept crumbs from the table cloth and picked up their empty glasses.

"What I'd suggest, Bob, is that you resign." Hargrove took on his kindliest expression. "Otherwise, you're to be terminated from the company within three days." He paused before reaching for his beer and finishing it. "I want you to turn in everything you're working on within an hour. I'm sorry, Lassiter, but we don't take chances."

Hargrove's expression was almost beatific. He turned toward the waiter who was, as the title implies, waiting. Hargrove spoke:

28

"I think we're ready to order food now. Aren't we, Bob?"

Airplanes always allowed Bill Mason ample time to think. After a certain point his mind could take no more of books, newspapers, magazines, meals, or the in-flight movie.

Today, somewhere between New York and London, his thoughts drifted to Robert Lassiter. How long had he known the man? Nineteen years, was it? Nineteen *already?* Odd, he thought, how Lazz drifted in and out of his world. Lassiter seemed to punctuate his life. After all, they were on the same side in the same business. A form of combat, it was. And no closeness between men ever matches the closeness developed in such circumstances.

Mason had been blassed with a window seat in the Pan Am 747. The flight was not crowded. No one sat with him.

Lassiter, he pondered again. Lazz. Turning up again, tracing him to New Jersey, then meeting him in New York.

"I got problems," he had said. "Real problems this time."

"They retired me, Lazz," Mason had told him. "You know that. A nice pink slip after all those years in China."

"I know," Lassiter had answered. "I need you anyway."

Lazz had seemed somewhat shaken, even three thousand miles from his immediate problems. Self-doubt was doing him no good. The man, earlier on in his career, had been the very prototype of quick wit, steady nerves, and quiet cunning. No longer.

"Bill, this one's going to bust me. I've felt this coming for a long time. I can't handle it."

"Captain Queeg retired me, Lazz," Mason repeated helplessly. "I don't see what I can do." Queeg was one of the nicer terms the retirees had for their director.

Lassiter was shaking his graying head with its thinning hair. Mason could see the new lines in the man's face. It had never occurred to Mason that his mentor could— to say it bluntly—fail. That he could grow old. Like an old coyote losing his teeth, he was near the end.

"They're letting go all the wrong people," Lassiter said. "Don't they realize what they're doing?"

Congress was on the Director to open the agency to

their inspection, show them the company books, account for every dollar being used for covert actions. And above all the Superspook—the agency's sixth head in five years—was to trim, trim, trim. Squeeze each nickel until the buffalo yelped. And get rid of the deadweight. Result: eight hundred employees permanently furloughed from clandestine operations. Furloughed to the sidewalk, all within a few months. The notices had been short and sweet: *"This is to inform you of my recommendation to the director of personnel to effect your separation in order to achieve the reduction ordered by the Director of Central Intelligence."*

That put eight hundred ex-spies, men and women, sour as hell at their former employer, all on the street at once and wide open to blandishments from God knew who. Bill Mason had been in the first wave of those released.

Bill turned the conversation back to its original direction. "Where are you based now?" he asked Lassiter.

"Europe. London. That's where I want you."

"I'm a China hand, Lazz. Europe isn't—"

"You worked two tours in Europe," Lassiter interrupted. "Don't kid me. I got you assigned to Europe, for God's sake. That's where you started."

"I prefer the eggroll assignments." He paused and added, "Unfinished business, you know."

"Oh, I see. Your own vendetta. You against nine hundred million Chinese."

"Maybe."

Lassiter pondered his next words. "Look, Bill. A network's a network. You know rot when you smell it. Jesus. Is sitting on a beach so much fun?"

"No one shoots at me. No one dumps me in the enemy's lap."

"It could be arranged."

"I mean it. I'm happy. I've got a woman. I've got a job. I'm getting a good severance from the agency and I sleep eight hours a night."

"I'm giving you a key," Lassiter had insisted. "An apartment key. It's in London on Leffingham Street. A safe house. Be there on September sixth. It's life and death, Mase. You're the only one I can trust completely."

And on and on he'd continued, making his case on a graffitied park bench behind the Public Library, then continuing at a Third Avenue bar that evening. Lassiter had spun a tale of vulnerability and deception, one which angered Mason just to hear it. Lassiter, of course, hadn't made a transoceanic trip just to talk. He had assessed the character of Bill Mason long ago. Mason couldn't hear a story like this one and sit on the sidelines.

"I'll spell the whole episode out for you," Lassiter had promised. "The whole thing. I'll give it to you move by move, step by step. I'll tell you exactly the type of game it is. Then it will be revelation time, Mase. *By name. I'll tell you exactly who we're looking for.*"

Then Lazz had fulfilled his promise.

Mason looked out the airplane's window and into the darkening sky. They were above Ireland now. He closed his eyes, five miles up in the air, and his mind propelled itself back still farther. Back to 1958, when he'd first seen Robert Lassiter. Jesus, nineteen years.

It had been at school. Kenfield Academy, Kenfield, Massachusetts. Preparatory grounds of future presidents— of companies and occasionally of nations. First day back on a sultry September afternoon.

The dining hall. Cool Mr. Lassiter, a new instructor of history as it happened, took table seven in the dining hall. Lassiter was a young man then, in his mid-twenties and teaching history to boys in their mid- and late teens. And while most of the other teachers were immeasurably older—they'd been at Kenfield since the last glaciers went through, it was reliably rumored—there was something different about Lassiter.

Something. He'd gone to Yale, but so had half the faculty. He'd been in Korea. That was something. Most of the faculty seemed World War Two vintage. And, oh yes, while in Korea with the Marine Corps, Captain Lassiter had picked up Chinese. Spoke it pretty well, in fact, meaning, to the boys, that in any big city he could get his shirts laundered properly.

Yet, there was more. Maybe it was generational. Lassiter was young to be at Kenfield. He was hardly a parent image, more like an older, wiser brother. *In loco fratis* as opposed to *in loco parentis*. He could, of course, referee a soccer match and keep up with the play, outskate anyone on the hockey team as assistant coach, come up with the meaning of any word any boy could find (*"Don't you bastards have dictionaries any more?"*) or verify lurid tales about and footnotes to any aspect of European or American history (*"Yes, I hear that is how Catherine the Great*

31

died," or "No, John Dillinger was buried intact, *once the bullet holes were stitched up.").* Lassiter, or Lazz, as the boys nicknamed him among themselves, was a compendium of knowledge, useful and useless, off-color or on-target but ceaselessly fascinating. It was thus inevitable; certain special relationships developed.

It was almost as if Lazz was plumbing the depths of certain boys, looking for a certain quality in their character, something which he alone was somehow going to transform to good use. He was, of course, disliked by many of the dinosaurs on the faculty. And when he began growing a beard over spring vacation (A beard? At Kenfield, where there were not even any Democrats?), his pull with the headmaster dwindled considerably. But by then Lassiter seemed not to care. He jauntily announced in May that he'd not be back. He'd found something in Washington.

Yet certain friendships persisted.

For some reason, in his new employ, Lassiter was constantly riding the trains between Washington and Boston. "The Northeastern Corridor," he called it. "Where ninety-six percent of this country's brains are located. Another three percent are scattered and the remainder, they're in jail," he'd say without smiling. Along the Boston-to-Washington route were New York and New Haven, where he stopped frequently. "Good to keep track of some of the Kenfield alums," he said. And he did—at Harvard, Yale, and Columbia.

The fifties ended. 1960. The inhabitants of the Northeastern Corridor found one of their own elected President. Trouble was, he was a Catholic and, worse, a Democrat.

Bill Mason, meanwhile, was at Yale, and during his last two years there he saw Lassiter with increasing frequency. Bill one day realized that in his choice of major, his hand had been guided. He enjoyed his major, liked it actually, but realized that it had been Lazz who'd steered him toward it—Far Eastern Studies. Well, no one majored in *that.* Original, certainly, and damned fun at cocktail parties where Republican bores from Long Island, with the help of a few Scotches, would press a forefinger to the corner of each eye, tug backwards and create a slant-eyed effect. Ha, ha. What did one do with a major in Far Eastern studies? Teach Far Eastern Studies?

32

Well, no.

1961. The Bay of Pigs. 1962. The Missile Crisis. Somehow Mason's future seemed vague. Law school? The Peace Corps? The Navy, the Air Force? Predictably, Lazz had been present with an answer. "For Christ's sake, Mase, you don't want to slog around ditches, with or without a rifle." Lassiter had an "in" and it would get Mason around the draft to boot. Government service of an unmentioned sort.

Unmentioned it was, until after graduation. Then none of it seemed so strange. Just as the British recruited their agents from the brightest young men at Oxford and Cambridge, so did the American intelligence community recruit from the upper echelon of its own universities.

Lassiter, seeing in Mason many of his own better qualities, had invited him to a New York apartment one afternoon during Christmas break. He first confessed that he himself, as a young man with high aptitude, an analytic mind, and a suitable family background, had been recruited by the Central Intelligence Agency ten years earlier while at the university.

"You've got graduation staring you in the face," Lassiter then warned. "Better know which way to jump. Got anything yet?"

Mason hadn't.

Cautiously, Lassiter went on. "The people I'm working for in Washington," he said, "they're interested in men with a knowledge of the Orient. Far East stuff," he added eloquently. "I've been watching you for five years, Bill. You're what they want. *Exactly*."

Bill Mason had listened. The pitch began.

"I guess State is expecting all hell to break loose over there at any time. Quemoy. Matsu. Taiwan. Indochina. The whole place is a mess. But intriguing, I suppose," he added quickly. "A few of the right moves, a few of the right young men in the correct places and who knows? We could have the Reds on the run all through Asia. Have to defend ourselves, you know, Mase. Can't have Uncle Sam looking like a candy-ass. Interested?"

"Yes," Bill Mason had replied. "I don't want to make a career of it, but I'll listen."

"Good," Lassiter said. He spent the rest of the after-noon explaining the details of what would be required of

33

Mason. Above all, Bill was flattered: He had been Chosen. Two weeks after graduation it began.

There were first the FBI and polygraph tests. *Have you ever had homosexual relations? Have you ever passed official secrets to anyone? Have you ever stolen or damaged U.S. government property?*

Lassiter had forewarned him. "As long as you didn't smash mail boxes, steal exam answers, or bugger underformers at Kenfield, you'll be fine."

"None of the above," answered Mason.

"Even if you did, Bill, tell them. They want to hear the truth. It's a compulsion with them."

Mason passed, easily.

Training followed in Camp Peary, Virginia. It was discouraging: Everyone else seemed to have the same credentials and backgrounds except for a few naturally bilingual types from New York and San Francisco. Then Mason was assigned a desk job for seven months in Washington, The District. Paperwork which seemed to have little to do with anything. Reading, screening, and writing reports. Filing reports, then never hearing of them again. Time passed uneventfully until a hot August day in 1964, early in Lyndon Johnson's administration. Gulf of Tonkin Day, as it would be remembered. The section chief held Mason past the daytime hours, then presented him with a visitor toward nine in the evening.

"Congratulate me, Mase," Lassiter had announced upon arrival in his office. "I'm going to China."

Mason leaned back in his swivel chair. He looked at his mentor with an *Oh yeah?* glint in his eye. "Does that mean *I* am, too?"

"No."

"No?"

Lassiter gestured helplessly. "I cajoled and begged in every way but the people on the sixth floor weren't buying it. Too young, too inexperienced."

"So explain to me how I get field experience sitting at a frigging desk?"

"I've taken care of that."

"How so?"

"Europe, Mase," Lassiter grinned. "Lucky you. I got you assigned to France."

"France! My whole damned training is for the Orient!"

34

"Got to remember, it's the Defense Department we're dealing with. Military mentality. Don't look for logic."

Mason responded eloquently. "Fuck!" he said.

A week later he arrived in Marseilles, an unattached young executive looking for employment with a US firm. He took himself and his new legend to Paris where the General Motors office hired him. Settling in, he socialized as much as possible with other Americans in the country, his acquaintances including several journalists. That was his actual assignment. He was a raw-information assessor: taking whatever basic information was given to him by American reporters stringing for CIA, assessing it in conjunction with all other information received, and sending back a scaled-down report to Washington. Easy, Mason soon realized, though not terribly exciting. Yet you didn't relinquish a foreign tour. If you did you would never get another one; or at least never another good one.

After two years, at the end of the first tour, he signed on again. Twenty-two months passed. Little things began to happen. He suspected his telephone was tapped, but he couldn't decide whether his side or some other was doing it. Some of his mail, he felt, was getting read before it arrived; he sent things to himself, in a disguised hand, to be certain. Finally it all came into focus. He was being relocated. He could smell it coming. •

General Motors fired him. The day he cleaned out his desk, a liaison officer met him on the Boulevard Haussmann and pushed into his hands a ticket for a flight to Los Angeles. He would leave in two days. No explanations given.

In Los Angeles he was given three days' stopover and another airplane ticket. This one for Honolulu. Now it was becoming clearer. He was told he would be met in Hawaii and briefed.

He was. He was met disembarking from the flight. His new superior was completely stone-faced and unexpressive as Mason disembarked and picked up his luggage. Eventually the man couldn't hold it in any longer and broke out in a wide gloating smile.

"Well," Lassiter said, "you always told me you wanted to see the world."

"You're a conniving bastard. No. You're worse."

The two men laughed and embraced warmly, exchanging profanities and insults.

"You'll like Taiwan," Lassiter said off-handedly.

A hand was on Bill's arm, shaking him gently. Bill opened his eyes, waking suddenly. He had the sense of having been dreaming about China.

"Sir. Excuse me, sir?"

Mason groggily looked into the pretty Anglo-Saxon face of a brown-haired, blue-uniformed flight attendant. For a moment, through his slightly bleary eyes, she looked like Julie Heasman.

"Sir, would you care to fasten your seat belt? We'll be landing shortly."

"Of course." He returned her smile and watched her for a few moments as she continued down the aisle. He wondered how long he'd been asleep.

He felt the aircraft descending. He looked out his window, shading his eyes from the inside lights.

He could see Heathrow, and, in the distance, London.

5

Mason sat on the edge of his bed and held open his palm. Refreshed after a night's sleep in a hotel, he thought of the safe house, the third-floor apartment in which he was scheduled to meet Lassiter. In his palm he held a pair of keys. The keys would admit him to the apartment. He would go there at noon and he would wait. Lassiter had promised to join him by two o'clock.

He stared at the keys. In a ritual that had become commonplace since his severance from the agency in March, he wondered what he was doing with his life.

It was different now. He was a man of thirty-seven, not a recent Yale graduate of twenty-two. The horizon was no longer limitless before him. His contemporaries had long since forged their careers. The Silent Generation, they had been called. Accurately, he thought. Silently they'd all set to their work, burrowing their way upwards into corporations, starting families, sinking into the comfortable affluence of the American upper-middle class.

Mason had been silent, too, but in a different manner. He'd served the system which he'd been brought up in and which he believed in. It was the sort of thing a young man did in 1962. Fifteen years later, no one could figure out why.

And now, he wondered, what was there? He had his severance pay and a pink slip—money but no career. Once again he'd be dependent upon Lazz, waiting for Lassiter to suggest the next move, once the connection was made in London.

He stood from the bed and slid the keys into his pocket, realizing the fragility of his situation. In this coming operation, whatever it was, he wouldn't even be officially involved. He wondered. Was that what they'd planned all along? They, meaning Washington. Captain Queeg and all the intellectual admirals now running the

37

agency. When an attorney loses his job with a firm, he can go elsewhere, either setting up for himself or joining another office. Same with a business executive. Ditto with a secretary, sheet metal operator, truck driver, or carpenter.

But what does a spy do? Defect?

What are his options? An agent spends fifteen years in black intelligence, operating abroad at immediate personal risk if apprehended; then he's put on the street. What skills has he to use in the civilian world? What can he do besides retire or join the other side?

The safe apartment was in Islington. Mason walked half the way, then took the Underground to Kings Cross Station. It would have been just a few more minutes' walk to 42 Leffingham Street, had he ever arrived. From the time he rounded the corner to a residential block of bay-windowed houses, he knew something was wrong.

There was a cluster of people, passersby they appeared to be, standing in a half-moon shape around a spot on the sidewalk. It was the type of helpless crowd which surrounds victims of traffic accidents. They stand, watch, mumble among themselves, and try to edge out each other for a view. They are as unhelpful as they are helpless.

Mason, counting the street numbers from down the block, quickly realized that the growing knot of people was before number forty-two. A police car was standing at the curb, its doors open. Bill could see, above the heads in the crowd, the dark blue helmets of two London patrolmen.

"Someone said it was a woman," Mason heard a voice say. "She jumped."

Heads nodded and an old gentleman pointed to the top floor of number forty-two. It was a taller building than the rest, with dormer windows and a gray exterior. A sixth-floor window was open. Definitely not the third floor. Mason was greatly relieved. *And a woman*, he told himself. *It was a woman.* Young? Old? Fat? Thin? Beautiful? Ugly? No one knew.

Mason stepped to the edge of the crowd and craned his head. He could see very little. Only a group of gray Metropolitan London Police blankets over the body. A thin stream of liquid flowed from the corpse. It looked like blood mixed with heaven-knew-what. Judging from the contours of the blankets, the corpse was twisted obscenely.

Mason eyed two open sixth-floor window panels which jutted outward. Beige curtains were dangling and fluttering—torn.

"Give us some room, please. Give us some space."

Mason looked to his left. A municipal ambulance had quietly arrived and two sleepy-eyed attendants climbed out. They moved through the assembled crowd carrying a yellow, plastic body bag. They stretched out the bag and laid it beside the victim, then lifted away the blankets.

Something unexplainable happened, something to do with the psychology of spectators, for as the coverings were lifted away and the broken body gradually came into view, the orderly crowd broke. They crowded in around the body, forming a circle.

Mason moved forward, also. As the final blanket was pulled away, he found himself looking over a short woman's shoulder.

"Gruesome, it is," he heard her say. "Absolutely gruesome." But she never averted her eyes. Then the final blanket was lifted and the body was clinically hoisted into the body bag.

The stark, horrible realization was then upon Bill Mason.

"Not a woman at all. It's a man," someone said.

Lazz. His dead eyes were vacant. A thin red line ran across the front of the skull. The body was preposterously twisted, broken like an old battered doll's. And the head, swaying on its broken neck, wobbled sickeningly toward Bill.

Lazz.

Above all there was an empty feeling, an overwhelming sense of loss.

Mason stayed as long as anyone, watching the body being removed. He said nothing. He scanned the dispassionate faces. He recognized no one. If anyone else there had known the deceased, it didn't show. But then, it wouldn't have.

The ambulance door slammed and the driver leisurely pulled away, with the corpse safely packed. The two police officers walked back toward their car.

"Where will they take him?"

Neither replied to Mason's question. He repeated it. This time he was heard.

"Don't think they'll bother much with the 'ospital," said the taller one.

"Did he say anything?" Mason asked as they got into the police car.

"Yes, sir. 'E said 'ouch' when 'e 'it the concrete."

The two officers laughed. Then their car's ignition whined and finally caught. The police car pulled away and a small sanitation van arrived to take its place. A single man hopped out. He methodically pulled a large broom from the rear of his truck, walked to a water standpipe halfway up the block, and opened it, releasing a fast gush of water into the gutter. Mason watched the water as it gurgled down toward where Robert Lassiter had died.

The sanitation man walked toward the spot. Then, for three or four minutes, he swished the broom through the stream of water where blood stained the sidewalk. Mason watched with fascination and horror. A few minutes later, with the concrete drying and the sanitation truck pulling away, all trace of Lassiter was gone.

To look at the fatal spot, it was as if nothing had happened. The street had been cleaned. The neighborhood would continue, as would the city, and the inconsequential death on Leffingham Street would be forgotten within hours.

For Bill Mason, it would not be so easy. The image of Lassiter's battered skull, rolling off a broken neck, was emblazoned in his mind. After walking a block Mason sat down on a curbside bench.

He was vaguely aware of traffic passing him. His face bore the vacant look of a man who has stopped caring and has entered a long, deep, personal narcosis. He thought again of Lazz and of the detailed story he'd told in New York a week earlier. But now Lazz was gone. Permanently.

He rubbed his chin and drew a breath, summoning the energy to stand. He'd return to his hotel and think. He wondered, had he and Lazz made a mess of their lives?

He walked toward Kings Cross Station, retracing the steps he'd taken less than an hour earlier. His head was down, his eyes were on his feet.

What kind of man had Lazz been when the end came, he pondered now. He'd seen the man only a handful of times in the last years. There was that horrible China thing, a meeting on Mason's return from Asia. Then New Jersey, then New York. A man can change considerably in the course of one year. In the course of several, he could become a different person.

He descended a long escalator to the Underground. He waited aimlessly on the platform, eventually boarding a train bound toward Westminster. He was jostled by the crowd inside and threw an angry elbow at someone in return. He was in no mood to be pushed. The recipient of the elbow recognized Mason's temper and moved farther down the car.

The train jerked and pulled out of the station. Mason stood deeply absorbed in his own bitter thoughts. Then something tickled his nose and he sniffed. He was again aware of his surroundings.

Mason smelled something behind him. He turned.

A pair of West Indians were smoking, holding the cigarettes in their cupped palms so that no one would notice. They laughed to each other and were systematically tearing at the seams of the bench upholstery until the grayish-white stuffing was starting to spill out.

Often a man notices things subliminally, by an accumulation of small perceptions which take a moment or two to travel from the eye to the brain where the implications are sorted out. So it was at that moment in the London Underground. Mason had turned away from the two vandals in disgust when he realized what else he'd seen.

Unless he was mistaken, there was a face which he'd seen before. Mason wanted to turn around and look. But he didn't. Not yet.

Where, he thought.

Within a few moments Mason had pegged it.

First in the street. The man had walked close by him when he had entered Leffingham Street. And then again outside the building in the mass of people surrounding the fatal section of pavement. Why hadn't Bill noticed it at the time? In a strange way, Mason felt flattered. He'd acquired a shadow.

It was suddenly bright outside the train. Euston Station. The West Indians continued to smoke and yank at the stuffing of the upholstery. They were forming it into little balls now, rolling it in their hands, flinging it in each other's faces and laughing.

The train slowed and came to a halt and the doors opened. Mason repositioned himself, facing toward the man who had followed him.

For the briefest instant, there was eye contact. Now Mason was certain. The man looked away, turning so that he faced away yet could watch in the glass of the window.

"God damn it," Mason muttered to himself. The train was very crowded. It lurched and started again. Mason considered the other man.

Not your typical Briton, he noted. The man was on the small side, maybe five seven, with closely cut black hair, a lean face, hollow cheeks, and an angular, almost prominent nose. He seemed younger than Bill, too. Maybe twenty-six. The man's upraised hand, holding the swaying strap, revealed a white cuff and suit jacket beneath the beige trench coat.

The train rumbled on. Bill checked his watch. One forty-five. Good, he told himself. There would be time.

He looked back up and caught the smaller, darker man turning his head away again. Whoever it is, Mason thought to himself, he's doing a damned lousy job of staying inconspicuous. But how many others were there who were doing a better job? Again the windows were bright. The train pulled into the station. Time to find out. Bill's reaction was not at all one of fear, it was a feeling of anger. A friend of nineteen years, one who'd come to Bill for help, was dead. As the shock began to subside within him, cold anger took hold.

The train came to a complete stop. Bill delayed a few moments, until the people outside were starting to embark, then pushed his way through them at a leisurely pace. He followed the signs to the escalator. He read the lingerie ads on his ascent to the street, never looking back. With his experience, he knew he had company. He could feel it.

On Dolnay Street the air was damp. Mason turned to his right and walked. He made sure to remain prominent. Half a block away he stopped and bought a newspaper, stood with it for a moment to remain in view, then walked until he came to a public house at the corner. Mason paused in front of it for a moment, as if to make a decision, then entered.

It was almost two o'clock. The lunchtime crowd had thinned. It was a solidly middle-class establishment, favored

42

by neighborhood businessmen and a sprinkling of women. A filmy cloud of cigarette smoke hung in the air. Music, from somewhere, was moderately loud, as was the clatter of conversation. Mason moved to the end of the bar. He watched the mirror above the Scottish roast beef, turkey, and ham on the ledge behind the bar.

"Yes, sir?" a barman finally asked.

Mason eyed the bill of fare and the prices. He also watched the mirror. His shadow had followed.

"Roast beef sandwich," said Mason. "And a lager."

At the other end of the pub his new companion had ordered bitters. As Mason waited, the darker man moved behind him and sat down by himself at a booth.

The barman set a fork, knife, and paper napkin before Mason and drew the lager.

"I was wondering," said Bill, picking up the stainless steel knife, "would you have something slightly sharper? These things, well, sometimes I have a terrible time cutting with them. Weak grip, I guess."

The barman gave Mason a steak knife. The sandwich arrived. Mason paid, took everything in his hands and turned. He walked to the booth immediately behind his shadow. He set down his sandwich, his beer and his fork.

At the last second he slid into the other booth, forcing his shadow down the banquette and against the wall. The handle of the steak knife was firmly in Bill's fist. He pressed the point of the knife to the man's ribs, just below the heart.

"All right," Mason growled. "Who are you and what do you want?"

The other man kept his hands flat on the table where they could be seen. A professional touch, Mason observed.

"You crazy fool!" snapped the man. "You think I didn't know you'd seen me? How many times did I have to catch your eye?" The accent was British, vaguely working-class, but with a hint of something foreign in it. "Put that damned thing away! Unless you're going to use it on the roast beef!"

Mason pressed the blade more adamantly. "You haven't answered my questions. Shall I draw blood?"

"Only if you feel stupid enough. My name is Auerbach. David Auerbach. I was your late friend's liaison officer. Now if you'll listen to me, you'll find I'm the only friend you have in Western Europe."

Mason never looked in the other direction until he heard another voice.

"Sir?" a man asked belligerently. A large shadow blocked the overhead light. "Any problems here, sir?" Mason looked back. The two men from behind the bar were standing there, each with a billy club in his hand. They were glowering down at Mason and the entire pub was silent, forming a semicircle behind them and regarding the two combative men in the booth with fascination.

"I'll call the police," someone said.

Auerbach laughed, convincingly.

"No, no, no," he pronounced, waving off all assistance. "No need. My mate here's just having a bit of fun. Come on, you silly wanker," he said to Mason, "put that away. The good people are getting cross."

Auerbach mirthfully pushed the knife away. Mason, seeing little choice, allowed his hand to be moved. He tried to join the game and grinned stupidly.

"What can I say?" asked Auerbach, whose voice had a slightly nasal squeak to it. "He's an out-of-work actor. Actors are crazy even when they're working. Now, mind, William, keep your paws off the bloody cutlery and behave." Auerbach raised his eyes to the barmen, hoping to dismiss them. "Bring my friend here a plate of chips, too. The chips are first class here. You look hungry, William."

The barmen, while not wholly satisfied, were nonetheless convinced that there would be no blood on the floor. So they let the matter pass, while vowing to keep an eye on the American. "Actors," one muttered. Wordlessly, the second barman moved the roast-beef plate from the empty table to the booth now occupied by Auerbach and Mason.

"Service with a smile," observed Auerbach as the food arrived. "First-rate pub, this. Glad you could meet me here, Mr. Mason."

The barmen were gone, as was everyone else. Auerbach spoke to Mason in a different tone now, as if to take him into a confidence. "Sit tight," he said. "We need to talk."

"Someone should do a lot of talking," said Mason sourly.

"I quite agree. Trouble is, someone has. If you sense my meaning." He paused, then added sympathetically. "Sorry about your friend Robert. He didn't fall, you know."

"I'd guessed that much, already."

Auerbach motioned to the sandwich and a side plate of chips which had just arrived. "Eat, so we can get out of here."

Mason was about to protest that he wasn't hungry, but suddenly realized that he hadn't eaten since the airplane the day before. He began to eat.

"Do you know who I am?" Auerbach finally asked.

Mason considered the answer. "I know who you claim you are." He definitely recalled Lassiter mentioning the name—the British liaison officer in the Vassiliev case.

"He was going to introduce us today," Auerbach said. "At the apartment on the third floor. You were to arrive at noon. I, an hour later. Robert, between one and two."

"Who threw him out the window?" Mason asked. Chewing, he looked up. "For that matter, what was he doing there early?"

"You might just as well ask what *I* was doing there early."

"I was going to."

"I wanted to watch people going and coming from that building," Auerbach said. "I didn't want any uninvited guests. Guess you know we've had our problems lately. Things have gotten sticky."

"Who threw him out the window?"

"I don't know."

"Make a guess."

"I couldn't."

"Damn you," sneered Mason. "You know more than that. Lassiter's dead and you're playing word games. I don't know what you want out of me, but you're not going to get it."

Auerbach studied his hands for a moment, then looked upwards again as Mason took a final sip of lager. "Mr. Mason," he said, "you need me more than I need you."

"Is that right?" asked Mason sarcastically.

"Do you have a job? Do you have sufficient money? Is your passport in perfect order? Do you have a visa? Do you wish to stay longer than six months?" He paused. "Have you, for example, registered with immigration as a former US intelligence officer in Asia? Will you fly home? Or would you care to stay long enough to discover what happened to Robert Lassiter?"

Mason considered it for a moment. He was calmer

now. "Lazz was no one's fool," he said. "Whoever suckered him this morning was someone he trusted."

"Of course," nodded Auerbach. "You were wondering if *I* had anything to do with it. Naturally. Well, draw your own conclusions."

Mason had already drawn his conclusions. Auerbach stood no more than five seven and was, in fact, on the slight side. No way that Auerbach had overpowered Lassiter. Not alone.

Yet other aspects of the man bothered Mason. He sounded English but didn't look it. And he was young. Getting a good view of the man now, Mason assessed his age at twenty-five or even less. Auerbach was both too young and too foreign to be a trusted intelligence agent. Yet that's what he claimed to be.

"You're looking at me strangely," Auerbach said.

"I'm suspicious by nature."

"Aren't we all? Are you paid at the bar?" Auerbach asked. "Time for a walk." When Mason seemed slightly hesitant, Auerbach added, "If you care to. Don't have to, you know. But I think a chat would be worthwhile."

They walked westward. Auerbach announced their destination as Regent's Park. Mason knew the trick. Auerbach wanted wide open space in which to talk.

They passed a white Rolls Royce with what was obviously an Arab chauffeur-bodyguard. The license plates said Lebanon and gave a low number.

"See that?" asked Auerbach somewhat loudly. "That's a byproduct of British socialism. Arab princes leaving a thin film of oil all over the city. Crazy Palestinians shooting at each other. The city's become a circus of foreigners." He looked to Mason, the American. "No offense intended."

"None taken."

"There are welcome foreigners and unwelcome foreigners. Not hard to spot the difference."

After a brief wait for a light, they crossed Albany Street.

"And you can?"

"Can what?"

"Spot the difference."

Auerbach laughed. "Can't *you?* Really?"

"What's it got to do with British socialism?"

"Everything," said Auerbach with genine bitterness. "You can't afford to be British anymore. But then," he added with hesitance, "I didn't bring you here to talk politics. I want to talk about Mr. Lassiter. I *am* sorry, you know. Genuinely. Over there." He pointed to a bench away from the gardens and several steps away from the walkway. "That will be perfect."

In another minute they had seated themselves.

"Your plans?" asked Auerbach.

"Jesus Christ. I was planning to meet—"

"Yes, yes, I know. But there isn't time to think of what you were going to do. There's the present and the future. Robert told me a good bit about you. Experienced man. Very trustworthy. You were pink-slipped, was that it?"

Mason nodded.

"So you're out of work."

"I came to help a friend."

"You still can."

Mason was silent. "How?" he finally asked.

"Do you root, Mr. Mason?"

"What? Root? Root for what?"

"I root for the English-speaking world, Mr. Mason," Auerbach said with a piercing stare. "I hope you might, also."

Auerbach spoke with a frightening toughness now, almost a religious passion, in the tones of righteousness which belong only to those who have been converted. "I'm not English, as I'm sure you've surmised already. But I have two eyes, two ears, and a brain. I know what side the gods are on."

"What the hell are you talking about? I thought you told me. . . . What the hell, *Lazz* told me that you were an officer in British intelligence. Now you tell me you're not English. What are you? Martian?"

"I consider myself *British*, not English. My father was naturalized. Came here from Hungary after the war —Second World War——not that either of us remember it. My father was a tailor. The Communists took everything the man had. His home, his store. A violin that had been in the family for two hundred years. He came here, married, and worked hard. I worked hard, too. Read political theory at Oxford. After my studies were complete I found a job."

"Doing this?"

"I enjoy it."

47

"You're young yet."

"Aren't you?"

"I don't feel young," muttered Mason. "I feel disgusted."

Mason's words were met with a shrug. "So you're turning soft in your old age. It happens. You see too much; you don't forget enough. The thrill goes. They were probably right to sack you."

Mason's eyes were fiery.

"Look at it objectively. You just said you didn't enjoy it anymore. Why keep on a man who's just going through the motions? With me, it's a holy war. I *hate* the other side. If it were a shooting war, I'd enlist. But it's not. It's quiet trenches, psychological barbed wire, and political hand grenades. Do you know what they consider to be my specialty?"

"I couldn't guess."

"Interrogation of defectors. But it's been a slow season, Mr. Mason. Nothing. So they linked me with Robert Lassiter. Told me to show him the ropes, guide his hand as much as I could in England. Found himself a nice hot Russian, he did. But you know what? He trusted the wrong person somewhere. That's who you and I are going to find."

"How do I know it's not you?"

"You don't." He pondered the point. "I could bring you into our headquarters building. Let you see that I'm received there. I don't want them knowing who you are, though. I—"

"You're setting up your own network, that's what you're telling me. You want me, since I'm out of work back home, to go to work for you. Payroll, housing. The works. You're incredible, Auerbach. What the hell's in it for me?"

Auerbach laughed. "Don't be so coy. It doesn't become you. You know what's in it for you. A job, lodging, money. Not great money, but good money. And, since it seems to matter, you can finish what you came to England for. Help Lassiter finish his case. This may have been his last day on this bloody planet, but you've got a way to go yet."

Mason thought about it. He watched a trio of children playing on the lawn. He could still see Lazz's head rolling off his shoulder, the empty eyes wildly focused.

"Who was running who?" Mason asked. "Were you running Lassister or Lassiter running you?"

"*I* told you and *he* told you. We worked with each other. Separate but equal, to use an American expression."

"And what's in this for you that's so important?"

"The satisfaction of a job well done."

"For God's sake," muttered Mason. "Think I don't see through you? You're a young climber. You're twenty-five, twenty-six, an immigrant boy, first-generation flag waver. Probably too smart for your own good, abrasive as hell and out to earn a reputation. Son of a Jew tailor kicked around first by the Nazis then by the Russians. Grow up in England, work hard. Join the foreign office, weasel your way into counterintelligence, and dust off an act that's too English to be English. Now you're out to bag a top Russian. And I know why. Because normally you're a small cog in an interrogation machine. You listen to parts of defectors' stories, help add them up, never see the full picture yourself, try to distill what it means politically. Right?"

Auerbach didn't flinch. Mason continued.

"Now, because you're young and inexperienced, they tossed you out free lance to work with Lassiter. They figured Lassiter wasn't working on anything of importance, but someone had to watch him, anyway. So they gave it to you, never dreaming that Lassiter would hit something. But he did. And you did. And now you want me to help you bring it home. You need me to help you find your Russian. For your own glory, of course."

Auerbach thought about it. "That's about ninety-six percent accurate," he said flatly.

"What part's not accurate?"

"I'm not completely sure that we're dealing with Russians, Mr. Mason. That's why I'm deeply anxious to enlist your help. Your help in particular."

A moment passed.

"What are you babbling about now?"

"As your John Foster Dulles used to say, 'the yellow peril.' You're a China expert, aren't you, Mr. Mason? Something of a Sinologist by profession. Maybe we can even discover who blew you in 1969. Just maybe," he said, pronouncing each syllable slowly.

Thoughtfully, Mason stood. Auerbach had no idea whether the American was going to walk slowly away or turn and punch him. Bill did neither. Instead he paced forward slowly, ruminating, his arms folded, his eyes creased and squinting as the thoughts flew through his mind.

For a moment he could see the lake, the swans, and the flowers of Regent's Park's west end. But his thoughts were far away. He turned.

"All right," he said, softly and just a trifle grudgingly. "You've got me."

A thin smile flickered across Auerbach's lips.

"You can start," Auerbach said, "by making sure that our late friend doesn't end up in the wrong place. Ditto, his possessions. Claim the body. I'll give you the address. Won't be any mistake, but you might want to get there before anyone else does. Know what I mean?"

6

"I think women are the stronger of the sexes," Sarah said. When Paul Frost smirked good naturedly, she quickly added, "No, *really*. Women are the natural survivors. I've learned that just by examining my own feelings. Suicide" —she would say the word now—"suicide would never occur to me. Any problem can be approached." She shook her head thoughtfully. "Suppose it had been me instead of my husband. Could *he* have recovered as quickly?" She shook her head again, as if to give a definitive answer, unpopular but true.

"We all learn to get by," Reverend Frost suggested, "to pick up and go on."

She shook her head, almost breaking into a smile. "Women are the *born* survivors. On the big things, Paul, we don't fall to pieces as easily. We're stronger. Forgive the rash generalization, but it's true."

"Sarah," he chided gently.

How odd it is that life is often a counterbalancing series of exits and entrances. Someone arrives, someone departs; someone dies, someone else is born. A death creates a vacancy among the lives that it touches. The vacancy remains until someone arrives to fill it.

Reverend Frost had stepped into Sarah Woodson's life not more than three days after Brian's funeral. Her husband had been buried in the old churchyard behind the town's single Presbyterian church, the one the Woodsons had attended every other Easter and each Christmas but had never bothered to join. Old Pastor Booth had not been picky about such things and there were plots available.

Booth had had a number of things on his mind or he might have sought to comfort the young widow himself. But lovable old Booth's health wasn't all that good, either. The more charitable called it heart trouble, while others suggested cirrhosis of the liver as the actual problem, pointing out that Booth had spent many years in friendly acquaintance with spirits of all sorts, both Holy and neutral grain. Pastor Booth had many times been suspected of combining the two on Sunday mornings, before roaring into sermons.

No matter. The man had something. Call it inspiration, show business, or call it divine guidance. Whatever, it held together the congregation. The Catholics had *their* colorful Irish clerics, so why couldn't the Maryland Presbyterians have one?

It was to the considerable relief of the congregation, in any case, that, during the summer of 1977, Paul Frost had arrived, fuzzy-cheeked and fresh from divinity school. Frost, it was said, would give The Ailing One a lift, take some of the work load off Booth, and, in particular, try to relate to some of the younger people in the community. Sarah Woodson, recently bereaved, counted among the latter. Hence, a few days after her husband's demise, Frost had arrived at her door, asking how she was getting on and whether he could be of any help.

Their minds had met. He had called on her many times thereafter. Their relationship had flowered, in a most platonic manner.

"Sarah, Sarah," he chided, shaking his head and making a tisking sound with his tongue. "A doctrine of female superiority? Is that what you're into now?"

"You don't have to agree. It's a free country."

"I don't *dis*agree. I wouldn't dare!"

They both laughed.

"Where's Priscilla?" he finally asked. "Still at school?"

Sarah Woodson nodded. She had passed the point now of crying when alone. Laughter came easier. Paul had helped.

"Tell you what," she said as they sat in her living room in the crisp September daylight. "Want to go for a walk?"

Paul Frost hardly had to think about it. "I'd like that," he answered.

She would like to have gone out with just a sweater and knit skirt, but the weather, though sunny, was more suggestive of the season that would follow, not the one just passed. So she flung an old tweed jacket over her shoulders and walked to the back door.

Paul Frost opened it. She kept forgetting that he was a minister. He wore street clothes, a red-and-black flannel shirt and neat khaki trousers, that made him look more like a well-scrubbed college student than what he really was—the assistant pastor of the local Presbyterian church.

"Sure you won't be cold?" she asked.

He shook his head.

"Men are never cold," she observed profoundly.

They walked across the back lawn, she with her arms folded, he with his hands in his pockets. The sky was flawlessly blue. He made a comment on the beauty of the afternoon. She stole a sidelong glance at him and was struck by how young he looked. His face bore a fresh youthfulness. He was light-skinned, with something of an Anglo-Scottish complexion, and his blond hair had slight waves to it. His jaw was firm, his shoulders square.

"Over there," she said, raising a gold-braceleted wrist to point. She indicated a path into the woods. "That's the starting point. All the trails begin and end there."

She was aware again that she hadn't followed it since her husband died. Today she would break the spell. Today it was surprisingly easy.

The leaves crinkled beneath their feet. He followed her along the trail, certain that she used to take it with her husband.

"You're looking well and acting well," he said, glancing her way. "I'm very glad, Sarah."

She shrugged ever so slightly. "You think it's the end of the world when it happens. But it's not. You were right that first day we talked. The world does continue."

"And financially?" He asked the question gingerly, confident that he knew her well enough after the last few weeks.

"I'll manage. We—Priscilla and I—we should get by, with a little cutting here and there. I may go back to work." She thought for a moment. "Brian's company has been very good to us. They've helped."

"ITW, is it?"

"Yes," she said. "I guess somewhere out there a few of these big corporations have a heart after all."

"I guess they liked him," Frost said.

"They?"

"His company."

She nodded. "He worked hard. Too hard probably.
53

Who knows?" She sighed, shaking her head. "Maybe it was some problem at work that had him so upset—"

"Which way?" he asked.

She looked up. They were at a fork. Before she could choose, he asked, "Do I hear a stream?"

"There's one down that way."

"I'd love to see it."

"You're my guest, Paul."

They took a narrow path between a row of oaks and maples, kicking through leaves and twigs as they went. The distant gurgling of a brook grew more audible.

"Know what they used to do?" she asked. "ITW?"

"What?"

"It's a big company, you know. Gigantic. Sixty-eight thousand employees nationwide. When they had a particular problem in engineering or computer operations, something which didn't make sense to the engineers immediately involved, they would send out a memo on it. To everyone. 'Open problems,' they were called."

"Sorry," he said. "I don't quite follow."

"Everyone in the company received a memorandum on the problem," she explained. "From the top executives to people in the mailroom. Anyone was free to offer suggestions. Naturally, if anybody offered the right suggestion to solving the problem, he or she was rewarded, either by promotion or outright bonus. That way they had sixty-eight thousand brains concentrating on the same problem. Clever, isn't it? See that?" she motioned. "A snapping turtle."

They were beside the brook. She chose a comfortable large rock to sit on, sweeping her woolen skirt beneath her. She indicated a thumb-sized turtle head in the water, moving slightly as the flippers paddled beneath the surface, water rippling in its wake.

"You've got good eyes. I would have missed it," he said. "How do you know it's a snapping turtle?"

"Brian told me. He recognized them all. The snappers drove out the other turtles. A bit larger and tougher."

He sat down on the fallen trunk of a large tree. Birds chattered overhead, distressed by their presence. The turtle chose the moment to duck its head under water and disappear.

"Did your husband ever tackle any of them?" Paul Frost asked.

Excuse me?" She looked from the stream to him, as if a trance had been broken.

"Those, uh, riddles that the company sent around? Did Brian try them?" As he spoke, she looked away again.

"You know Brian," she said, almost with a smile. "Or maybe you didn't. Always working on open problems—constantly. Right up until the end. Spent too much of his time on things like that, probably."

A moment passed.

"It's still difficult," he said, very deliberately. "Isn't it?" Her eyes rose to his. "Becoming adjusted, I mean."

"Of course," she said, almost without emotion. "You spend so much of your life with a man. Then he's gone. Under so strange a set of circumstances. . . ." She shrugged.

She looked at Paul Frost appraisingly. He was about eight years younger than she, Sarah estimated. She wondered in passing if they looked it, whether the two of them, appearing together, would strike the onlooker as a man in his twenties with a woman who's older. Or, she pondered, did they look like a couple—a *young* couple?

"I think my husband had an affair once." The words slipped from her mouth almost as if she hadn't realized what she was saying.

He turned toward her.

"I don't know why I said that," she murmured. "I'm sorry."

"Obviously you've been thinking about it." There was a long pause and then he asked. "Was it recent?"

"No. Not recent at all. Maybe about three years after we were married. I'm not sure who she was. I'm not sure I knew her. Someone he met through business, I think. I don't know. I was guessing at the time."

He seemed uneasy. "How did you. . . . What made you think . . . ?"

A wife has a way of knowing," she said. "You can feel it. He was away a lot, working late frequently. Didn't seem as affectionate as before we were married, or as he was later in our marriage. It bothered me at the time. Made me feel, somehow, cheapened—compromised. Does that sound silly?"

"No," he answered, sensing that that was the response she wanted. "It was an intrusion into your marriage. Your reaction is understandable."

"After a while I forgot about it. Maybe I had imagined

the whole thing. But it seemed to end, at least in my mind. Gradually the whole concept, of his being untrue, faded. I forgot about it until just recently."

"Should I ask why?"

She thought about it before she answered. "Because it was one of the two things he did in all the time we were married that I could never understand. Only those two things in all those years. The other . . ."

"Was his suicide."

She nodded. She tried to smile, but there was an edge of melancholia to her voice, as if being in these woods, where she had come so many times with Brian, had precipitated her mood.

"I guess deep down I'm still a little confused. Time," she said. "All I need is more time."

She looked at Paul Frost critically. Her mood seemed to snap, to change instantaneously, as if she was suddenly aware that she'd talked too much, revealed too much.

"Hey" she said. "Why am I telling *you* all this? You're younger than I. And never been married, right?"

"Correct."

"Ever come close, Paul?"

"No."

She was pensive for a moment and they both turned toward the sound of a pair of squirrels chasing through the oak branches above them.

"Can I ask you something that's none of my business?" she said.

"Shoot."

"Why'd you become a minister?"

"Silly question," he said. "Divinity school is much easier to get into than law school."

She looked at him quizzically, then broke up laughing, realizing that he was kidding. "If you weren't a minister, I'd curse at you!"

"Curse if you like. I know what all the words mean."

In fun, she raised a fist as if to strike him. She was aware that he was handsome, indeed, far more attractive than a young minister had any right to be.

"So that the church doesn't have to finance a new set of teeth, I'll answer your question."

"Please."

"A matter of faith," he said, picking up a stick. "I've

56

always had a curiosity about things, basic things—meanings, explanations. In high school I started to read philosophy. From there I moved on to theology. All the while, to tell you the truth, I thought I'd become a lawyer."

"Why a lawyer?"

"Why not?" Paul shrugged. He prodded an acorn with the stick. "I was interested in civil liberties, poverty work. You know, all that 1960s crusading stuff. I figured law was the best means."

She nodded, listening intently.

"Confession time," he said. "I even applied to law school. Got accepted to four out of eight places. Pretty good batting average."

"Why didn't you go? To law school, I mean."

"I did."

She appeared surprised.

"For six weeks," he said. "University of Wisconsin. Long enough to know that it wasn't for me. You see, I had spent most of my free time, in high school and college, reading philosophy and theology. I missed it. Law school was all torts and cases and principles." He made a silly, distasteful face and laughed. "A lot of bull."

"So you quit?"

"I left." He tossed the stick aside. "I don't really think of it as quitting. Finished six weeks of the first term and had a three-day break while exams were being corrected. Went back to my apartment and collapsed from fatigue. Woke up ten hours later and picked up a book I'd been trying to get to for eight weeks. A humanistic interpretation of the Letters of Paul. That's when I knew. I mean, that's when I really knew, Sarah. It was something I wanted to commit my life to. It's where. . . . How do I explain it? I felt at home there. I suppose it sounds like hogwash about having a calling." He hunched his shoulders. "Call it that, if you like. Later that year I applied for divinity school. I was accepted." He paused, looking at her. "And here I am, your friendly assistant pastor."

"Interesting," she said. She was struck by his total lack of material consideration. She'd never known anyone quite like him.

"It's a good life," he said. "Really, it is. My basic needs are met. I don't want anything more. I'm able to help people, albeit in a somewhat different way than I

57

would have ever expected. And I can read all the theology I want," he added with a boyish grin.

"It's very selfless."

"Not at all," he declared. "It's such a high that it's almost a *selfish* thing to do. It's gratifying to help people and relate to them on a human-to-human basis. What more could one ask for out of life than to be happy with what one's doing?"

"But, what about the real religious aspects of it?" she asked. "Frankly, my husband and I were never very religious. Not in a formal way."

"I accept God and I accept Jesus," he said simply. "Always have. Always will. In that respect, my life has been constant since day one. Of course, day one wasn't *that* long ago," he laughed, his grin broadening to lighten the conversation.

She was playing with a twig, her fingers kneading the bark, as if to examine it in detail. She was thoughtful about what he was telling her, until she was suddenly struck by how many other long and pleasant hours she had passed in this same spot, talking with her husband. She on the same flat rock, Brian on . . . well, exactly where Paul Frost was, not that he knew it. A vague sense of deception crept up on her, somewhat as if she were somewhere she shouldn't have been.

"We ought to be going," she said. "Priscilla will be home soon. She'll wonder where I am."

"The only real career choice I have to make," he said, hoisting himself to his feet, and offering her a hand to help her stand, "is where I want to go."

"Excuse me?"

"A decision," he said. "What type of parish do I want: a comfortable suburban church where the golf courses are more popular than the pews on Sunday mornings, or maybe an old church in an inner city, where I'd be more needed."

"I thought you were staying on with Pastor Booth."

"Oh, no, not at all," he said. "Which way is it? To the house, I mean? Sorry, I'm lost."

She indicated the direction.

"I'm just temporary," he said. "Helping along for a few months until Pastor Booth is back to a hundred percent. Then it'll be off to somewhere else."

"Oh," she said flatly, "I see," and wondered if her voice betrayed any emotion. She hoped that it hadn't because, above all, she didn't want him—or anyone else—to get the wrong idea.

7

The mortician's office was in Bayswater, on a side street of little note and even less style. It was nestled between a licensed turf-accountant named Liebling, a man whose venetian blinds shrouded his plate-glass window, and an Italian restaurant called Rodolpho's whose window was adorned by wine bottles in straw baskets. Mason arrived early in the morning. As he stepped from the taxi to the curb, a light drizzle was beginning. A day had passed since Lassiter's death.

He entered without knocking. The empty green-walled anteroom was bedecked with day-old flowers showing early signs of wilting. From a door opening onto a back corridor there appeared a small bespectacled man with a rodent face and a thin ring of hair crowning a balding head.

"Yes, sir?" asked the man expectantly. "May I help you?"

"I telephoned earlier about a Mr. Lassiter. My name is—"

"Mason. Mr. Mason. Of course, sir. I'm Albert Lasko."

Lasko offered his hand. Mason accepted it.

"Terrible thing, really," said Lasko. "A plunge like that. I'm very sorry." There was an uneasy pause, after which Lasko said, "How might I help you, sir?"

"I came to inquire about the body. What, uh . . . ?"

"Plans have to be made?" asked Lasko. Mason nodded. "I'm awaiting instructions, sir. What I need, ideally, is the next of kin." He looked at Bill Mason hopefully. "You knew the deceased well?"

"Fairly well."

"I noticed that Mr. Lassiter wore a wedding band."

Bill was struck by the statement. He did not think of Robert Lassiter as a husband, though a decade earlier he'd been one for five years. Odd that Bob still wore the ring of a woman who had discarded him, Bill reflected. But then, the divorce had been her idea, not Lassiter's.

"Unlucky in love, I'm afraid," Bill explained.

"Sir?"

"His wife divorced him several years back. I have no idea where she is. I know she remarried. Changed her name."

"Of course," Lasko nodded with disappointment. His expression changed as if he'd suddenly thought of something. "Sir, did you wish to view——?"

Mason was shaking his head. "I merely wanted to know what arrangements might have been made. And by whom."

"Ah, I see. The truth is we're awaiting instructions."

Lasko nervously removed his glasses as he spoke. He wiped the round lenses with his necktie, thumb and forefinger, then tucked the tie back into his belt.

"Waiting to locate a relative, I should think. Meanwhile, it's taken care of."

"Taken care of?"

"Well, yes," replied Lasko making it sound obvious. "His company, the one he worked for."

"What about them?"

"They've made the appropriate arrangements. Tobacco concern, I believe they are. Paid in advance. Mr. Lassiter's remains may stay here for sixty days, pending notification of the family. When a relative is found, further instructions will be acted upon." He paused, then said, "You know, sir, a London interment could be arranged. I know of——"

"No, London wouldn't do. I think Mr. Lassiter would have wanted to return to the United States."

"Oh, yes. Of course. I see. I keep forgetting. He was American, your friend."

"They told you, didn't they? The company?"

Lasko smiled. "They didn't need to. I knew. Odd though, when we get Americans here—we do occasionally, motor accidents and such, you know—they are normally recognizable immediately by their clothes. I suppose your friend had worked over here for a while. English clothing, down to the underwear, shoes, and socks. Most foreigners stick to their former dress habits. But not your friend. Not on his final day on earth."

"Then how did you know he was American?"

"The mouth, sir," he elucidated. "Not accent, of

61

course. Are you feeling strong? I'd like to show you some-thing."

"Please do."

Lasko turned and led Mason through a dimly lit cor-ridor to an adjoining room which was considerably damper and colder. It was a clinical room with a coffin-sized ex-amining table in the middle, no windows, stark overhead lights and a cold storage vault occupying all of one wall.

Lasko looked at the vault pensively, as if to wonder where he'd put something. He opened one drawer, then shut it. "Mouth. Teeth," he said. Then he opened the drawer he actually wanted and said, "Ah."

Lasko's back was to Mason. There was a considerable sprinkling of dandruff across the Englishman's shoulders.

"Teeth," Lasko proclaimed proudly.

"What?"

Lasko was opening a small case the size of a pack of cigarettes. "Teeth," he repeated. "A mouth tells you a great deal, sir. Dental work differs from nation to nation." Lasko turned over the box into his hand and presented three of Robert Lassiter's molars: left side upper. "Knocked out when he hit the sidewalk," said Lasko with sympathy. "Cut off at the base, as you can see. Notice the filling. American silver. Lighter than English, higher silver content than the continent. Not bad dental work, though. Good dentist. The mouth had a very American look to it." There was a pause. "Western United States, maybe," he said. "Right? Maybe California. Right?"

He looked at Mason expectantly.

"I wouldn't know."

"Sir?"

"He traveled a lot. I don't know what dentist he might have used."

Lasko sighed, his game spoiled. He dejectedly placed the teeth back in the box. He was refiling it when he spoke again.

"What are we to do, sir?" he asked. "With your friend, I mean?" He raised a finger to his lips. "He's right here, you know."

Lasko reverently patted a larger drawer of the vault and indicated the number five. "If only we had a relative. The man's personnel records at the tobacco company were incomplete. Tragically." Lasko shook his head. His small dark eyes seemed genuinely sad. "Bloody bureaucracy," he said. "Have to fill in forms before you can even breathe in England these days." From somewhere he produced a legal-sized document which Mason saw had Robert Lassiter's name at its head, next to the printed words, FULL NAME OF DECEASED.

Bill Mason looked at the antiseptic steel casing which formed Drawer Five, the penultimate resting place of a middle-aged self-doubting spy named Robert Lassiter. So this is what it had come to for Lazz. A boy from a good family. The best private schools, a go at teaching, then recruitment into career patriotism. A failed marriage to a woman he probably still loved. A career that crashed before his eyes. Now he was reduced to a mass of flesh and bones reposing in a yellow body bag in a second-rate mortuary in London. This, thought Mason, would never do.

Somewhere rain was hitting a window. The building was otherwise still.

"Sir?" Lasko asked, breaking the silence.

Poor old Lazz, Mason caught himself thinking for the first time in his life. He turned toward the mortician. "Maybe we could speed things along?" he suggested.

Lasko frowned, not quite understanding. "Which is to say . . . ?"

Mason motioned toward the form in Lasko's hand, toward the blank space beside the deceased's name where it said NEAREST RELATIVE. "Do you have a pen?" Lasko nodded. "Then start writing."

Hesitantly Lasko uncapped a fountain pen and leaned on his examining table.

"Nearest relative," said Bill, as if dictating a letter. "William Mason. New—"

Lasko was not writing. "Sir?" he asked plaintively, as if to question the suggestion. "Sir, really . . . ?"

"I think it might be easier for everyone," Mason said. "Much easier."

Lasko drew a deep breath. He began to write. M-A-S-O-N," he spelled out and asked, "Address?"

Mason groped for one. "New Jersey," he said. "Delwood, New Jersey. Care of Robertson, Beachside Road." He thought for a moment. "Make it F. O. Robertson."

Lasko wrote obediently. Within a few moments it was finished.

"Now, sir, the arrangements for shipping the body to America—?"

"Instructions to follow."

Lasko looked at him with utter incomprehension.

"You said the company would pay for sixty days," said Mason. "My stepbrother has fifty-nine of them remaining. Right?"

"Correct, sir," Lasko said. There was an expression of sad tolerance on his face.

"I'll tend to it as soon as humanly possible," said Mason. "Well within your sixty days. Don't worry."

"Yes," said Lasko, who no longer looked Bill in the eye. He methodically completed the form as best he could. Then he reversed the paper on the counter and asked Mason to sign it.

Mason scrawled a signature in the appropriate space. His overwhelming urge was simply to leave. When he raised his eyes again and set down the pen, Lasko was looking away, contemplating the end of the vault, searching perhaps for a more isolated drawer in which Lassiter could be his guest for the next few weeks.

No further words were spoken. Moments later Bill Mason passed through the front door and out into the rain. There were no taxis.

He held his coat close to him, wished he'd had a hat, and had ventured half a block when he heard a voice calling from behind him.

He turned. It was Lasko.

The mortician had thrown on a raincoat, raised an umbrella, and was hurrying after him, calling him by name.

"Mr. Mason, Bill Mason," panted Lasko as he caught up. Lasko's glasses were wet from the rain, as was his bare forehead. "I almost let it slip my mind. Quite the unusual, and I nearly forgot."

"Forgot what?" Bill looked downward at the man and felt his head getting soaked. He saw an envelope in Lasko's hand.

"Quite the oddity," said Lasko. "You being the proclaimed stepbrother," he said with implied cynicism, "could instruct me what to do."

"About what?"

Lasko fumbled with the envelope. It was bulky and wrinkled, as if it contained some kind of mechanism or mechanical instrument. On it, in the dim light, Lassiter's handwriting was visible.

64

Bill, read the notation on the envelope. *Take this to be repaired.*

"I suppose he was going to give it to someone," Lasko suggested. "Someone named Bill . . . ?"

Mason nodded and took the envelope. "Of course," he said. "I'd forgotten." He could feel the envelope's contents—a watch.

Mason was back in Auerbach's flat. He sat in the armchair in the living room, shades drawn, holding in one hand a kitchen paring knife and in the other hand the electronic watch which Lucille Davis had given Lazz.

Mason looked at it carefully. He rapped it sharply. No, it didn't work at all. And Lazz had been so pleased with it the last time he'd seen him.

Mason turned the face of the watch upside down and held the back of it to him. He loosened some small screws. He wedged the paring blade into a crack in the casing, pried, and then blinked quickly as the casing of the watch split in half.

He caught all the pieces in his palm and could easily see that the watch's interior had been hollowed out. The empty compartment didn't afford a vast amount of space, but not that much space had been necessary. The hidden contents, six silicon chips, were not that large at all.

8

She peered through the peephole. She had never seen the man who'd just pressed her doorbell. The large blond woman reluctantly opened the door a quarter of the way. "Yes?" she asked. A checkered apron covered the wide front of her body and her right fist played with something in the apron's pocket.

"I'm looking for Dr. Davis," he said.

Lucille Davis's frame filled the partially open doorway. She was every bit as tall as the man who stood before her. He appeared to be American, seemed slightly younger than she and was not at all evil looking.

"Who wants to see Dr. Davis?" she asked, trying to decide about him.

"My name is Bill Mason," he said. "I'm a friend of —I was a friend of Bob Lassiter."

She looked at him appraisingly for another moment. The door opened wider and Bill Mason was impressed with the woman's corpulence.

"*I'm* Dr. Davis."

"You?"

"I have a brain and a vagina," she said. "They both work. Do you want to talk with me or do you want to take a hike?"

He apologized and said he wished to talk. She allowed him in.

She admitted him to an apartment which suggested a type of sustained transience. The furniture was inexpensive and worn; obviously she'd been there for a few years. The walls were white and showed long-accumulated grime; the area above doorknobs bore fingerprint smudges. The apartment's construction was as flimsy as the furnishings.

It was the appropriate interior for such a typical, new, white high-rise which, due to its lack of character, could have been anywhere in the world. By chance it was in London.

Lucille Davis's heels missed the cheap Indian carpets on the wooden floors. Her shoes were heavy against the wood. The carpets' colors clashed, unless you happened to like orange with green and purple.

The focal point of the living room was a large desk before a window at the far end. Papers and books were in a selective disarray both on the floor around the desk, and upon the desk itself. A typing table, dwarfed by a large electric typewriter, stood to one side. Despite the sunlight outside, the lights were on everywhere. An aging air conditioner hummed and rattled.

"I've met a lot of men named Bill," she said. "Never liked any of them. Sit down. Who sent you here?"

"No one," he answered, even before he was seated.

She was on the sofa, looking at him with total distrust. He sat across from her in a wicker chair which sagged when he sat in it. He had taken her favorite seat. Bill Mason was aware that her hand was still in her apron pocket.

"Are you a God-damned spook?" she asked.

"I worked with Bob."

"So who the hell didn't?" she retorted. "Sorry," she said, though clearly she wasn't, "but I think Bobby worked for a shit outfit. You can quote me."

"There's no one to quote you to."

Her large face was midway between a scowl and a grimace. "Fat chance," she muttered. "I don't like you. On principle." Her hammy fist emerged from the apron pocket that was embroidered with a small cloth caricature of a pussycat. She held a silver-handled ice pick, an instrument of many functions; it sported a five-inch spike.

"Mason, was it?" she inquired skeptically. "Your last name?"

He nodded. "I'm not carrying a weapon."

"Foolish on your part. Bob never mentioned any Mason," she said rudely. "But he didn't talk names much." She kept her grip on the ice pick. With the fingers of her free hand she toyed with the spike's fine point. "I'm a busy woman, Mr. Mason," she said. "Know what I'm doing?"

"I'd hesitate to guess."

"I'm cleaning my freezer," she said. "And between

67

cleaning my freezer and chipping ice off frozen vegetables I occasionally do some work." She indicated the desk. "Absorption of split neutrons into the U-235 isotope at macroseconds. That mean anything to you?"

"No."

"Of course not," she said. "You're a spook. Not paid to understand. Well, damn it, tell me your story, Mr. Mason. What brings you here? Be forewarned: Frightened fat ladies learn to carry ice picks when there's so much crap going down."

"I want to talk about Bob Lassiter."

"My freezer awaits me, as do my isotopes. Bob's dead. They've deep sixed him somewhere. What else can you tell me beyond that?"

"I came here to ask, not tell."

"I have no answers. Not for spooks."

"I thought you were his friend."

"*Did* you?" Her weight shifted on the sofa. She crossed her legs and the squashed pillows reacted. "Now who would tell you a thing like that?"

"Bob."

She was silent. For a moment he thought he caught something extra in her blue eyes.

"Dr. Davis, I want to know why a man goes out a sixth-floor window so unexpectedly."

She laughed mirthlessly. "Only so many reasons available," she said. "Three, in fact. You're a big boy. You know them."

"Maybe I don't."

She inclined forward. "Lesson One. Dr. Davis's Law of Gravity. Bodies outside of windows are pulled to the sidewalk below. Pulled to their death. Okay so far? Now, why are they out of windows in the first place? Three fundamental possibilities: Jumped. Fell. Or pushed." She leaned back. "Which of those do you like in Bobby's case?"

"I find all three unsettling," he said.

"Very good," she countered, "a spook who knows to avoid a direct question. I'll ask again. Did Bobby jump, fall, or was he shoved? You were his friend, you say. Maybe you can tell me."

He glanced beyond her to the kitchen; the refrigerator's freezer door was open. "I guess I owe you a brief history lesson," he said. He was about to give it when something unexpected slid against his leg.

He glanced down as a cat's bushy tail brushed his wrist. A black-and-white Angora, overstuffed like its mistress, glowered at him—slanted green eyes sunken into an indignant triangular face. His hand moved to pet the cat; the animal stalked away.

"That's Barney," she said flatly. Somehow it made the scene complete. "Settle down, Barney."

"I knew Bob since 1958," he began. "Since school. Before college. He was spending a year on the faculty. I was a student. Later we worked together."

"You were spooks together."

"China," he said. "And Southeast Asia."

"What years?" she asked, obviously checking.

"Sixty-eight to seventy-two for me. Sixty-four through seventy-one for Bob."

"Good answer. You did your homework."

He continued to talk, telling her how he'd been discharged in March of 1977: "Fifteen years of service rewarded with the bum's rush and a one-way ticket to the sidewalk." Subsequently he had been in this job and that job, including one during the summer in which he swam a lot, absorbed sun, and got tracked down by his old friend Robert Lassiter.

"Bob located me in New Jersey," he said. "I had avoided him when I got canned. But Bob pursued me, figuring I might just show my face in New York City."

"Eight million people and he just spots you like that?" she said. She whistled, mockingly. "A man of vision, I'd say."

He looked her straight in the eye.

"Years ago Bob and I made an arrangement. If we ever got in trouble and had to keep an invisible profile, we would have several meeting places, depending on the location. In New York it was Bryant Park. The time was always the same. Thursday, one fifteen P.M. Not so hard to find someone if you know where to look."

"Son of a bitch," she said. Her tone of voice started gradually to change. "So *you're* the lifeguard. Bobby mentioned a lifeguard."

"To me he mentioned a physicist."

The woman ran the heel of her hand across her fore-

69

head, wiping sweat from her dark eyebrows. "Where'd you say you were from?"

"Originally?"

She nodded, looking at him very inquisitively now.

"Medford, Massachusetts," Mason said. "Haven't been there in years."

"I'm from Arkansas, myself. Little Rock. I'll bet you can probably tell by the accent. Huh?"

Mason shrugged. He recognized the tactic. She was stalling, talking about nothing while she decided about him.

There was a lull while Lucille Davis reached to a bowl on the bamboo coffee table. She tossed an imported Frito into her mouth and munched.

"Lord, lord," she mused. "That man really left tracks, didn't he? What else did he tell you?"

"He told me he had serious problems. Fatal problems for a man in his line of work."

"Meaning?"

Bill Mason explained: Lassiter had headed a network in London concerned with Soviet counterintelligence. Lassiter had had an English liaison officer—unnamed, said Mason—and an immediate American superior who commuted back and forth between stations in London and Spain.

Lassiter had been in London since 1971, with the exception of one brief troubleshooting stint during '76. He had returned to the States to whisk to Washington a young Englishwoman he had recently recruited. But once back in London, in the autumn of that same year, Bob had received a tip from a certain American physicist conducting research in England. Subsequently Lassiter had sniffed out a rather strong and repellent scent. The definite stink of a Soviet network, operating within the academic community and beneath diplomatic cover. It seemed that a computer-systems analyst named Edward Colbourne, late of the ITW Corporation, had traveled each year from Baltimore to Mexico City to attend what were ostensibly business and engineering conferences. Unfortunately Colbourne's personal conduct had been something less than exemplary in Mexico. Something to do with a Mexican woman and her unwanted pregnancy which, since she was a practicing Catholic, developed into a Mexican-American baby.

Lucille Davis listened attentively, with the aid of another corn chip.

"At one engineering conference," said Mason, running clinically through what was almost common knowledge (meaning the newspapers had the story), "Colbourne fell into a conversation with a man who gave his name as Beckman. Beckman said he was Dutch. Beckman struck up a friendship with Colbourne, gradually angled around to proclaiming that he was a corporate recruiter in the employ of the RCA Corporation. And, as further meetings occurred, Beckman either located or created a vulnerability within Mr. Colbourne. Drawing on one motivation or another—Lassiter never discerned exactly what it was—Beckman had seduced Colbourne into passing blueprints, product designs, marketing plans, and ITW parts to him in Mexico. A fancy position with RCA was part of the original bait, naturally enough. But by the time the final delivery had been made, a set of silicon chips, Colbourne was all too aware who Beckman really was. A man named Vassiliev."

"The Russian that Bobby arrested eleven days ago," she said.

Mason nodded.

"You're telling me more than he ever did."

"He told me in New York that they took some silicon chips out of the Russian's apartment."

"They might have. Bobby never said."

He considered her response. In the kitchen, something gurgled in the defrosting refrigerator. It unnerved both of them momentarily.

The chips, he explained, had been like a Chinese puzzle. Examining the chips from different angles, one was led to different conclusions, some of them contradictory, all of them aggravating. Or, as Lassiter had asked over and over, was it all a red herring? Red in the non-political sense, Bill said. Did those damnable bits of silicon mean anything at all?

Maybe not, but consider the implications if they did. Colbourne had passed them on from ITW. What else had he passed?

The circuits were the highly sophisticated kind used in both US surface-to-air missiles as well as cruise missiles in development. Surely the Soviets had similar technology. Surely there were more sophisticated parts of each missile that the Kremlin might have liked to inspect? Why then, the fascination with blank computer circuits? The IC chips hadn't even been programmed. If they were blank, they contained no secret. They were merely memory banks which had not yet acquired a memory.

"Why would someone steal a secret which didn't even exist yet?" Bill asked rhetorically.

"Why then, indeed?" she replied.

Mason gestured helplessly. "One way or another, Lazz went out of a window as a result of this case. There's another 'why.' Failure. Did he miss something? Blow something? Was a pink slip coming and he couldn't take it? Or had he succeeded too well? Had he unearthed something and—?"

"—and somebody stopped him."

Mason rubbed his chin for a moment. "Bob was too experienced to walk into a trap with strangers. Someone he knew . . ."

"And trusted?"

Mason nodded. "Know what he told me?" he asked. "He said his network was rotting under his nose. Someone had tipped Vassiliev before the arrest. It was tearing him apart. The Russian had known Bob's move even before Bob had decided to make it. Figure that."

She thought for a moment, then ran her hand through her blond hair. There was darkness at the roots. Mason flirted with an idea. For the last few days had she let herself go? Since when? Since Bob hit the sidewalk? She looked as if she hadn't been outside for days, now that he thought about it.

She looked him squarely in the eye, as if anger was simmering.

"I'll tell you something, Mr. Mason," she said. "Bobby wasn't any quitter. He was a sticker. He wouldn't have jumped out of a window just because things had taken a bad turn."

"That leaves us with 'fell' and 'pushed,' " he said. "I knew him to be rather careful around heights. Sure-footed."

"That leaves us with 'pushed.' "

There was a long moment.

"I can't help you, Mr. Mason," she answered. "Honestly, I can't. I don't know anything."

"Maybe he might have mentioned—"

"Nothing," she said sadly. "He rarely told me anything."

"I guess you liked him," Bill Mason said, trying a new tack.

He almost admired how stubbornly she withheld any betrayal of emotion.

"I liked Bobby," she said flatly. "But I'm very clinical about my personal relationships. I have my research, Mr. Mason. I'm not a romantic."

She stood with complete self-composure and turned her back to him. He watched her amble toward the kitchen.

Her mood changed. She stood in the kitchen, looking into the freezer compartment, and made a dyspeptic face. "Thaw, damn you," she muttered with annoyance, and gripped the ice pick in a solid fist and hacked at the ice in the rear of the freezer. Mason could hear the small shards flying away.

He followed her, and stood behind her at the kitchen door.

"They ought to make one that self-defrosts," he said.

"They ought to make a lot of things."

He glanced at the kitchen counter. A few dairy items were warming: milk, butter wrapped sloppily in wax paper, and several containers of yogurt all huddled in a group near the sink. A few frozen dinners were thawing, also.

"I guess you'll miss him," Mason suggested.

"Miss him?" she said, sparing the impacted ice for a moment. "Miss Bobby? Sure. One always misses a lost friend." Her eyes were doleful for the first time. "You know, he wasn't a bad guy. Bobby had principles. You don't find that too often these days. Especially in his line of work. *Your* line of work, Mr. Mason."

Mason said nothing, knowing that a silence would serve better than a direct question.

"Not like some people," she continued slowly. She slammed the pick into the rear of the freezer. The chips of ice splintered before the powerful hands and fell in small slivers. "Success," she mumbled. She looked at what she'd done, then turned back to Mason. "Bobby had principles. Ethics. Sense of duty, sense of country. Yeah, for sure, old-fashioned ideals. The kinds of things that no one talks about much any more. Patriotism, you could call it."

She pushed a loose strand of hair back from her eyes. "Sounds like bullshit, but it's not. Bobby was a *man*. I miss having a man around." She whacked the ice again. Angrily. "Bobby and I believed in all the old-fashioned stuff," she affirmed, permitting a smile. "You an atheist, Mr. Mason?"

He shrugged.

"I believe in God," she continued. "Bobby did, too." She exhaled a deep sigh. "Yeah, of course. Sounds corny, doesn't it?"

Her attention drifted, then suddenly her round face lit up.

"Know what we used to do? Bobby and I?"

Mason waited.

"The aviary," she said.

"What?"

"Oh, listen. Bobby and I used to take long walks all over this city." She enjoyed the memory. "Sometimes we'd go arm in arm, like a couple of teen-agers. One of our favorite places—I guess, our all-time favorite place—was the London Zoo. Bobby liked the bird house."

Mason began to grin uncontrollably. Yes, it sounded right.

"I swear," she said. "The man must have liked feathers or something. We'd go into that bird house and watch our winged friends for hours. So, know what Bobby did? Started doing bird calls. Had it up to fourteen identifiable species before . . ." She looked at Mason. "Sound like the man you knew?"

"It does," Mason said.

She laughed. "Hey, do you know what a sight we must have been? Here's this man in his mid-forties, a Langley spook yet, walking arm in arm through London with his chubby, blond physicist girlfriend. Can you picture that, Mr. Mason? Imagine if the Russians were following Bobby. I'll bet the KGB is *still* trying to figure it out. Bet they've got half those birds wired now. Wired or stuffed."

"Maybe," said Mason without meaning it.

She shook her head. The expression became bittersweet to match the memory.

"What did he think of Frank Hargrove?" Mason inquired.

74

The smile was gone. She looked back to the freezer. "Who's Hargrove?"

He said nothing. She kept chipping.

"Hated his fucking guts," she snapped. "Bobby despised the man."

"Ever met him?"

"Me? Lord, no!"

"Why'd Bob hate him?"

She laid down the pick and stepped back from the freezer. It appeared finished.

"I only know what I hear," she warned. "Secondhand information. Hargrove sits in an armchair, Bobby said. Sits in his damned office and oversees virtually every network between Gibraltar and Scotland. Sends out other people to bleed, die, hide on rooftops, set up wiretaps in drain pipes, and plant microwave units in car trunks. And the 'chief' sits in his office deciding who to recommend for a layoff or who to fluff up for promotion. He doesn't know what's happening in the field, Bobby said. Never did. He's been behind a desk for fifteen years and his brain has gone soft. Hey," she said, "you have the credentials to get in his door. Why don't you go see him yourself?"

"I can't find him," Mason said. "Hargrove's difficult to locate."

"Since when?"

"Since about an hour after Bob Lassiter fell out of a window. Sorry," he said, correcting himself. As he spoke she turned fully toward him. Her eyes were bloated, and watery, resisting tears. "Sorry," he said again, a softer voice this time. "Not 'fell.' Pushed."

Mason's assertion nudged her over an emotional brink. Somewhere the dam broke and the tears were cascading down her cheeks. She hugged him for comfort. He helplessly embraced her, letting her head fall on his shoulder.

"God damn it," she blurted between sobs and gasps, "I loved that ornery son of a bitch. God knows I did. God knows!"

She was saying something else, too, something about Bobby being the only man she'd loved in her life. But her pent-up feelings had nearly turned to hysteria. She was crying uncontrollably and Mason couldn't understand her.

75

9

Sarah Woodson opened her eyes and looked at the dimly glowing face of the clock-radio beside her double bed. Three fifty A.M. She wondered why she was awake.

A noise downstairs. She lay absolutely motionless and heard it again. Absently, until she caught herself, she wanted to send Brian to see what it was. She lay there, now knowing what had awakened her, and wishing she'd heeded her sister's suggestion that she buy a dog.

Then she heard it again. A thin film of sweat was spreading over her skin. She was more awake now and she could place the noise. It was the sound of someone walking, sneaking around downstairs. Someone moving around, trying very hard not to be heard.

Oh, God! she thought, what would she do if she heard the footsteps ascending the stairs? What *could* she do? Scream? Who'd hear it, Priscilla?

Priscilla!

Sarah flung off the blanket and swung her feet onto the cold floor. She thought of throwing on the light.

No, too sudden. Might make the intruder panic.

She stood, listening so intently that she could hear herself breathing. She felt her heart increase its beat. She buttoned the top button of her nightgown, and moved to her doorway. There was a telephone in the hall.

She heard the noise again. Was it a footstep? A door? Now, listening from a different angle, she wasn't so sure. Oh, God, if only she wasn't so sleepy and tired, maybe she could make a rational judgment. She stepped softly into the hallway. She desperately wanted a bright light but was afraid to put one on.

There was a dim light in the hallway from a forty-watt bathroom bulb which remained on all night. She moved to her daughter's door and opened it.

"Priscilla?" she whispered.

Sarah squinted. She could feel the sweat through her nightgown now.

She saw Priscilla's body. The girl was in bed sleeping in her normal position, barely moving as she breathed. There were two noises downstairs, again like someone moving, or examining something.

How long would it take if the police came immediately? Fifteen minutes? Twenty? Never before in this safe, comfortable house had she known such fear. Never the stark, unrelenting fear of a violent physical attack in the darkness.

She heard the loudest noise yet. Like something softly banging something. *A hip against a table?* She moved to a position near the top of the stairs. She could see nothing. She moved another few inches toward the head of the stairs, and nearly jumped when her hand touched something.

The something rattled and moved—it was the telephone table. She picked up the receiver. She wanted to dial but didn't, retreating instead as far as the cord would allow. She held the telephone to her ear, waiting. The operator would come on the line eventually.

She heard the noise again. *Oh, God, hurry! Hurry!* She expected to hear a creak on the stairs.

Something clicked on the other end of the telephone. "Operator."

"Operator, please," she whispered, bunching up part of her nightgown and trying to muffle her voice. "My name is Sarah Woodson. I'm a single woman in a house. There's an intruder. Downstairs. Please, call the police and—"

"I'm sorry, madam. I can't hear you."

Sarah was on the verge of panic.

As she repeated her words, she heard another noise, in a different downstairs section this time. The operator clicked off. Sarah had no idea whether the message had gotten through or whether she'd been dismissed as a crank.

If only someone were here with her. If only Brian were. . . . Paul, she thought. Paul Frost. Oh, Jesus, why not? He lived closer than the police. She didn't know what he'd be able to do, but he'd do something. He was a man, after all. Maybe even the mere presence or arrival of another man would—

She groped for the telephone again. What was his number? She thought. Her fingers began to fidget with the dial. She dialed four numbers, letting the dial slip back silently each time.

She thought her heart was going to stop. A door opened behind her and she heard a human voice.

"Mother?"

She pressed down the telephone and whirled.

"Mother what—?"

"Priscilla!" she hissed.

The girl was awake, not understanding, and reaching for the hall light. She flicked it on.

"Mother, what are you doing?"

In a near frenzy, Sarah rushed for her daughter, eyes wide with fear. She pushed a hand over the girl's mouth.

Mother and daughter, eye to eye. Priscilla with no understanding of what was happening, Sarah trying to point and indicate that something—someone—was downstairs. But the hall light was on. And whoever had been down there would have seen it and heard Priscilla's voice. Sarah turned toward the stairway expectantly, waiting to hear the first footstep.

None came.

Priscilla looked at her mother with puzzled, slightly fearful eyes. Sara mouthed the word *listen*. They stood perfectly motionless. Seconds passed. Sarah's courage rallied. It was as if she had imagined the whole thing. And yet she was sure she hadn't.

Beneath the hallway table was her sewing basket. She took from it a pair of shears.

Priscilla shook her head. "Mother, I don't hear anything," she whispered.

"Wait here. If you hear a struggle hide."

"Mother." She was growing more frightened now. "Don't go down."

But Sarah was already on the stairs, each step creaking. She turned the stairway corner half expecting to see a man waiting.

She reached the bottom of the stairway. Nothing. Her hand groped for the light switch. She threw it on, illuminating the entire living room. Her eyes swept across the room, her hand forming a sweating fist around the shears.

Nothing. No one.

Not a sound.

She took another step.

She heard a click and froze. She looked toward it.

The front door was slightly open. The screen door on the other side was locked, presumably, but a draft was sweeping through the living room. It caused the door to move an inch or two, according to the currents of air, and tap—or bang—against the door frame.

A window on the other side of the room was open half an inch. Sarah remembered having opened it. Its drawn shade was clicking. A current of air blew in through the slightly open door and out the window.

All this a draft? she wondered.

With more confidence she walked to the darkened kitchen and turned on the light.

Nothing again.

She went from room to room, even opening closets, satisfying herself that nothing had been touched, that no one was there, that everything was in order.

The basement, she thought.

She opened the door, turned on the light and peered down. Then she inspected it herself, shears in hand. Nothing. No one.

When Sarah came back upstairs, Priscilla, in a bathrobe now, was standing in the living room.

"What is it?" the girl asked.

"My imagination. I guess," Sarah answered. She exhaled. Sure enough, the screen door was locked from the inside and, evidently, the latch on the main door had failed to catch. "Have to have that fixed," she said. "This time, really. I must."

"Mother, did you think someone was down here?"

"I didn't know what I thought."

"Silly," said Priscilla, with the mild contempt that only a child can show for a parent. "Who'd come and rob *us?*"

"I don't know."

Sarah checked the screen door's lock to her satisfaction and turned on the outside light only to find a vacant green lawn. Then she closed the latch and pressed it firmly now. Her nerves were uncoiling. Her eyes felt tired.

"All this for nothing," Priscilla said. "Moth-*ther!*" she scoffed. "Sometimes, I wonder. I have a test tomorrow."

"Let's both get some sleep," Sarah said, and wrapped her arm around her daughter and walked her to the stairs.

79

She had just turned off the stairway light when Priscilla, looking over her shoulder, said excitedly, "Mother! A car!"

Sarah whirled, her heart jumping. She saw the lights unmistakably, as the car pulled into the driveway. And it wasn't a normal car. There was enough moonlight for mother and daughter to see the upper contours of the vehicle, and its odd attachment on the roof.

"The police," Priscilla said.

They were responding to the message passed on by the operator. Sarah met them at the door and asked them in. They were two wide-shouldered town cops. She was frankly glad they had come. She apologized profusely, explained that there were just the two of them, she and her daughter living alone, and that she had been awakened by a noise downstairs. Well, she'd jumped to conclusions. Nothing but a faulty doorway. She would have it fixed and not bother them again.

Once convinced that there was no real trouble in the household, the police told her to forget it. It had been little trouble for them to come. If ever in doubt, call.

She thanked them and they left.

Ten minutes later she clicked out her night table light, lay perfectly motionless and, against her will, listened.

She heard nothing but crickets. Priscilla slept safely in her own bedroom.

Her eyes became used to the darkness again. Against her will, she was listening. Her eyes refused to close.

Funny thing, she thought. That door. She was sure she *had* locked it. In fact . . . she now recalled . . . she had. She'd pressed it securely and had been satisfied that it had locked. At ten thirty, just before going to bed.

She sat up suddenly because now she knew she *had* heard something.

She threw off the sheets and walked downstairs again, more boldly this time, as she was certain the house was empty. She moved through the dark rooms easily, knowing where everything was and not hitting anything. She walked to the back door.

She waited for a moment, then switched on the outside floodlight over the garage, the one she and Brian used to catch the raccoons in the garbage cans.

She looked quickly across the back lawn and her eye went to a movement. It was distant, back maybe fifty yards among the trees and woods. But it had been unmistakable. The figure of a man in dark clothing ducking down into the brush. She'd seen it. Or hadn't she? Were the tired eyes playing tricks?

For ten full seconds she watched the spot. Nothing.

Then she moved quickly to the den and opened a closet which had been closed since Brian had died. She pushed her arm through a row of his old coats and reached to a twenty-two calibre target rifle he had kept, one which he'd taught her to use.

She loaded it—six bullets—and walked back to the living room, the image of a frontier wife.

She watched the spot where she had seen the man. She watched it for several long minutes and flirted with an idea of firing a few shots at it in random fashion. Had it not been for Priscilla, she might have.

Instead she sat down in a chair in the living room, a place where she could see both front and back doors. She laid the rifle over her lap.

For as long as she could, she stayed awake, two hours at least, nodding several times, and actually sleeping ten minutes here and there at a stretch.

It was a smokey pub in the east end of London, the type of semi-respectable place where workers and blue-collar family men stop for a few hours on the way home, then stay for a few more.

Mason, displeased with both the locale and the dirty-fingernailed ambiance, stood at the far end of the bar, his foot against an aging wooden rail, while a noisy group of workingmen argued coarsely at the other end.

Mason felt considerably out of place. He knew Auerbach had planned it that way. The Englishman, by way of Budapest, was no one's fool, certainly not Mason's, and was obviously a man adept at all sorts of ploys, particularly the psychological ones. A kid from the northern London slums, Auerbach had invited Mason, the product of genteel Massachusetts breeding, to meet him here. Mason knew the game. If there was any advantage to be had, Auerbach wanted Mason not to have it. Better to recall to Mason's mind who was employing whom. And why.

"The little runt," Mason grumbled. And almost on cue, at fifteen past eight, Auerbach walked in. Mason sipped from a shot glass. He considered what fun it would be someday, when this was finished, to break Auerbach's nose. There'd been a time when British Secret Service seemed stodgy and stuffy with "old boys" from the damned "network." Now Mason wondered with whom he'd rather be dealing. The "old boys" were at least predictable. A man knew where he stood.

Mason watched Auerbach.

The younger man crossed the room, hesitating only to place a passing hand on the shoulder of a bull-necked laborer at the end of the bar, a man who must have been the age of Auerbach's father, though Mason was only guessing.

The touch elicited a grin from the man, tweed-capped and with a face faintly resembling a bulky bag of groceries.

"Davey, boy! How's me young lud? Still working with British Railways?"

"It's a living, Peter."

"Trains is worse than ever, Davey."

Auerbach shrugged. "How's your Bess?"

The man made a sour expression and his friends laughed grandly.

" 'Asn't spoken to 'im in a week, she ain't," said the shortest in the bunch.

"Spoken or nothing else wid 'er mout'," added another. There was a chorus of male laughter from all but the last speaker, who, having hardly finished, received Peter's rejoinder: a full-force elbow in the ribs.

Auerbach moved to the end of the bar, joining Mason.

"Solidarity with the proletariat," sneered Mason. "How quaint. You're a thorough phoney, you know that?"

"Of course, I know it," said Auerbach. "But *they* don't know it. That's all that matters. What are you drinking?"

"Irish whiskey."

"In *here?*" Auerbach rolled his eyes slightly. "I didn't know they stocked it."

"They do."

"I'm surprised."

"I told them I knew you. Do we have anything to talk about?"

"Did you claim your friend's remains from that pederast mortician? Lasko, is it?"

"I saw him."

"And the body?"

82

"Resting comfortably."

"Good. Finish your liquor. We're taking a ride."

"To where?"

Auerbach had the annoying habit of facing away when asked a direct question. He would also pause for several seconds sometimes before giving even the most routine answers. But surprisingly Auerbach turned squarely back toward Bill and replied with candor, and with what might have been taken for affability.

"Remember, old man, I said it was the slow season? Defectors," he explained in a low voice. "I lied. Got one fresh. Alive and hot. Has a story to tell that will have your hair crawling. I don't suppose you'd be interested."

"Where is he?"

"Sorry." Auerbach smiled.

"For God's sake. What I am going to do? Send up a smoke signal from here?"

"We're keeping him out of the city. Out in the sticks, if you will. To tell you the truth," he added slowly, "we don't really want the pushy Yanks to know we have him. Not yet."

"So why do you trust me?"

Auerbach smiled. "You'll see. Coming? Finish your bloody liquor. It'll be late when we get there."

10

Strange about Auerbach's foot.

Auerbach's right foot had appeared perfectly normal when used for such activities as walking. Once inside Auerbach's car, however, a deep green Triumph Dolomite, the right foot turned, as it touched the accelerator, to concrete. God had blessed Mason with the fastest chauffeur on the eastern shores of the Atlantic. Not that he appreciated it.

Auerbach, silent at the wheel as they boarded the motorway leading west from London, seemed bent on defying all laws of time and distance. He drove at an insane speed, particularly on the M4 once past Windsor, and served as an acute embarrassment to the Jaguars and TR-7's which he overtook. Auerbach, in fact, appeared to take great glee in roaring up behind expensive touring cars, flashing his lights madly, then passing. A societal vendetta, Mason assumed. If there was such an animal as a safe reckless driver, Auerbach was it.

Mason sat on the left side of the front seat, a Britishism to which he'd never grown accustomed. He braced himself with a foot against the floorboards. Not that it would do any good at a moment of impact.

Mason finally spoke. "Hungary was it?"

"Hungary what?"

"Where you were from."

"Yes. Why?"

"Thought it might have been Belgium, that's all," said Mason. Belgium, or somewhere in Massachusetts, he mused.

"What's that mean?"

"It means you're not driving, you're flying low. Where are we going, Auerbach? Are you trying to get us to Ireland by midnight?"

"I didn't know you were a humorist."

"I didn't know you were a maniac. Now, what's the mystery? Where have you got your God-damned defector? Where are we going?"

"Outskirts of Bath, old man. Hope you like Georgian architecture."

Mason frowned. He looked at Auerbach whose slightly sinister eyes, fortunately, never swerved from the motorway.

"What have you got? A Russian?"

"An East German, not that it makes a difference."

"Why Bath?"

"Why *not* Bath? Who'd look for him there? It's ridiculous, I admit." His eyes squinted slightly. "I keep track of my quarries, Mason. Very close track."

Auerbach tightened his death grip on the steering wheel. Then Bill felt the car give an extra lurch and, incredibly, the concrete foot was flat on the floorboards. They accelerated. They were doing one hundred.

Half an hour down the motorway the dark English countryside was still flying by and they were rocketing in and out of occasional pockets of mist. Auerbach addressed Mason very lucidly.

"Tell me, old man," he said, "ever give any thought to going over to the other side?"

Mason turned his head slowly and regarded the man at the wheel. Auerbach's eyes were riveted straight ahead. In the back of Bill Mason's mind, the image seemed a perfect metaphor of Auerbach: eyes straight upon the destination, traveling too fast in the meantime.

"What the hell does that mean?"

"Defecting yourself," said Auerbach. "Going onto the other side's payroll." When no response came immediately, he expanded, as if it weren't already clear: "Surely you must have a certain bitterness toward your former employer."

Bill spoke each syllable evenly and with precision, obviously insulted: "It never crossed my mind."

"Just asking."

Another twenty minutes of tense quiet passed. Then Mason tartly muttered, "You're a crazy bastard, Auerbach." After the British secret service agent had chuckled appreciatively, they spent the remainder of their journey in a chilly silence.

Auerbach took two wrong turns within the city of

Bath and lost about a quarter hour correcting his mistake. Mason suspected that the mistake was intentional, making it much harder for him to remember where they'd been. They'd passed the Royal Crescent twice, going the same direction each time, but it was much too dark by that hour—pressing eleven—to admire Georgian architecture. Or for that matter, any architecture at all.

Within twenty minutes they arrived, as promised, somewhere on the far outskirts of Bath. Mason guessed that they'd gone through the city to reach the other side of it.

When the car finally stopped, they were in front of a dilapidated house which, unlike its neighbors, had every shade drawn and every light on. There was a short driveway into which Auerbach pulled. He led Mason to the doorway, knocked three times, then three more, then twice.

"Three, three, and two, huh?" Mason noted aloud.

"It means I'm selling brushes door to door. Cheer up, Mason. You'll like this, actually."

"So far I've loved it. I enjoy having my life imperiled needlessly."

Auerbach responded with a forced grin. The door opened abruptly. A huge hulk of a man eclipsed the doorway. He answered to the name of Louis.

Louis was white-shirted and dark-haired. He wore his shirt open two buttons below his neck to reveal a garden of chest hair and he wore cheap black-and-red-checked pants which looked as if they'd never encountered a hot iron. He was the largest man Mason had seen in England. Six five, probably, and wide.

Louis glanced quickly at Mason and Auerbach, whom he dwarfed, then looked back to Mason. Louis wore a brown shoulder holster which, since it carried hardware, was viewed by Mason as being more than ornamental. It reminded him that he had no sidearm himself. It doubly reminded him that probably he had been crazy to come here.

Louis mumbled and permitted them entry.

"We can start any time," Auerbach announced, crisply indicating that he was in charge. "Where's the Hun?"

"He was sleeping," Louis replied as they walked single file through the foyer and into the house.

"Get him."

Auerbach flopped on a tattered sofa in the living

room. He made himself comfortable by hoisting one of his feet onto the coffee table in front of him. His shoes were muddy. Mason chose a lone corner chair across from Auerbach.

Auerbach produced a bottle of Scotch from the floor beside the sofa, poured himself two fingers' worth in a glass, and offered the same to Mason, who accepted.

A second man appeared, obviously Louis's companion and fellow sentry. He, too, had clearly not been chosen for his ectomorphic build. He responded to the name of Edgar and his knuckles barely missed scraping the floor.

Then there were footsteps on the stairway. Louis was leading a man downstairs. Louis introduced him simply as Rudolf and took up a vigil outside on the front steps, accompanied only by a box of cigars and a bottle of liquor. He was told to sit there until summoned, while Edgar disappeared toward the rear of the house.

Mason recognized the arrangement: another of Auerbach's private undertakings. The German was his. Louis and Edgar were, also. Babysitters, keeping the Hun warm until Auerbach had decided what to do with him.

"Comfortable?" Auerbach asked. "I want my guests to be comfortable."

"Come on, Auerbach. Get on with it."

Auerbach grinned slightly. Mason was sorry that he had said anything. Auerbach had him on edge, exactly where he wanted him, and Mason had confirmed it.

Mason felt a spark of resentment flash inside him and might have retorted sharply, even in front of the German, had the Englishman not kept talking. Somehow Auerbach sensed moods and weaknesses. He knew just how far each man could be pushed—foe or friend.

Auerbach ran through the rules of this particular game:

"You know how it works, Mason," he said, suddenly very serious. "We've debriefed the man thoroughly and in the most exacting detail. We've taken him over his career several dozen times, from the moment he was recruited to the moment he defected. We like to think we know as much about this man as he knows about himself." That self-serving smile appeared again, and he added, "Maybe more."

"Sodium pentothal?" asked Mason.

"Yes," said Auerbach with disinterest, "and, if you're impressed by such things, a polygraph test also. Covered all the usual ground. Trust me."

Mason hunched his shoulders in acquiescence. No use challenging Auerbach on the point. Auerbach had a story that he was dusting off. Mason might just as well get on with hearing it.

Mason glanced at the German.

Rudolf didn't look like what defectors should look like. He didn't appear frightened or shaken. Only tired. Nor was he a gray bureaucrat who had filched a bunch of documents, microfilmed them, stuffed them into a valise, and taken off for the border. Rudolf was a young man who had probably not yet seen thirty candles on his birthday cake. He was handsome, in a working-class manner, with large bones and blond hair. He looked as if he might have been a ditch digger who had cleaned up his act and become a bouncer in a fancy Munich night-club. Mason studied him for a moment and perceived a slightly witless look through the eyes.

Maybe it was boredom. Mason knew what the man had been through over the past few days. Or weeks. Rudy, Bill thought, looked distantly like former President Ford.

Inevitably Auerbach, being a debriefing specialist, would have taken him over the tiniest details of the man's life, twenty times, maybe thirty, working on him hours at a stretch, waiting for a slip. He would have worked the story frontwards, backwards, both ways from the middle, helter-skelter, and scatter shot, inquiring how the man was recruited and trained, where, why, by whom, and when. Rudolf would have had to regurgitate all the answers, the important ones and the unimportant ones as well. Field assignments, tradecrafts, projects, collaborators, bankers, safe houses, mobile drops, spotters, cut-outs, stables, commanders, case officers, locations. For fun, if there was such a thing, Auerbach would have asked him such questions as eating habits in locations Rudolf had claimed to have been, methods of financial support, names and sexual preferences of secretaries and office hands. It was, spiritually speaking, like an X ray, an exploratory operation, and an enema all combined, except it was worse. For Rudolf, not for Auerbach.

"Just out of curiosity, Auerbach," Mason asked, "Where'd you get him?"

"I bought him." Auerbach cracked his fingers.

"Money, huh?"

"Does he look like a pro-West intellectual to you?" Auerbach sneered, as Rudolf watched and listened. "He likes blue jeans, cars, television sets, and western women who take the pill. Materialistic subversion, you could call it. A man of limited intellect, though he's done his homework learning English. No political interest whatsoever, but a fine, fine memory." Again, the smile. Auerbach spoke freely in front of Rudolf. "Somewhat patriotic, though. Wouldn't take pounds, wouldn't take dollars. Wanted West German marks." He raised his eyebrows.

"So he's a closet economist. Let's get on with it."

Mason glanced at his watch and was horrified to see it was five minutes past midnight. He had an incipient headache and Auerbach kept jabbering.

"The debriefing took place over fifteen days," said Auerbach to Mason. He chose his words carefully now. "Twenty-four August through seven September. Significance?"

"The days immediately before Lazz died."

"You're learning." Auerbach's tone had changed quite abruptly. He was a cold professional. The jibes were gone, as were the attempts to gain petty advantages. His voice was clipped, his eyes slanted and intent. His mood was analytical. He'd taken on the air of a private tutor.

"We're going to cover a small part of what Rudolf was kind enough to tell us. It bears upon you, Mason, and it bears upon your late friend. We came upon it somewhat by accident, but now that we have it, well, you know how these things are. It suddenly fits. I'm ready."

Mason nodded. He took a sip of Scotch. Rudolf drew a breath, preparing to unravel whatever he had to say.

"Let's hear it," urged Auerbach. For the first time that evening, Mason was in accord with his new employer.

11

As stories went, it was pretty much of a three-fisted one. Mason listened with a mixture of fascination and contempt, wondering how many of his own counterparts, men like Rudolf, had spilled out their own guts for the other side. Selling out for money. If only people acted for philosophical reasons, he reflected. Life would be so much less complicated.

"Rudy have long memory," Rudolf announced as a benediction, indicating by his use of third person that he would be a character in his own story. "Rudy remember."

You wouldn't be here if you didn't, Mason agonized silently. Talk, damn you, talk.

"Start with a bit of background," said Auerbach.

Rudolf nodded, a quick obedient forward jerk of the head. The blond hair was a little out of place now and, as he began his monologue, he swept a forelock from his eyes and thick brow. He leaned forward slightly so that he was only about four feet away from Mason. Mason smelled the halitosis from there, and eased back in his own chair. It was going to be that type of evening, Bill thought.

"Background," Rudolf proclaimed flatly.

The German began. Mason feared he would be listening to a life history before the defector approached anything of lasting interest.

Rudolf, twenty-six, had not been anyone's idea of the ideal Aryan youth. The illegitimate son of a coal miner's wife, but not of the coal miner, he'd been raised by a poor mother as the youngest of five children. There'd been no father in the house. When he was nine, the mother had deserted the family, and Rudolf had been placed in a state-supported foundling home with one hundred other children. It had been all downhill from there.

Rudolf spent his early adolescence in and out of

90

trouble with the foundling home, then graduated to trouble with the police. Neighbors learned to cross the street when they saw him coming. Little wonder. At sixteen he was in a reformatory for setting a dog on fire. At seventeen he was in jail for repeated public drunkenness. At eighteen he was in for petty robbery coupled with not-so-petty cracking open of a magistrate's skull. Worse, he seemed pleased with himself and all the attention heaped upon him. His picture had even been in the newspaper.

Someone suggested that army discipline might do wonders for him. Hence, within a week of his next release from prison, he found himself drafted into the East German People's Army. Surprisingly, Rudolf *did* respond to discipline, or at least was cowed by it for a few years. When the time came to reenlist, he reenlisted. He now had a clean, in fact *good* military record. Another two years passed and he applied for special duties, not even knowing what that meant. It merely sounded good. He was becoming restless.

As it happened, the East German Army had places available for heavy-hitting types who followed orders and didn't complicate matters by thinking too much. Rudolf filled the bill. He received special training as a military policeman, then as a military guard. Excelling and enjoying himself for the first time in his life, he was subsequently trained as a Consulate guard.

When an opening came for two guards at the East German Consulate in Geneva, a mission to the United Nations organization in Switzerland, Rudolf's name was one of twenty-three on a list of prime candidates. To be sure that favoritism had no part the names were written on slips of paper and dropped into a jar. Rudolf's was one of the two selected.

So, off to Geneva. For the first time, at twenty-six, Rudolf, the thick-browed juvenile delinquent, entered the western world.

It was a reawakening.

His first assignment at the consulate was as a street guard outside the main building. It was an overwhelming post for Rudolf. For eight hours a day, six days a week, he would watch western society. Beautiful young women escorted by men no better looking than he. They drove fast, sleek cars, smelled of expensive fragrances, and dressed in glorious, revealing clothes. They—the men and the women—looked as if their sins came easily, often, and were eminently enjoyable. Promiscuity seemed to be its own reward.

With basically nothing to do all day on his post, Rudolf began to think.

All through his teen years, if he'd wanted something he had simply taken it. His bully-boy mentality told him that he could do it. But Rudolf did recognize superior force when he encountered it, such as the discipline of his own army. One step out of line, he knew, would land him back in the workers' paradise, never to see the West again. This time, he recognized, he would have to graduate to means more subtle in order to obtain his ends.

At the same time, Rudolf began to see more of the East German Ambassador to the United Nations.

The Ambassador, Igor Hesselman, a balding Communist Party autocrat, was disliked and feared by everyone who worked within the Consulate. He was one of the old-line Stalinists disappearing from Europe, whom everyone wished would disappear faster. He was also something of a hypocrite for a man who represented a puritanical regime.

The consulate maintained a stable of young women in Geneva, attractive young frauleins whose only purposes were those of sexual entrapment. They bore no overt links to the Consulate whatsoever, but, rather, had moved to West Germany, then to Switzerland. Their mission was to secure employment with gentleman friends in sensitive jobs where information from other consulates, embassies, or diplomats could be filched. Hesselman had a strange sort of loyalty test for them. From time to time, to prove their devotion to the party and to the Democratic Republic of Germany, they would be escorted to meet the ambassador privately. The old man would lean on them for sexual favors of an unspeakable variety. Any woman who declined could expect a quick trip home, with a worse fate to follow.

Two emotions began to work on Rudy. He had stood at the doorway in Geneva long enough to see young men his own age with gorgeous women, western clothes, and cars. And he'd seen his own ambassador abusing attractive young German girls for his own pleasures. So much for political concerns. What was most incredible was that Rudolf, who hadn't had sex for seven months by this point, was able to control himself. Perhaps he was a shade smarter than anyone had given him credit for.

"Rudy do not like the ambassador," interjected Rudolf very concisely as he looked directly at Mason. "I would like pour steel into his eyes." Rudolf grinned dumbly. It was supposed to be a joke. Sort of. Mason felt a compulsion to grimace and rub his own eyes. He resisted, slowly blinking instead.

"Rudolf used to work in a steel plant outside Dresden," said Auerbach softly, as if that explained everything. Auerbach mentioned a tiny incident dating from the time when Rudolf, as a teenager, had worked in an iron mill. It seemed there was a larger man who day after day gave Rudy a tough time. Rudolf never said anything. One day the larger man's arm had a collision with a pair of orange-hot pincers. He never troubled the teenager again. Moral, concluded Auerbach: Don't fuck with Rudy.

The defector continued.

"Rudy stand around say nothing all time," he explained. "But Rudy think. Rudy want good life in West, also."

Well, who the hell didn't? Mason thought.

"So Rudy not so dumb. He work hard, be good German soldier at work. Get access to vault. Want something for sell. Get access every official document in whole consulate."

Mason, with wide eyes, looked to Auerbach. "Oh, Jesus!" he mumbled.

"Yes, indeed," Auerbach said merrily. "Our friend here cleaned out their vault. Everything. And they don't even know it."

"What the hell do you mean, they don't know it? You've got Goldilocks sitting here in England, missing from his guard position at the Geneva Consulate, and you think they don't smell something?"

"His disappearance has been *covered*," Auerbach said, treating Mason's question as a minor nuisance. "We'll get to that. You're distracting him. Let him talk."

It was a long process, Rudolf explained—access to the vault. Much like obtaining keys to a forbidden kingdom. And yet, given the fact that Rudolf was a man of limited ingenuity and little formal education, he had accomplished his mission with relative ease. Perhaps it was single-mindedness; perhaps it was simple-mindedness. More probably, it was naïveté concerning what he'd set out to do. He had no idea of the enormous amount of luck he would need to pull it off. Yet somehow he muddled through.

Obtaining clearance for the filing vault was little problem. He showed no visible interest in the vault, other than considering it a piece of furniture which was to be treated with deference. So naturally, he was considered ideal as an inner-consulate security man. He was allowed inside with senior officers only, then was allowed to fetch and replace file envelopes for other embassy officers. It was during this time that he learned the combination to the second of the three locks. The third and innermost combination he learned four months later, a piece at a time. That left only the first lock, a delicate key mechanism, yet the most rudimentary of the three devices.

It was all so simple from there on, Mason realized. So easy and childlike that it took a childlike mentality such as Rudolf's to cope with it. The man just went into an amusement store and bought some molding clay. Rudy carried hunks of the stuff in his uniform pockets for weeks until he had the opportunity—three seconds when no one else was near—to press a young diplomat's vault key against the flat surface of the clay.

Four days later he found a locksmith who would make the key. From there, the East German Army noncom had entry to one of the most sensitive vaults in Geneva.

Rudolf smiled to Auerbach and Mason. He seemed pleased with himself.

"Rudolf considers himself a patriot," said Auerbach after the appropriate interval. "He has decided that the West German system, which allows him much more personal luxury, is a better system. He's pleased to help us win."

"Of course," uttered Mason. Win *what?* was his private thought. But Auerbach was rattling onward.

He guided Rudolf past other matters which Mason instinctively would love to have known: How much was removed from the vault? What was in it? Mason didn't ask, as he knew Auerbach wasn't about to tell. What Auerbach was leading up to, however, followed quickly. It was information concerning an East German alert on a Soviet spy caper which had gone on the rocks.

94

Mason's ears perked. The particulars, Rudolf proudly explained, had been culled from three folios pilfered from the embassy and photocopied.

"Jesus Christ," muttered Mason incredulously. He was convinced by now that the line which delineated genius from idiocy was thin, thin indeed.

Music sounded faintly in the background and for a few seconds it shattered Mason's concentration and returned his mind to the shabby living room where they sat. He looked nervously in the direction of the noise.

"Louis has a transistor radio," said Auerbach softly. "I told him he could listen to it if he wished." The German glared at Auerbach indignantly. "It's Rudy's radio, actually," added Auerbach. "The damned Kraut was at my heels for a radio from the first day we arrived here."

Mason nodded. He was aware that the room was very warm and that a certain tedium was building, the tedium of listening to Rudolf's fractured English and Auerbach's subtle coaching.

But even Auerbach was deeply into the tale being related. And against his own better inclinations, as Rudolf nodded furiously in accompaniment, Auerbach began to steal some of his defector's thunder. He started to tell part of what followed himself.

Perhaps, Mason guessed, it was to make sure that the account would not deviate and would cover only what Mason was meant to hear.

No matter. Mason listened attentively.

"As you probably know, the East Germans—except for this one here—are pretty damned faithful to the Mama Bear in Moscow. The intelligence services, I mean. The German people hate the Russians, always have and always will. But their intelligence people are faithful to the Soviets. Mark me well on that."

Mason nodded. Auerbach had told him nothing he didn't already know. Yet.

"So here's what we picked out of the Geneva vault. An East German operative, just back from the Far East, spun an eerie little tale about a Soviet spy operation. Seemed the Russians had bought off a top American, a straight cash deal, and had infiltrated a US operation against the Chinese." Auerbach smiled.

The defector's eyes changed their expression and lost

their intensity. "Rudy thirsty," he announced, with a look of disinterest.

"Later," snapped Auerbach.

"Beer," Rudy grunted, glancing around.

"Oh, for God's sakes!" snapped Auerbach violently. "This is the last time I recruit a sausage maker. This one keeps two breweries in business all by himself."

"Beer," repeated Rudolf.

Auerbach sprang to his feet and stomped to the kitchen. He threw open a cabinet and took down a bottle of beer. Failing to find an opener he lodged the bottle's neck on a doorknob, whacked it firmly with his hands, and brought the frothing bottle back to the German.

Rudy guzzled down three or four loud gulps and made an expression of distaste. "Warm!"

"It's all you're getting, mate," Auerbach said sourly. "This isn't the bloody Connaught. Now just sit tight and nod or you'll be damned well on your way back to Dresden."

Rudolf took the hint. Auerbach was back into the story, as if nothing had happened. Louis's music was louder now, accompanied by increased static. He had switched to, of all things, an Irish station.

"Once upon a time, not so very long ago," announced Auerbach with undue cuteness, "there was a spy network in the Orient. In China, in fact. A career CIA officer was running it. Sal Roberts, I think was the name. Roberts was a damned fine spy, I might say, trusted only people who were tried and true, as the cliché goes. This is maybe about ten years back."

Mason felt anger brewing.

"Sorry if you won't like the story, Mason. But it's direct from our East Prussian files."

"Get on with it."

"Roberts headed a network. Ever since the Nationalist Chinese had lost in 1949, an occurrence never predicted by the Asia sages in your State Department, there'd been virtually no intelligence nets within China. Nothing worthwhile at all. Not surprisingly, of course. Pretty hard to drop a round-eye in downtown Canton. But with Asia heating up, Washington was pressuring the Nationalists to help land infiltration networks. Am I right, Mason?"

"So far."

"So Roberts was sent to China. Hong Kong and

Macao, actually. Those were—still are—the open ports simply because the Red Chinese never wanted to close them. Too much money and trade going in and out. But that's a tale for another evening. The fact is that Roberts was training Nationalists in the ins and outs of infiltrating and establishing networks which would stay in China and work locally in key cities, keeping an eye on the Red Guard, Mao's public announcements, all that. If an eye could be peeled on goods at railroad stations heading south, military goods for Vietnam in other words, that would be fine, too. Well, Roberts instructed his infiltrators, men and women. And he had help too. A younger man named Williams."

Mason had a headache. A four-alarm one. He looked at Auerbach's gleeful face. Rudolf noisily drained his beer bottle and went to the kitchen to retrieve another.

"Well, this Williams was quite something," said Auerbach. "Had a real flair for what he was doing. An adventuresome lad. Too adventuresome. Wanted to have a look at mainland China himself. So after the operation had been functioning smoothly for many months, with recruits being put ashore by junk and small merchant boats somewhere south of Kowloon, Williams started to accompany his landing parties. Rather rash, wouldn't you say, Mason?"

"Rather rash," Mason affirmed drily. Then he added bitterly, "Downright idiotic."

"I'd say so. But, you must remember about young Williams. There were many things he didn't know. He didn't know, for example, that Roberts wasn't really heading the network."

Mason leaned forward silently. He had been reaching for the Scotch but his thirst was already evaporated.

"No, indeed," pronounced Auerbach, sensing now that he had riveted his guest's attention. "Roberts had kept secrets from Williams. Company policy, unfortunately. Roberts was reporting to another American, a man named Donald Furman, who happened to be the district chief. *His* orders were not to let anyone know he was on the premises. Not a man to thumb one's nose at."

Auerbach moistened his lips and aimed for the conclusion.

"Furman was a cagey old beast. He'd been shunted aside from time to time for promotion. This was a man who'd been shot at for his country. Took the snubs rather

97

hard. Hard enough to be bought. Bought off for cold cash."
Auerbach nodded toward the German. "Just like our mate
here. He received a glorious hunk of cash each month.
Not major information, mind, but just enough, when fused
with other items, to tip the hand on every movement that
the American network was making."

"If I believe this, I'm pretty angry," uttered Mason.

"I'm certain you are. Because pretty soon luck ran
out on the American operation. The nets inside China were
too good. Uncle Mao is taking one of his Olympian dips in
the Yangtze and the American-trained Nationalists are
hanging around taking snapshots. So the pressure started
to come back the other way. The Chinese wanted the outsiders rolled up. They got them."

"Through the Russians," said Mason. A statement
and a question.

Auerbach nodded. "Solidarity with the worldwide
socialist movement. All that claptrap, at least in those days.
The Chinese leaned on their sometime pals, one supposes,
and got the information they needed. Probably a swap.
However, Furman wanted to drop a real prize into their
yellow hands. A US spy. A real live Yank spy. So Furman
kept in touch with Roberts, the older agent. Furman
waited until one night when Roberts revealed that Williams
had gone with a landing party. Within five hours it was
over."

There was a deathly silence in the room.

Auerbach finished. Sino-Soviet rift or not, someone
somewhere was working at least two ways from the middle.
A whistle had been blown. Furman, the American on the
Soviet payroll, had alerted the other side, whoever that
was, of the black-intelligence operations. The landing party
had a welcome which they could have done without. The
Nationalist Chinese were summarily executed. The American was placed on trial for espionage, in private, and convicted. Williams, as he was known, was imprisoned. Diplo-
matically, the timing wasn't bad. A few years later, also
in secret, Kissinger visited China as a precursor to the
President. The thaw would commence. The American's
life sentence for espionage would be four years. It would
be the single days that seemed like a lifetime.

"Good story, isn't it?" Auerbach finally said.

"The ball's in your court," replied Mason sensing his

own emotional vacuum. "This isn't the story I recognize, but you can play the point."

"Not much to play. You heard the facts. Dénouement time, Mason. Let's fill in the blanks. The younger man—Williams. The one who went to prison in China. Who was that?"

"You know who it was. Stop playing."

"Don't be so damned stubborn. I want you to say it."

Somehow the words were not easy. "That was me," Mason said in a low voice.

"The slightly older man, the one who had unknowingly set the younger man up for a fall. Who was that?"

"Lassiter," said Mason. "Robert Lassiter."

"And Furman?" pressed Auerbach. "Who was Donald Furman?"

"I met the man once. That's the name I knew him under." Mason's expression was pensive. Troubled. "Why would the Soviets have blown me to the Chinese?" he asked almost rhetorically. "Christ knows, they were at each other's throats at the time."

Auerbach shrugged dramatically. "Who knows?" He stayed with the central point of the evening, however: "Would you recognize Furman again?"

"Perhaps. It's been a while. Depends how the man has changed." He pondered it for a moment. "Yes," he concluded. "Yes, probably."

Quickly Auerbach reached to an envelope on the table beside his chair. He ripped it open, scrutinized what appeared to be two photographs, and handed the first one to Mason.

Mason took it in his left hand and glanced at the photograph for only a few seconds.

"That's him," Mason said solemnly. "No doubt."

"Circa 1969," said Auerbach. "Taken by a British agent in Singapore. Now try this one, taken last year."

Another glossy photograph, eight by ten, was offered to Mason. With growing fascination and bitterness he took the second photograph. It showed a well-tanned man walking in a London park. The picture had been shot from somewhere above, probably a window of a tall building. There were other pedestrians in the picture, as well as benches, and pigeons. The telephoto lens had struck again. Mason studied the picture of the man said to be Furman, somewhat older now, but no heavier.

"Yes, all right," said Mason. "That's him—Furman."

Auerbach smiled as if Mason had just proven something important. "And that's why you're here tonight. That's why, along with the whole story that's been told to you, your friend Robert Lassiter went out of a window."

"Sorry. Why?"

"Furman," scoffed Auerbach. "Furman, indeed. That man worked with Lassiter longer than you ever did."

"That," he said in a hushed voice, "that is Frank Hargrove."

From there it was a matter of mopping up, though in this case, given the Hargrove-Furman-Lassiter connection, the mop would have to be particularly absorbent.

To Mason's tired mind, it all seemed to follow a textbook form. Thrust, parry, counterthrust. Or in terms of physics: for every action, an equal and counterbalancing reaction. Physics? His mind drifted to Lucille Davis for a moment, proving how tired he was. Classic patterns.

It had begun as straight-out espionage: establishing missions in China for the gathering of otherwise unknown information. Covert operations, or black intelligence, as they liked to call it back at the Farm.

The straight-out intelligence work in China a decade earlier had provoked a counterintelligence effort. It was not a certainty, Mason reminded himself, but apparently the Russians or *some* Russian had assisted the Chinese. Their counterintelligence effort had entailed infiltration, an infiltration which *might* be persisting to this day, given the fact that Hargrove was even now the bureau chief in London.

Might? Mason wondered. Hell, Lazz had hit the concrete, hadn't he?

There were a few matters of which Mason could be sure. But one of those few, without question, was that it was now a counter-counter game. Espionage, then counterespionage, and now (too late) counter-counterespionage. And what was he doing it for? For Lazz? For himself? To prove an invisible something?

Mason took a deep breath and exhaled slowly. Something mattered somewhere, but he wasn't sure what it was.

A few minutes later Louis was in the room, as was Edgar. Return of the noble savages, thought Mason idly. The baby sitters would put Rudolf back to bed and tuck him in—no good-night kisses—though the latter didn't seem much in the mood for shut-eye. Rudolf, in fact, was developing an unquenchable thirst, and was now dropping unsubtle hints to Auerbach about how he'd someday soon like to sample whatever could be arranged in the line of young English country lasses.

"I'll think about it," Auerbach told him absently, much like an annoyed parent who has decided to withhold the allowance for another week, just to prove who depended on whom.

Then they were out the door, Mason and Auerbach, with not another word to Rudolf. They stepped into the cool night, heading to the car. Both men were thinking differing thoughts on similar subjects.

"Sometimes I think he's a sociopath," said Auerbach, buckling himself into the front seat of the Triumph. He waited for Mason to open the left side door, slide in, and do the same. "Other times I'm certain of it. Our Rudy, I mean. Our secret Hun."

"I thought you said he could be believed."

"He can be. Everything he's given us double-checks and triple-checks. So why would he lie about this?"

"Because maybe this is more important than everything else," Mason suggested impetuously.

"Possible," Auerbach granted. "But *he* doesn't seem to think so. Sodium pentothal and the polygraph. Remember?"

Mason rolled his car window down, needing the air after so long an ordeal in the stuffy house. The neighborhood was soundless except for a few trees rustling very slightly.

Auerbach turned the key in the ignition. The auto roared to life. It recurred to Mason what kind of ride he was in for, and for the second time the same night.

"You forgot to tell me," Mason reminded him as the Triumph eased onto the street. "Why don't the East Germans know that Rudy cleaned them out?"

"Oh, yes," said Auerbach. "We made it look good once we bought him. Had him develop growing disagreements with the ranking military officer in the embassy. Finally one thing led to another and Rudy—he downright enjoyed this, mind—our Rudy hauled off and blasted the major in the mug." Auerbach laughed. "Broke his nose and jaw, I hear. Not bad for one shot. Then our boy rushed off to the Canadian Consulate where we arranged to have some of our maple-leafed brethren waiting for him. Rudy asked for asylum in the West. Got it rather rapidly, I'd say."

Mason was nodding. The pieces fit togther. "All right, Auerbach. I'll give you credit for this one. It smells right."

"Speaking of smells, the man's breath was bloody horrible, wasn't it? Like a wheel of overripe Camembert. You Americans know all about body odors and ways of disinfecting them. I want you to suggest something before I have to interview that Hun again. Mouthwash. Maybe something with mint, not one of those medicinal ones."

Mason looked at his driver. Auerbach *wasn't* joking. They were passing through Bath again, headed for the motorway. Most of the city's lights were off, except the yellow street lights which reflected onto the stately Georgian buildings, and the stop lights. Auerbach eased through the red ones. In a few more moments they'd entered the motorway and Auerbach's foot was against the floorboards again, the accelerator lost somewhere in between.

Maybe it was because he was so tired, but Mason wasn't half as terrified by the high speed ride back to London. Maybe it was because he had done it once already, lost his virginity for speeds in excess of ninety-five, and knew that there was a chance for survival. Or maybe it was simply that his mind was elsewhere. In China. In London. On Hargrove. The only really cruel touch to the return trip came about half an hour after boarding the M4.

The sky became pale gray, turned pale blue, then was bright with morning. Mason knew that he'd spent the entire night in company which he disliked intensely. In a way it had been like spending an entire night with a prostitute, except in this instance there had been four of them.

12

A numbing fatigue had overtaken Mason.

It was more than simply tiredness. It was a mental and physical exhaustion, following closely the night spent on Bath's outskirts, a night which Mason thought of, for lack of a better name, as the Night of the German Occupation. It was not the sort of tiredness cured by simple sleep, a cup of coffee, or a pot of tea. To Bill Mason it felt like a depletion of the spirit.

Why? he wondered. Depression had overtaken him before and probably would again sometime. But why had it caught up with him now? Mason examined his feelings and the events of the last few days. He sat in the living room of a two-and-a-half-room flat in Chelsea, a safe flat to which Auerbach had led him, installed him, and told him he could keep indefinitely.

"Thanks," Mason, circles under the eyes, had said.

"Courtesy of the Labor Government," acknowledged Auerbach. "Curse their socialist asses."

"I'll take it," said Mason.

Auerbach had told him to remain available—stay visible, in other words. The Briton would make the next contact. Instructions complete, Auerbach pushed a plain white enevelope into Mason's hands.

"Open it when you get upstairs," Auerbach said. "Enjoy."

Upstairs, and with the door closed, Mason had torn away the edge of the envelope and allowed the contents to slide out. Three hundred pounds sterling: two fifties, the rest in fives and tens. As easy as that, Bill Mason had found a new employer. He threw the envelope on the foyer table. He tried to ignore it.

The apartment was faded, but comfortable. It was appointed with outdated, oversized furniture from the

1940s, the type of graciously decrepit old pieces that one found at estate sales and Goodwill stores.

Mason spent an hour in the afternoon looking for the inevitable electronic ears. He found only one, concealed behind a ventilation grating in the kitchen.

"Bugger yourself, Auerbach," Mason breathed into it, and gleefully smashed it with an iron frying pan. He enjoyed for a few seconds a sense of accomplishment. Yet he knew no one planted *one* bug.

Julie Heasman had insisted that he snored. Now Mason could turn to Auerbach for verification, except that his landlord did not come around.

On the first day after the Night of the German Occupation, Mason slept for ten hours, rising in time to go out for dinner and then taking a long walk through nighttime London. He ended in a quiet pub, minding his own business and sipping brandy until closing time.

He watched himself in the mirror behind the bar. Observing himself as if seeing a stranger, he saw a man deeply troubled about something. The vision disturbed him. He took a long, slow walk home. It was only now that he recalled that he hadn't shaved in two days. So at two thirty A.M. he reacquainted himself with a razor.

Another day passed and the fatigue persisted. It was then that he suspected that it was something more, a real depression. And not a mild one. By the third day—still no Auerbach—he'd fully recognized the anxiety that afflicted him. Yet there was something ineffable about it. He remained indoors that afternoon and tried to define it.

He felt betrayed, a sense of having been double-dealt along the line. By Lazz? By the CIA? By Hargrove? For that matter, by Auerbach?

He wondered why he remained loyal to anyone. Join the other side? he thought idly. Like Rudy, be a traitor to one side and be held in contempt by the other? Well, defectors got what they usually asked for . . . and deserved.

Those first three days in the apartment he wandered the city. He would start from Chelsea and follow wherever his feet took him: Maida Vale, Notting Hill, Hammersmith, Finsbury, Brent. His body clock, off since the night with Rudy, gradually returned to something approaching normal. But he ate little and drank too much. He considered looking for a woman, for sale or for free, but quickly concluded that it wasn't worth the trouble; he wasn't that interested anyway.

He found a small nuance of pleasure just being in the midst of crowds, noontime on Regent Street or evening in the West End. But when his spirit tired and when his feet followed suit, he returned to the flat Auerbach had so kindly provided. He heard one of his neighbors. Apparently there was a young woman in her twenties who lived next door. So what?

The flat itself overlooked a small park, a nameless square which was gray and brown, with concrete, spindly trees, and fallen leaves. Old people gossiped at the near end during the day. In the late afternoon children's gay voices could be heard past his closed windows as they played at the other end. Mason would absently contemplate them. Then he would settle back into a ragged but comfortable green armchair and turn his attention inward.

What had left him with the spiritual emptiness? Lazz's death, perhaps, the unceremonious death of his friend. But there was more than that. His firing from the CIA? Yes. Being dismissed from his career does little to inflate a man's self-esteem, particularly when one's been trained to do nothing else. But that was a lingering sensation that had dogged him since early in the year. What about Rudolf? Old Rudy. Or *young* Rudy, more accurately. "Well, Mason, what do you think? Another fine example of German engineering, what?" Auerbach had asked facetiously during the white-knuckle ride back to London. Mason hadn't even answered.

Maybe that was it—Rudy's story of how Mason had been betrayed in the Orient. Betrayed by . . . someone. Hargrove? Certainly Lassiter had unwittingly aided in his capture by the Chinese. When the network was bagged, Bill Mason had been the prize trophy.

He felt the taste for brandy but had none in the flat.

He pondered Rudy's story. Yes, he finally decided. That was it. Or a large part of it. He didn't know whether Rudy was to be believed or not. His tale made sense, at least in that it was coherent. Even the fact that the story was out of the East German files. No secret service in Europe was as amicable with the Russians as the East Germans. It made complete sense that the East Germans would have sent an alert to Moscow to confirm the existence of a newly discovered operation. As someone in Langley had once explained to Bill, in terms not intended to flatter, "When Moscow eats beans, East Berlin farts. And vice versa."

Auerbach, Lassiter had explained before his death, was trustworthy. (As Hargrove had been? Bill wondered.) Did that make the defector's story credible by a sort of osmosis? Did that also mean that Hargrove had been responsible for Mason's capture in China? And for Lassiter's death? Was the whole CIA setup in London rotten because Hargrove, an alleged double, sat on the top of it in the district chief's chair as head of intelligence in Western Europe?

Wouldn't Captain Queeg like to know about *that!*" Bill actually said aloud. Then he shut up. Though no one was in the room with him, he was highly embarrassed. He'd been talking to himself.

All of this was in prelude to his fifth day alone, a Tuesday.

Bill Mason slept late, lying in bed until almost noon. There was no ringing telephone, no knock at the door. Lying under a single blanket and a sheet, he listened to the passing traffic. He could tell the buses from the diesel taxis and the gasoline-engined cars from the gasoline-engined taxis. His gums hurt. Too much brandy the night before; he had finally purchased his own private supply. His mind was inexplicably on a case Lazz had described to him years ago, a case in which a trio of East German fieldmen had sought to smuggle out of London a disaffected member of their consular staff, one who'd had too-close contact with officials of the United States Embassy.

The East Germans had stuffed their unconscious countryman into a steamer trunk, marked it diplomatic, and tried to send it air freight to someone's grandmother in Leipzig. Only they forgot to poke enough airholes. A lock broke somewhere and out tumbled a full-scale diplomatic embarrassment. Quite dead. "Show me a trunk murder," Lazz had remarked, "and I'll show you a sloppy packer."

Or perhaps a trio of sloppy packers.

Bill threw off the blankets, showered, dressed, and went out to track down a morning newspaper and some lunch.

He cursed Auerbach. Bill was being manipulated. Auerbach was trying to indicate who controlled whom simply by showing who chose the proper times for appearances and vanishings. And similarly, Mason was being left in the cold open air so that he would welcome the sight of David Auerbach when he finally did appear.

"Son of a bitch," mumbled Mason as he bought his morning *Herald-Tribune*.

"Pardon, sir?" asked the newsagent.

"Nothing, nothing," snapped Mason rudely. "I talk to myself."

Mason stalked off in the direction of Piccadilly. He felt the confused man's gaze upon his back.

On an odd impulse he wandered a side street in the theater district and saw something which he would never have entered in the United States: an American-style cafeteria. But the wooden signboard on the sidewalk actually made the place look appetizing. He walked through a glass door and entered upon a small island of plasticized American culture. It was someone's idea of an American cafeteria and it wasn't all that distant from the original item. Surprisingly, the beanery was busy.

Mason took an orange plastic tray, a paper napkin, and aluminum tableware from a dolly and started through the line. He was aware of a smattering of German being spoken around him, as well as the inevitable inflections of the American South and Midwest.

People pressed close as he checked out with the cashier, paying one pound twenty-five for a sandwich, the contents of which were slightly mysterious, and for a fruit salad which was more straightforward. Picking up his tray, he jostled the tray of a small dark-haired woman behind him. She righted it quickly but a bowl of hot tomato soup jumped off and hit Mason's leg just above the left ankle, spilling completely and soaking his pants cuff, sock, and shoe.

"Oh, my God," she said with horror. "I'm so dreadfully sorry! My fault completely!"

She looked at his ankle in utter terror. Mason felt the heat of the soup seeping through to his flesh. Not knowing what else to do, she dropped her tray on the counter and obsequiously bent down to his foot. She brushed clumsily with a handful of paper napkins. Mason pulled his foot away.

107

"Don't worry about it," he said, wishing to avoid an absurd scene. "I'll rinse it off."

She stopped brushing, looked up at him, and rose. It dawned on him that she was American. She was awkward and small, with jet-black hair pulled straight back. Her face was round and intense and her coloring was too white, as if she hated sunlight. She was in no way attractive, but looked, through some movement of the eyes, as if she might be extremely bright.

An attendant appeared and helped Bill Mason to a washroom where his sock and shoe were rinsed. He declined further aid, putting the damp garments back on. What the hell, he remarked to the befuddled attendant, it was raining out anyway.

He returned to the table where he'd left his tray. The woman who had spilled the soup was waiting. Mason grimaced and sat down.

"I'm so embarrassed. I'm so sorry," she said. "I don't know what to say." She blushed. "May I pay a cleaning bill for you? May I do that, at least?"

If you really want to help, Bill thought, you can go away.

"It's not necessary."

"But I must do something."

"You've done enough already," he said, milking the implication. "Thanks, but no thanks."

He estimated her age as about thirty, give or take a few years. She wore a wedding band but no diamond. Her fingernails were short and uneven; she bit them. He concentrated on his food and ate, thinking he had won.

"American, aren't you?" she asked.

He looked at her for a long second. "Yes."

"Where from?"

Rudeness would soon graduate to outright profanity, he thought.

His left foot was uncomfortable. He could smell the soup. "New York." A lie. He didn't look up.

"Funny," she said. "I hear Massachusetts in your voice."

He glanced at her and made no response. Go to hell, he thought. My foot stinks of tomatoes and you're analyzing speech habits. Worse, she was doing it accurately.

"Cincinnati," she said. "Ohio."

"What?"

108

"Cincinnati, Ohio. That's where I'm from." She offered her hand. "Essie," she said. "I'm Essie Kelman."

With annoyance he set down his fork. "Pleased to meet you." He shook her bony hand and reached for his fork again.

"Don't you have a name?"

Oh, my God, he thought. Now she wants me to screw her. He looked up at her and thought never in the coldest of winters would that happen.

"Yes. My name is Bill. I'm also not in a terribly good mood and the dish of soup on my foot hasn't really improved it. So I'm not in much of a mood for conversation. All right? Nothing personal."

She looked slightly hurt; he didn't care. He went back to his fruit salad, now wanting nothing more than to finish and leave. A minute of blissful silence passed before she broke it.

"What kind of work are you in?" Her voice was as welcome as ten long fingernails scraping a blackboard.

"Unemployed. Hard core." He ate more quickly.

"What kind of work *were* you in?"

He gave no answer.

"What kind of work are you looking for?"

"Madam." His voice was icy now, angry but controlled. "Last time out, I was the downstairs piano player in a Brooklyn whorehouse. Before that I was a blacksmith. Next, I'd like to be an astronaut. If you can't offer me anything like that, why don't you offer me a few minutes of peace and quiet instead?"

He glared at her for a half-second, then finished his fruit salad.

She tittered with laughter five full seconds after he'd spoken. "You got a real upside-down sense of humor, Bill," she told him. "Where'd you acquire it? China?"

He stopped chewing. "What?"

"China," she repeated. "I'll bet you've been in China."

She leaned back. He noticed that she hadn't touched the meager amount of food she'd bought. He pushed the tray away and folded his arms on the table before him.

"The soup I'm currently wearing. It wasn't an accident, was it?"

"I wouldn't know," she said. "Your elbow hit my tray. Did you do it intentionally?"

"It wasn't an accident, was it?" he repeated.

109

Now she was silent.

"How long have you been following me?" he asked. More silence.

"For days," she said finally. "Off and on." A coy smile. Her teeth were crooked.

"What the hell do you want from me?" he snorted, visibly angry. "And who are you?"

"I—or, I should say, 'we'—would like you to pick up where Robert Lassiter left off." She posed the next part delicately, or so it seemed. "Robert had other employment besides CIA and the tobacco-company cover. What we're offering is a straight business deal. Same as your friend was doing."

"Who is 'we'?" he asked nastily.

"Middle Eastern News Service," she said. "We're a nonpolitical news and information bureau based in—"

"Never heard of you." It was an accusation. "And Lazz—Lassiter never did, either."

There was a manila envelope in her hand, a large one, and she spoke cryptically about documents, Lazz's signature on checks and on a contract.

"You're lying," he said, trying to seem the opposite of what he was: interested. "I've never heard of you," he repeated.

She grinned broadly. "Ah, but Bill," she said, annoying him with her false familiarity. "We've heard of you. Come on," she said. "Let's talk."

Bill knew a recruitment when he smelled one. He looked her coldly in the eye and he wondered where her back-up was, in case she got into trouble, and whether or not there was a wire between her rather meager breasts.

"All right," he said. "You talk, I'll listen. But there's nothing in the world you can give me."

It was an odd pitch, unusual because it was almost straightforward. And as unfitting a location for a business proposition as the cafeteria was, Essie Kelman forged ahead with it. She *was* very bright, Mason noted, and there was a certain zealousness to her mission.

The Middle Eastern News Service, she explained, was a news and an information service—she stressed the latter—attempting to provide an objective summary of events from Algeria to Israel.

"We have offices in Tel Aviv and Cairo, Jerusalem,

Bengasi, and Tunis. Had one in Beirut, too, but the building isn't standing any longer," she said. The latest set-to between Christians and Moslems had taken care of that.

Impartiality was paramount. Mid-East News was trying to provide objective commentary and reportage from a moderate standpoint of Arab and Israeli opinion; a sane middle ground.

"All I see is craziness on both sides," Mason said. "Where's the profit in sanity?"

"There isn't any," she said bluntly. "We lose money. Lots of it." She seemed happy about it.

He waited for an explanation.

"I'm not hiding anything from you," she said. "It's Saudi oil money that finances us."

"And you're openly offering me something on a Saudi payroll?" he asked incredulously, as if the mere concept was ridiculous.

"Yes," she said. "Why? Do you still have a conflict of interest?"

He didn't answer the question. "How'd you get on to me?" he asked. "I don't even know what this job is yet. What makes you think I'd want it?"

She elaborated. The job was that of consultant. Sort of. Mid-East was out to hire someone as an analyst of US diplomatic or covert maneuvering. No past classified information would be requested or expected. No conflict with principles of present or former careers. No names. Merely an insight into American or English intelligence maneuvers, by someone who'd been on the inside.

"Look," she said. "I'm American, too. I wouldn't ask you to do something treasonous."

I'll bet, he thought. She went on to explain how only half the people in Mid-East were Arab. A proper balance to form a proper view, a search for a sane middle ground for middle eastern policy. She was repeating herself.

"And what's in it for your Saudi benefactors?" he asked.

"Isn't it obvious?" she said. "The Saudis are businessmen. All they care about is oil prices. It's to their advantage to encourage an atmosphere conducive to world oil trade."

"So they can gouge in peace," he suggested.

She let it go. "We all need oil," she said defensively. "Look what happened to them in 1974 during the oil

111

embargo. They lost millions by not being able to ship to the West."

And they made it back just as fast by spiraling the prices upward, he thought.

"I wouldn't know," he replied.

She began to talk glowingly of the fine people she worked with, how they paid her a modest fortune to work easy six-hour days and how, if he didn't believe her story, he could come into their London offices and meet her superiors. Or, if he was still skeptical, they would be happy to fly him to any of their offices in Europe or North Africa. For starters, she said, they would gladly arrange a detailed briefing in Tunis in five days' time if Bill was interested.

"Suppose I told you," he said, "that you and your damned Arab friends could go to hell on a camel?"

She shrugged. It was Bill Mason's turn to torment her. Any recruitment involving an initial trip to Tunis was problematic at best. Some former Company employees had been short-sighted enough to fall into what were euphemistically known as camel traps. Shortly after arrival, prospective employees disappeared into the desert air, and thereafter suffered devious means of persuasion (North African specialties being considered among the most persuasive) so that they'd impart from their souls every tiny detail of their previous employment. Legend had it that a handful of burnoose-clad specialists in hot, sandy nations had built solid careers extracting western intelligence information in this manner. And somehow all of it filtered back to the Mother Bear herself on Dzerzhinsky Square in Moscow.

As to the western agents themselves, the shells of them would be seen in the more squalid streets of North Africa or sometimes even South America inevitably nursing hungry addictions. It was a game played by the heavy hitters, only.

But to Mason what was most perplexing was the candor with which Essie Kelman was spelling out recruitment. Why make it *quite* so obvious? What did he have that they wanted? Essie Kelman, bless her, probably didn't even know, herself.

"—did they pay you?" she was asking him.

"Sorry?" he said.

"How much did they pay you? Your last employer."

112

He picked a figure close to the truth. "Thirty-five thousand a year."

"I'm sure Mid-East would double it. On principle."

"Sounds like fairy gold to me." She seemed to miss the analogy. "Turns to dust in the morning, follow?"

"I'll show you something," she said.

She opened a manila envelope. "Your mentor," she said, to demonstrate how much research someone had done. "Robert Lassiter."

She handed him a short two-page contract, along with a series of checks. The contract was an agreement between the late Robert Lassiter and the Middle Eastern News Service for services as an advisor-correspondent. The checks, dating from late 1973, were each for two thousand five hundred dollars per month, until the February 1976 check when the figure became three thousand. The contract was signed, the checks endorsed and processed.

Essie Kelman was wearing a smile smug enough to punch in. "Surprised?" she asked.

He examined the signatures. Excellent forgeries. Mid-East was doing it the whole way. "A little," he answered.

She waited for him to say more. He continued to peruse the contract and the checks, paid through Lloyd's Bank in London.

"It's a lot of money, Bill," she said eventually. "Think about it. All taxes taken out, very little work." She paused as if seeking something new to add. "If you wished, an initial sum of money could be paid into a Bahamian bank."

He handed the papers back to her.

"It's all very nice," he said coolly. "But I don't need money. I don't know what you want from me, but it will take more than money to get it."

Mason had Essie Kelman by surprise. "More than money?" she repeated, her white brow furrowing.

"A friend of mine went out a window," he answered. "Maybe your friends can help me. Am I clear?"

She considered it. "I can convey a message."

"Convey whatever you want," he said, "but I don't want to see you again. I want to see someone farther up the ladder. Then we can talk."

Her hands fumbled slightly with the documents as she placed them back in their envelope.

"I have nothing else to say," he said. "I think I know who I'm looking for. All I want is proof."

She waited until she was certain he was finished. "Come by here tomorrow at one," she said. "A man will introduce himself as Mr. Rasheed. His real name is Ali Fahrar. He'll ask you for the time, then introduce himself. You'll give your real name and you'll tell him you're American. He'll ask if you've been in London before. You'll say you haven't. You'll ask him if he has and he'll explain that—"

"Not here," Mason interrupted.

"What do you mean, 'not here'?"

"Frankly, the place depresses me."

"Then you pick something."

He thought about it for a moment. "The east end of Sloane Square. Two in the afternoon."

"Consider it an appointment," she then said very soberly. "I'll give you only one other word of advice."

"What's that?"

"Be there."

Yet, within the same city, Lucille Davis, Ph.D. in physics, was having her own headaches. Oh, the isotopes were behaving properly and predictably, but human nature was not so easy to harness. There was a big aching hole in her life, caused by the absence of the man closest to her. Lucille had taken to leaving her research closer to five in the afternoon; it had been her habit to work till seven. Returning home, she would stop at a fish store that she always passed and buy her cat a nice slice of swordfish or salmon for his dinner.

As a meal for Barney, fish succeeded. As a bribe for extra affection from the cat, such gestures were hollow. Barney was getting on in years and curled up in a large fur ball toward eight in the evening, no matter what had been on the menu.

So Lucille was very much alone, abandoned in a sense, somewhat the way Mason had been. She and David Auerbach might have gotten together and solved a few of each other's problems, but then they didn't even know each other, had never met, and, hell, she was in advanced physics and he was in the spook business.

She had had a spook or two too many as it was, and when sleep failed she began taking long, depressing walks through central London at night, spending too much time standing, staring, and thinking on Westminster or Lambeth

Bridge, not talking to a soul, just to get it out of her system or put it on a back shelf mentally.

But she couldn't.

She pictured herself at the center of an isosceles triangle, fenced in by her late, beloved Robert Lassiter at one point, young Bill Mason—he seemed young to her—at another point and that son of a bitch Frank Hargrove at the third.

Thoughts of Hargrove sent her stomping home in a fury, bursting through the door so abruptly that it scared Barney, who had seen many such tirades in the past. Lucille turned her rage upon the defenseless freezer compartment of the refrigerator. The appliance wasn't working right so the frost build-up from day to day was enormous, allowing Dr. Davis ample opportunity to get out the trusty old icepick and smack it into the ice until the small dark watches of the morning, or until it was all hacked bloodlessly away. Whichever came first.

Sadly, the insomnia worsened until it became chronic; the nighttime walks through London, centered around any one of the bridges, became routine.

13

Leaving Essie behind, Mason began a journey that took the better part of two hours, though he traveled no more than two and a half miles from where he'd begun.

After a confusing pattern of walking, underground routes, buses, and slipping in and out of three stores and one movie theater he arrived at Bramford Street in Islington, convinced that he was traveling without a shadow.

He looked for the number fifty-four and was happy to see, from the display window, that the proprietor of the small curio-and-antique store was still listed as Maurice Bobbs. Mason entered the store.

There were two other customers, a man and a woman speaking German. Bobbs, a Jamaican of medium height, short gray-black hair, and matching heavy brows, was behind a counter of silver jewelry. He paid little attention to the Germans. He glanced at Mason, and looked back to the rings they were examining. There was no sign of recognition, no greeting.

Bobbs, with the contempt of a London antique dealer who deplores his merchandise leaving the country but sells it anyway, ignored his customers. He dealt icily with the Germans. Mason continued to browse, picking up small items and fingering them clumsily, drawing hostile glares from Bobbs. Finally the Germans left.

Mason approached Bobbs.

"I'm looking for something for a lady friend," he explained slowly. "Maybe you could help me."

"Perhaps."

"What I had in mind," Mason expanded, leaning on a glass showcase, "was something about thirty-eight caliber, lightweight, and with a silencer, if possible."

The merchant made a tisking sound with his tongue, shaking his head. "Oh, Billy boy," said Bobbs, finally

116

smiling, "I've warned you about playing with the heavy-weights. When will you ever learn?"

"Never, probably. Can you help me?"

"Man, do the little birds sing in the fucking morning?" Bobbs laughed. He put a sign saying OUT TO LUNCH on the front door and, cursing joyfully, placed his arm around his old friend and led Mason to his stamp collection.

"I don't have an awful lot in stock right now," Bobbs explained. The black man was hunched over a backroom showcase which was heavily reinforced with thick glass and steel bars. Bobbs worked on a combination lock, spinning it merrily. Then finally, with a key, he opened it. "Who's your trouble with?"

"Don't know actually. Russians, maybe."

Bobbs sighed. "Damned Bolsheviks," he said. "My father *told* me we didn't do enough to support the czar. Thirty-eight, you said?"

"Sorry?"

"Caliber." Bobbs glanced up. His eyeballs had a pink tint. There was a faint scent of liquor on his breath.

"Yes."

Bobbs removed several drawers of stamps. He reached underneath and came to a false bottom in the cabinet. He clicked something and pushed upwards. A false bottom opened. He slid out a shallow, neatly-maintained extra drawer. There were four compact handguns and assorted accoutrements.

"You're familiar of course," said Bobbs casually, "with the pistol laws on this troubled little island? Rather strict."

"I know how they work," said Mason. "A mandatory prison sentence for anyone convicted of carrying a concealed handgun."

Bobbs laid the tray before Mason. Bill reached for the weapons. Bobbs stopped his hand, wordlessly handing him a thin wool glove.

"Of course," Mason said. Properly gloved, he examined the four pistols, checking aim and weight on each, hefting them up and down in his hands. "Silencers?" he asked.

Bobbs nodded.

Bill gravitated toward a Walther special: a small,

menacing .38 with a rude little pug nose. It carried seven shots per clip and could be equipped with a silencer.

"With that one?" Bobbs asked flatly, "I like to think of that one as my Italian-government special."

Bill looked puzzled. "The Walther? Why?"

"Anyone hit with that little bugger will last as long as the average Italian government." Then there was a flash of Bobb's white teeth as he exploded in staccato laughter. Mason said the Walther would do nicely. Gently Bobbs took back the pistol from his customer.

Bobbs thoughtfully hefted the weapon in his own hand, then suddenly whirled and drew a bead on a porcelain pitcher sitting across the room.

"See that piece of ceramic junk?" he asked. "Souvenir mug from the last silver jubilee—1937. I could blow it to bits without aiming. I'd like to."

Mason knew Bobbs would have.

"Know why I don't?" asked Bobbs, lowering the pistol. "The fucking bullet would go through the fucking wall. Two walls. *Ten* walls." He whistled between his teeth, spun the pistol in his hand and firmly pressed it back on Mason's palm. "Ought to see what it would do to an engine block, man," he said. "A gen-uine engine block." He looked at Mason inquisitively and turned serious. "What's going down?"

"What do you mean?"

"I'm your main man. Trust me. Everyone is hardware shopping this week. Tell this poor old colored man what's happenin'." There was a disturbing glint in his eye.

"I don't know what you mean, Maurice. I'm not lying to you."

Bobbs cast Mason a long lingering stare. "War drums," said Bobbs. "I hear things, I feel things. Not one US person in London's CIA crib who's in a gabby mood this week. They's all nervous. No one wants no jive. They come to me to build their arsenals but no one says what's cooking. Get my meaning?"

"Some."

Bobbs scowled. "I've seen a lot of scar tissue in my time, Billy Boy. I smell turmoil. A pick-up, or we got a purge coming? You tellin' me you don't hear nothin'?"

"I don't know anything, Maurice. There might be trouble at the top of the London office. But I don't *know* anything."

Bobbs nodded his head sharply toward Mason's selection from the stamp collection. "Then what you need a piece like that for?"

"Preparing for a rainy day."

"Sure, man?"

"Yes."

Bobbs sighed. "Shame," he observed. "You're ready for a lot of rain." He shrugged. "I'll giftwrap it for you."

The stamps were quickly back in the showcase and the drawers back in place. Bobbs grabbed a set of three old books. He cut a square out of the inside pages. He sealed the gun and its silencer within, wrapped some bullets separately, then wrapped everything as one package.

"What's expected of you people these days?" Bobbs asked as he worked. "The front office puts men in the field, then Carter won't let them operate. Doesn't he know what it's like out there?"

Mason shrugged. "Maybe not."

"A lot of cowshit, if you ask me," said Bobbs. "Constitutional rights," he scoffed. "Open democracy," he mimicked. "Don't Carter know that the world is one big back alley?"

"When I'm in Washington, I'll tell him."

"You tell him that I remember when Kennedy sent us into fucking Cuba from Guatemala, then pulled away our air support. You tell him that Maurice from the Liberation Army remembers." He finished wrapping. "Hear there were layoffs," he said. "Who's going to do the dirty work now?"

"They've got this idea," Mason said. "More reliance on intelligence gathering and analysis than covert action. A triumph of technocrats over fieldmen, Maurice. Times change."

Bobbs lit a cigarette and blew out the somke with distaste. He scowled. "You take a man like Nixon. *He* knew how to exercise power. What he do wrong, anyways?"

Mason knew it was time to leave.

"Hey, Billy? How about those pink slips? What about you?"

"I'm all right," Mason said. "It's the older guys they're rifting."

Bobbs nodded and was enshrouded by his own smoke. He seemed pleased to believe that in the general bloodletting in Langley, Mason's job was secure. Bill he liked. A trooper. An old-fashioned type of guy.

"Enjoy your stamps," Bobbs said. "Lick them in good health."

Somewhere Maurice Bobbs had rattled a skeleton.

Mason couldn't place it as he left the antique store, his newly acquired books under his arm. He began walking. What was it Bobbs had said? Mason was leaving with lowered spirits. He entered the underground at Kings Cross Station. He stood on the platform waiting for a train.

Bobbs and his damned politics. That was it. Bobbs was the most personable crypto-nazi whom Mason had ever met. His grandparents had been Haitians, on his mother's side, and all of a sudden, one sunny day when Maurice was thirteen, the grandparents had simply disappeared into the countryside, courtesy of the Tontons Macoutes and Papa Doc's sledgehammer brand of patriotic reform. Bobbs had borne a vendetta against Caribbean dictators ever since. He hated them on either side, right or left. Totalitarianism smelled the same no matter how it was wrapped.

A slightly defective personality, Bobbs was. Mason had recognized it on their first two meetings. Langley, 1965; Washington, 1974. He did have his uses, however, even though he'd retired from covert work. Bobbs spoke Spanish, French, and English perfectly, was black, trustworthy, and not interested in women. They had converted him into an invisible quartermaster, providing supplies to various points of Company call. He was an incarnation of every American's Second Amendment right to bear arms. Yet it had been Bobbs's political pronouncement which had rattled Mason.

The train pulled in. Mason boarded.

What was the role of an intelligence service within an open democracy? How was Mason's former company to function in the face of internal bloodletting, massive dismissals, and a wave of public embarrassment and humiliation? How was the security and intelligence service of a relatively free and democratic society to protect its own freedoms while under full Congressional and Presidential restraint? How, while combating the espionage agencies

120

of the eighty-five percent of the world which was neither free nor democratic?

A sense of futility pervaded Mason's thoughts. The larger questions persisted. He couldn't rationalize the answers, much less give them words. Mason had gone into government intelligence in 1962 with at least the belief that somehow his side was better than the other, that his nation was more on the side of Truth and the Angels than the others.

Then, over the next years, he'd seen his own side use every lousy trick in the arsenal: blackmail, electronic surveillance, political tampering, coercion, drug experimentation on unknowing victims, burglary, even assassination.

Now they were being told to stop. What the hell did the idiots in Washington expect? Did they think spy satellites could do everything except sing and dance?

It was incredible. Bobbs had forced him to consider it again. That was part of the anguish. No longer did he even carry the little protection that the agency would give him. He was on his own: bitter, armed, on the outside. A young career officer flushed away like so much flotsam.

Maybe Essie Kelman was right, maybe Bill should do some thinking along a different line. Mason had been dismissed. What further obligation *did* he have to the organization which had betrayed him? And to Captain Queeg? It was laughable.

As he turned onto his street in Chelsea, the brandy bottle, as an evening's entertainment, loomed large.

Or maybe a bar, he thought. Make more of an outing of it. No, he'd go upstairs first, he decided. He would put his books away, at least.

He was up the stairs and opened the door to his flat. He heard something and stood perfectly still for a moment. But it was only the impassioned sounds of the young woman who lived next door. She had a visitor this evening, someone she seemed to get on with rather well.

Mason stepped into his flat, turned on the light, and closed the door. He threw both locks. He turned and his heart jumped. The man, gun across his lap, who'd been sitting in the dark waiting, spoke.

"Where the bloody hell have you been? I've been sitting here all day."

Auerbach. Finally, Auerbach.

"Out," replied Mason.

"Least you could have done was left me something to read." He contemplated Mason. "What'd you buy there, books? Could have used them for the last six hours. Let's have a look."

Mason put the package aside belligerently. "Go to hell," he said. "I don't owe you anything."

"No?"

"No. How'd you get in?"

"I used my key," said Auerbach routinely. "It's my flat, remember?"

Mason suddenly felt silly. He was about to ask about the weapon lying across Auerbach's lap when Auerbach spoke again.

"I have funny thoughts sometimes," he said. "Began to wonder if that was you in there. Next door. Putting it to the bird who lives there. She likes it, you know. Want some advice?"

"No."

"Never trust a woman. Fat women, thin women; beautiful women, ugly women. All the same. Can't be trusted. Never tell you what they really think. Or want. Case in point," he continued fluently, "they *all* like to be crapped on."

Mason eyed the kitchen, looking for his brandy and tolerating Auerbach's diatribe.

"Think of your own past, Mason. Think of the men and women you've known. The men who are the most insincere, the biggest cads, the biggest bullies, are the ones who enjoy the most sexual success. Women say they want tenderness. What they want is to be shat upon. Do you think there's one woman alive in the world who hasn't gone to bed with a man because he said he loved her, only to find out later that she was getting the same tired old line? Well, Mason? Right or wrong?"

"I wouldn't know," Mason responded absently. "I'm tired."

Auerbach looked at him with disappointment, drew a breath, and seemed as if he were about to continue. But he didn't. He changed the subject instead.

"Well, old man, no hard feelings, anyway. Your time has about come."

"For what?" Mason asked indignantly.

"For a bit of exhilaration," Auerbach explained. "For you to roll up the network Lassiter was trying to quash.

122

Another week or two, but they'll be full periods. That's all it'll take. You'll be in London long enough, won't you?"

Mason considered Tunis. Or France.

"Of course," he said. "Let's have a brandy. We'll drink on it."

Auerbach appeared sheepish. "Oh, ah, sorry about that," he apologized. "You'll be able to get more tomorrow. Nothing else here to do all day, hear?" He shrugged.

"What the damned hell are you talking about?"

"I finished your bottle."

Mason bristled. When Auerbach saw how his apology was being received, he sought to make light of the situation.

"Whoa, now, Mason," he said, standing and raising a hand. "We'll get a case of it tomorrow, if it's your pleasure. You don't know how glad I am to see you. Been waiting all day."

Mason eyed him suspiciously. "Business?"

"Got something to show you, old man. Hope you didn't just eat."

"Who is it?" Bill asked softly.

"A friend of yours," said Auerbach, suddenly sounding very tired. "Afterwards, you and I will have to have a chat. You've been holding out on me, haven't you?"

Mason was slow to reply. "Yes," he finally admitted.

14

To Bill Mason's eternal relief, Auerbach didn't drive. They took a taxi. The American had a hunch where they might be going when the vehicle neared Bayswater. The taxi turned onto the same street where Mason had left Lasko in the rain.

Auerbach paid, including a hefty seven percent tip, and the two men stood on the sidewalk. The night was damp but clear.

"I don't get it, Auerbach. Why here again?"

"Because it's time to check in with old acquaintances," Auerbach said. "Your mate Lasko knows how to keep his mouth closed as well as use his imagination on death certificates."

"If you say so."

They passed the Italian restaurant and Auerbach knocked on the mortician's locked door. Lasko appeared half a minute later.

The small, balding undertaker recognized Auerbach immediately and opened the door. Then there was a flash of recognition in his eyes when he took a hard second look at Mason.

"Ah, yes. Drawer Five's step-brother as I recall," Lasko said.

Auerbach was direct. "I want Mr. Mason to view your latest arrival."

Lasko's tongue slipped between his lips for a moment, moistening them. "Of course," he said respectfully. "Another relative?" He brushed the dandruff from his right shoulder.

"No jokes, Lasko. Just show us your corpse."

"Of course."

The path was familiar and the body had obviously been waiting for them. It remained a mystery to Bill until Lasko led them to the proper place and Mason first saw,

124

beneath the white shroud, the size and shape of the body. From then it should have been anticlimactic. But it wasn't.

When the shroud was pulled away from the head, Mason wasn't surprised to see the face of Lucille Davis, late doctor of physics and bereaved former lover of one Robert Lassiter. What stunned Mason was the horrifying twisted expression on the dead woman's face—that and the deep welts on her neck.

"Strangled," said Auerbach, without expression.

"Strangled with a bicycle chain," added Lasko, unable to resist eccentric details. "See?"

The mortician's stubby little index finger pressed to the woman's throat, indicating scars and scrapes and, in one spot, poking at a wound that bore the definite impression of a chain.

"Lassiter's girlfriend, yes?" asked Auerbach, raising his eyes from Lucille to Mason.

"Yes."

Mason was transfixed. He continued to stare at Dr. Davis's face until Lasko's hand pushed the shroud back over her.

"It's not a safe city anymore," Auerbach intoned. "She took long walks at night. Wandered into a bad area."

"What's the difference between a Pakistani and a gorilla?" Lasko asked.

Mason, startled and not having heard the question properly, turned and said, "What?"

"A gorilla doesn't mug people," snapped Lasko.

"All right. That's enough!" Auerbach reprimanded. "Put Davis away. My friend and I need to talk."

Auerbach took Mason by the arm. As Lasko tended to the body, selecting a large drawer for it, Auerbach led Mason into a separate room. He closed the door behind him. Mason observed the soundproofing.

"Davis was in the habit of taking long walks at night," Auerbach repeated. "Someone was waiting for her last night. In Lambeth." The Briton thought for a moment. "Can you shed any light on it? Looks like more than a standard smash-and-grab to me."

Mason grimaced. His mind harkened back to his meeting with Lassiter in New York's Bryant Park.

"I didn't think you'd know," Auerbach said. "But you've been withholding information on her. It's time we trusted each other, Mason. Just a trifle, perhaps."

Mason nodded. He was prepared. Since the first moment he'd seen Auerbach, Mason had anticipated the time when he'd have to trust him.

"Lazz made the type of mistake that forty-seven-year-old spies make," Mason said. "Put his trust in the wrong place."

Auerbach settled in to listen.

"Lucille was a plant of some sort. I'm still trying to figure who she belonged to."

Auerbach winced.

"Lassiter let his guard down with her," Mason said. "He was used to being distrustful of beautiful women who drifted his way. But when he encountered an overweight, sex-starved physicist, he let down his defenses." Mason looked back toward the closed door. "She didn't look much like a Mata Hari, did she?"

"She does now."

Then Bill began a monologue. There was no reason to hide details from Auerbach. Not now. Not with Lucille Davis dead. He began to tell what Lazz had told him.

The Vassiliev case, Lazz had suspected, had been blown open by Lucy Davis. A careless word here or there at a moment of weakness and Davis had learned that the Russian was going to be arrested. When Lassiter had come to New Jersey looking for Mason, Lazz had been convinced: His trust of Lucille had been his undoing in the Vassiliev case. "That woman's a plant!" a tormented Lassiter had revealed. "I can't believe I never saw it until now." Lassiter had sat on a Bryant Park bench and had been close to tears.

"Come to London, Bill. Help me trap her. Let me find out who she's working for," Lassiter had implored.

Mason, as always, had come when called.

Auerbach fidgeted with a fingernail and listened intently to Mason.

"When Lassiter hit the sidewalk," Mason told Auerbach, "I figured Lucille Davis had shoved him."

Auerbach was shaking his head. "She was giving a lecture on a Cesium-137 isotope in Oxford at the time of his death," Auerbach said. "I checked. No way she could have pushed him. She had three hundred witnesses to where she was. That in itself is suspiciously convenient."

"Then who pushed him? And why?" Mason brooded. "And who killed her? And why?"

"Theory time," said Auerbach. "Have one?"

The room was quiet for a moment.

"Maybe," said Bill, still thinking.

Auerbach waited. Bill began.

"Suppose Davis was assigned to say close to Lassiter," Mason theorized. "Nothing else. Just stay close and pass along anything she knew. But she became more attached to the man than anyone could have expected. Let's face it. . . . They had a physical thing going." Mason stopped in mid-thought and pressed a finger to the corner of his mouth. "You said she took long walks? At night?"

"Sometimes," said Auerbach. "She appeared depressed. We couldn't follow her all the time, damn it. No manpower. If it had been up to me we would—"

"Maybe that's it," Mason suggested. "She'd passed along enough information to get Lassiter killed. Lazz had been closing in on something concerning these stolen computer chips. He didn't even know what it was himself, but he was drawing close. Dr. Davis revealed that, not meaning to get Lazz killed. But she *did* get him killed. Afterward, she knew it. She may have felt betrayed by her own side, follow? And they probably worried, judging by her erratic behavior, that she was going to jump back to our side to avenge his death. Now," Bill concluded darkly, "they couldn't allow that, could they?"

"And in fact," mused Auerbach, "if that was the case, with Lassiter dead she'd also outlived her usefulness."

"We could try it on," Bill said. "It fits."

They were aware of Lasko moving something in the next room, making a lot of noise pushing furniture through a hallway. For a moment it distracted them and reminded them where they were.

"It's a pretty brutal outfit," said Mason, shaking his head, "whoever they are."

"KGB," Mason shrugged, as if that explained it.

"Probably, I suppose. But it's almost too bloodthirsty for them."

"Depending on what's at stake," Bill suggested.

Auerbach nodded. "That lets us drift back to Frank Hargrove, you realize," he said. He raised his eyebrows as if to imply an association of the previous subject with the current one. Auerbach held one hand in the other and cracked his fingers.

"Hargrove? How?" Mason asked.

"I refer back to my Sausage Maker's story," said Auerbach. "Rudy. His reference to Hargrove."

Mason understood the implication.

"Hargrove's gone," said Auerbach. "Disappeared from the face of the earth. Left his London office late on a Friday evening on his way, purportedly, back to Madrid. Never made the trip, old man. That's called AWOL. Or over the wall if you prefer."

Mason considered it. Somehow he wished Lazz were there. Somehow Lassiter had always had the rapier-sharp insight into defection games.

"My own guess is that the ground is shifting," said Auerbach. "We'll see the new alignment within a few weeks. We've got two dead in London and you've got the Soviets hot after some computer parts. Meanwhile, Hargrove chooses this time to up and leave. Well, use your imagination."

"Anything's possible," Mason insisted.

"Of course it is," laughed Auerbach. "Anything's possible, but not everything's probable. Tell you what, old man. We're groping for straws in the wind. The only solid piece left for us to play with is Hargrove. We have to find him."

"He could be in Moscow by now. Or anywhere besides England."

"True. But we're watching every exit. As best we can, that is. That's the game now, you know. Find Hargrove any way we can. After that we can figure who shoved the resident of drawer five out a sixth-story window as well as who tied a bicycle chain around our favorite physicist's neck."

The door opened slowly and it was Lasko again, whining about the hour and strongly suggesting that he might like to close his humble emporium.

Auerbach stood. Then Mason.

"Do whatever you want," Auerbach concluded. "If you want some back-up, ask me for it. Just let me know what you're doing. That's all I insist on."

Mason was silent, deep in thought, as they neared the door.

"And by the way," added Auerbach, "you can remain in the flat. Hope you're enjoying your stay."

15

"It was a week ago last night," she said. Then, thinking more about it, she corrected herself. "No, eight days ago. A week ago Wednesday."

"And this is the first time you've mentioned it?" Paul Frost asked, puzzled and frowning.

Sarah fidgeted with a cigarette. She had smoked too many of them over the last week. Even Priscilla had noticed. In a tiny fit of annoyance, she pushed the half-smoked cigarette into an ash tray and snuffed it, breaking it in half in the process.

"This is the first time I've been *sure*," she said. "Two days ago. Up till then . . . Well, you know . . . I was figuring I'd been imagining it." She shook her head. "Not now. Now, I know."

Frost sat across from her in the living room of her house. She occupied the chair she had sat in all that night eight days ago with the rifle across her lap. "Sarah, if you're so worried about something you should tell someone. Even if you can't tell me, you should—"

"You're the only one I can tell, Paul."

"Well, then," he said, seeking to mollify. "Better late than never. What's going on?"

She recounted the early morning hours when she had been certain there'd been an intruder downstairs. She told Paul, for the first time, how she had crept along the upstairs hallway, called the police, found no one, and dismissed the two policemen who had responded.

"Several minutes after they left I decided to make a test," she said. "For my own peace of mind. Turned the light on, looked across the back lawn"—she indicated the direction with her head— "and saw a man—the back of a man—ducking down into the bushes."

"Did you call the police back?"

"No."

129

"Should have."

She made a sour expression.

"You're a taxpayer, Sarah. Better ten false alarms than one time when you really need them and don't call."

"They would think I'm crazy," she said. She reached for another cigarette and lit it. He watched her, hands folded across his lap. As was his habit, he wore a sport-shirt, neat gray slacks, and a buckskin jacket. No clerical collar. She might have been talking to a brother rather than a minister.

"Why would they think you're crazy?" he asked.

She blew out the smoke with distaste.

"I brought them out here on what appeared to be a false alarm that Monday night," she said. "Then two days later I went to the police station. Told them what I thought I had seen. I could tell," she explained slowly, assessing Paul's expression to see if he believed her. "They were exchanging glances. Crazy lady, they figured. Well, they drove out to the house again that afternoon. They were nice about it, I guess. Went out to the area where I'd seen the man. Looked all around. Didn't find any sign of anything." She considered it. "Of course, by that time they wouldn't have."

"That's out where we were walking two weeks ago," he said.

"That's right. Near the path through the woods. I guess they thought my intruder should have left a calling card."

"Come on, Sarah."

"They agreed to send the police car by a few times each night. Lot of good that does."

"How often do they drive by?"

"At first three times a night. Then twice. Last night, once."

"Early? Late?"

"Early. They're all back in their barracks playing cards by two A.M. That's what I've heard. Rarely come out ever after that unless called." She frowned. "Why?"

"No reason. Just curious." He shifted the conversation's direction. "On the telephone before you said you'd found something."

"I have," she said.

"Do you want to tell me about it?"

She nodded and put out the most recent cigarette.

She was aware of the nicotine stains on her fingers and was embarrassed by the crowded mess in the ashtray. "Come with me," she told him. "Downstairs. The basement."

He seemed surprised. Sarah led him to the basement door, opened it, and let him follow her down several wooden steps. They walked through a corridor with dank cement walls, illuminated by a bare sixty-watt bulb. Then they entered a small cubicle converted into a work area. There was an old desk, sturdy but not much to look at, with a disorder of papers and technical manuals on its top. The drawers were open slightly, as if someone had closed them in a hurry.

"Brian used to call this spot 'Woodson's Warren,'" she said, turning to see that he hadn't lost his way. Paul appeared to be looking around with a certain wonderment. On the walls and on ledges hung several odd, unrelated mementos and souvenirs.

She reached to a wall and threw a switch. An old lamp went on, casting better light.

"This was Brian's work area," she said. "You know what he was like." She corrected herself. "No, sorry. Didn't mean that literally. You don't know. He was always thinking. He had that analytical, scientific mind which wouldn't stop. When Brian had a technical problem," she said, shaking her head in bemusement, "he couldn't get away from it. I mean, the problems gripped him. She paused. "Maybe you know the type of mind."

He nodded. "I do," he said. He was listening intently and glancing around the room, especially at the old mementos which lay idly by. Dust-laden lawn furniture, a retired dining room table, golf clubs from the 1950s, and a duffle bag, marked *Korea,* which appeared to date from when her husband apparently had been in the US Army.

"I think I told you once," she said, "about this policy ITW had. If there was a technical problem which defied their research specialists, they'd send around a memorandum to everyone in the company. They'd have sixty-eight thousand minds working on the one problem."

He nodded again. "I remember."

"Well, this is where Brian used to come and work on those things. He'd set up his desk here and pore over his journals, manuals and computer print-outs. Often I'd never see him for five evenings in a row. The only thing

131

that would stop him was if he came up with a solution, or if someone else did."

"Did he ever?"

"Maybe six or seven."

Paul Frost looked impressed.

"Brian was working on one when he died," she said. He nodded sympathetically.

She snuffed her cigarette. "Shouldn't smoke down here. Too much paper," she chided herself. "I'm getting distracted," she said. "That's not why I asked you down here." She turned away from him and looked critically at her reflection in a mirror which her husband had hung in the work area. The mirror carried the crest of McKenna's Irish Whiskey in green and gold paint across the front. She swept her hand across her hairline, pushing a lock of hair back from her forehead and searching unconsciously for gray. She pulled a bobby pin from behind her ear and reclipped her hair.

"The intruder was down here," she said.

"*Here?* Why here?"

"I don't know."

She turned back toward him. He was reaching to the large trunk upon which her husband's US Navy duffel bag had rested. Next to the duffel he picked up a long, sharp instrument. He grasped it in his right hand and examined it. It had the contours of a long steel dagger, but was in fact a World War Two German bayonet. He held it with the handle in his fist, much as someone familiar with the weapon might.

"I hate that thing," she said coldly, seeing what he had. "I asked Brian to get rid of it many times."

His fascination appeared broken and he looked up to her quickly. "Sorry? I was distracted."

"Brian's uncle was in the war," she said. "Brought back a lot of fiendish souvenirs." She paused. "Why are men always so fascinated with such things? Must be phallic."

"I don't know." He continued to hold the blade in his hand, appraising it. "You were starting to tell me?" he said.

"Two days after the intruder, I came down here to check the furnace. The furnace is in the next area of the basement, you see." She nodded in its direction. "That's when I noticed the papers."

He sat down on the edge of an old trunk. He continued to consider the weapon in his hand, looking at it with considerable thought, yet listening to her intently at the same time.

"Had they been neat when your husband departed?"

"No. They were messy then, too."

"Well, then . . . ?"

"Two days earlier I'd spent some time straightening the desk area," she said. "Everything was much neater." She turned back to Paul. "Someone was here looking for something."

"Any idea what?"

"Something he was working on?" She shrugged helplessly. "I don't know. I'm only guessing."

"Did you tell the police?" he inquired. "Fingerprints," he suggested. "Did they take fingerprints?"

"No," she answered. "No one knows. The police think I'm crazy with grief and seeing ghosts. I didn't tell them."

"Maybe Priscilla?"

"She hasn't been down here."

He nodded. "Where is she today?"

"School. She won't be home for two hours."

"Ah, of course. I'd forgotten."

"We're quite alone."

He smiled with self-effacement. "I don't think you'll get into too much trouble with just a member of the local clergy."

Her thoughts were elsewhere. "Maybe I should go through everything he was working on," she said. "Maybe I'll find something."

He stood and began moving toward her. Slowly. She looked back to him. "Paul?" she asked. "What is the utter fascination you have with that loathsome weapon?"

"This?" he asked, holding it up, blade first.

"Yes. *That.*"

"I'll tell you," he said. He moved to a position a foot or two from her. He held the handle of the knife in one hand and the blade extended outward. He held it upward so the light shone on it and so that she could clearly view the blade. He held it about breast high on her and she was aware again—she had forgotten—how the six-foot minister was a head taller than she. She liked men of his height. "Take a good look, Sarah."

She leaned over the blade.

133

"See the writing there?"

"It's in German." She saw Germanic lettering beneath an unmistakable swastika.

"Fifteenth Army of the Third Reich," he said. "Sixth Division under General von Salmuth. My father fought with the US First Army under General Bradley."

"So?"

"My Dad brought home exactly the same souvenir," he said. "Brian's uncle and my father must have been somewhere not too far from each other in the war. Funny coincidence, that's all. But as soon as I saw the knife, it rang a funny bell."

"I didn't know you spoke German," she said.

"Only a little. Seminary German. I'm Lutheran, recall." He laid the knife aside. "Hateful object, really. I was a conscientious objector during the Vietnam years." He looked back to her. "Oh, Sarah, I'm sorry," he said. "You called me down here to show me something. I've hardly been listening."

"Do me a favor," she said. "When you leave, take that knife with you. Do something with it. Thow it away, throw it in a lake, stuff it in the garbage. Anything. I want it out of the house. Bad vibrations," she said.

"Of course." He picked it up again and held it downward by the blade.

They were upstairs again, talking. She made tea.

"You *do* believe me, don't you?" she asked.

He sipped the hot tea. He took it strong and straight, without milk or sugar.

"Sarah, if you're so certain, then I belive you." He nodded. "You're an intelligent woman. I believe you saw something. If you're sure that you had an intruder . . . a burglar, well, maybe I or Reverend Booth should talk to the police. You have a right to feel secure in your own home."

She was shaking her head again. No, she said, the police simply were out of the picture. They didn't believe her. Talking to them wouldn't help. Besides, nothing was missing.

"Maybe you have mice," Paul offered between sips of tea. "Or squirrels. Or a draft of some sort. That could have messed up the papers."

"Paul," she said somewhat dejectedly. "None of those things account for the opened drawers. Or the man I saw."

She felt something hot in her left hand and realized that the cigarette she was smoking had burned all the way down to the end. She had seared her fingers. She dropped it clumsily into the ashtray.

Drafts. Mice. Squirrels. Who was he kidding? She knew what she had seen. She glanced at her watch.

"Getting late," she said. "Well, now you know. What's been bothering me, that is."

"I don't know, Sarah," he said. "I'm sorry to be a broken record, but it sounds like a police matter to me."

She shook her head. "I guess I'll just drop it," she said. "Pray he doesn't come back."

She felt like smoking again. She felt like blowing the smoke directly at him.

She'd done a lot of thinking over the last week. She'd come to three conclusions.

One: There *had* been a man in her house. She'd heard him and seen him. Two: He'd gone to the basement, looking for heaven knows what among her husband's belongings and workpapers. Three: The intruder hadn't found what he had come for. Hence, he would return.

Her voice suddenly took on a tired edge. She was weary of her guest. "Finished your tea?"

"Yes."

"I have to run, Paul," she said. "Grocery shopping, I'm afraid. When you leave, take the bayonet. I want it out of the house."

16

Mason spotted Fahrar long before he was approached by him. The American had watched Sloane Square from a shop window and had spotted an Arab of generous proportions. Fahrar, wearing a beige raincoat, had been stationed near the south end of the square for a quarter hour. It was Wednesday, quarter past two.

Mason ambled slowly through the square. Fahrar, mocha-skinned and wearing blue-tinted eyeglasses, viewed Mason with curiosity, then animosity. He allowed Mason to stroll past him, and continue to one corner of the south end.

When the American strolled back, Fahrar rose from a bench and strode casually toward Mason. When he was near, he stopped.

"Sir?" he asked, speaking with the accent of an Arab who'd learned English at good schools, "Would you have the proper time?"

Mason looked at his watch. "Eighteen past two," he said dully.

"A wonderful day for a walk," said Fahrar. "My name is Rasheed." He offered his hand, without friendship.

"Mason. Bill Mason. I'm American."

"First trip to London?"

"Yes, in fact. It is. You?"

Fahrar laughed mirthlessly. "No, no. Certainly not. I live here."

"Maybe then," suggested Mason, finishing the ritual, "I could trouble you for a direction or two."

"Of course."

The men fell into stride together and walked to a bench. Fahrar was an imposing man. His shoulders were unbelievably wide. His arms were so thick that there was no extra room in the sleeves of his raincoat. He appeared

136

not to have a neck, just a thick, battered head set atop his shoulders. His dark, moustached face was like a fist. His size was emphatic. He looked midway between a diplomat and a bouncer.

The sat down. He viewed Mason with vexation now. "I've been here two previous days. You have not."

"That's right."

The Arab looked at Mason. "Well . . . ?"

"Well, what? Am I going to offer an excuse? Is that what you're wondering?"

Fahrar was quiet in a way that indicated, yes, that was what he was wondering, and what he wanted. Or else he'd crush a certain skull.

"I damned well didn't feel like coming," said Mason. "I was making the acquaintance of a bottle of brandy."

"Very bad."

"I've been told that before. It doesn't trouble me."

"Follow me."

They crossed a pathway into the square. "Like to drink, do you?" asked Fahrar.

"I've been known to find joy at eighty proof, if that's what you mean."

Fahrar nodded. "Not a good habit, you see."

"Meeting you isn't much of a habit, either. In case you haven't noticed, I don't like people like you. A few belts of liquor help."

"You're free to leave."

"I just might."

"Why don't you?"

"I thought I'd hear you out," said Mason. "I don't have to like you to work for you."

Fahrar looked at him with aggravation but said nothing else provocative, no matter how obviously Mason irked him. Mason guessed Fahrar was probably one notch above Essie Kelman, but not in a position to make decisions himself. Fahrar's job was to lead Mason closer to recruitment, not to take bait or enter into an argument.

"A correspondent's job appeals to you?" Fahrar asked.

"No. But the money does. Come on, Fahrar. Who's kidding who? You know why I'm here."

Fahrar motioned to another bench in the square, led Mason to it and the two men sat again. "Perhaps we need to like you," suggested Fahrar.

"I doubt that very much."

"Oh? Why?"

"Because it's already evident that I despise you. You people are the nouveaux riches of the world, among the most belligerent and certainly the stupidest. I hear you put up a mosque in Regent's Park and then didn't even have it pointed in the right direction." Mason snorted resentfully. "Figures. Parvenu barbarians with money. Russian puppets, too." He looked at Fahrar to see how he was taking it. Fahrar was sitting and listening. It figured. "I'll tell you something else. I dislike myself for getting involved with you."

"Then why do you?"

"Maybe I'm stupid. Maybe I want to know why a friend flew out of a window."

"You are a malcontent," Fahrar observed sharply.

Mason laughed. "The decision's already been made. I have something you want. You have to tolerate me until you have whatever it is. Then I'll be ready for the junk heap."

Fahrar's reaction surprised Mason. He was shaking his head furiously. "Not so. Not true at all, sir. We have a future for you. A very good one."

"Oh, yeah?" Mason challenged. "What the hell is it?"

"You will see. In Paris. You will come to Paris?"

"Sure," Mason sneered. "Any time."

The Arab played with a pack of gold-tipped cigarettes, intentionally failed to offer one to Mason, then lit one himself. "What do you suppose you have that we, allegedly, want?"

"Insight. Information."

The Arab blew out the smoke and gazed straight ahead. "Yes. Maybe. A good guess."

"Guess, hell. I'm warning you, Fahrar," Mason spat out sourly. "Don't play me for an idiot or the whole deal's off." Fahrar looked him calmly in the eye. "I've been in games like this before. Been in them from both sides. I know how they work. You want me in your employ, then you better make me a damned good offer."

"What would you like?"

"For starters, I'm looking for a man named Hargrove."

Fahrar answered without hesitation. "We can provide him."

"I hear he's out of the country."

"He is in London. We are holding him."

"As your pawn, right? You're a son of a bitch, Fahrar. You pulled him in so that you could use him as a bargaining tool. Exchange him for something you want, right?"

The Arab blinked. A smile was his only answer.

The two men were silent, as a blond woman in jeans and a tweed jacket walked by. When she was beyond earshot, Fahrar continued. "There is work you could do for us in America," he explained. "Work which would be accessible to you."

"That's long range, Fahrar," Mason retorted. "You've got more immediate plans. Be specific."

"There are some computer chips," the Arab conceded. "Silicon. Integrated circuits . . ."

"And Moscow wants them back, is that it? After that Vassiliev clown was dumb enough to lose them?"

Fahrar stiffened. Mason could tell that Fahrar had nothing further to volunteer. "Are you prepared to come to Paris for discussions or not?"

Mason let Fahrar wait several seconds. "You put your recruiting pitch in a neat little bundle. There's just one piece missing."

"That is . . . ?"

Mason looked his contact in the eye. "If you think I'm going to cross borders on my American passport, you're nuts. Get the message?"

"What could I do?" Fahrar gave a shrug of naïveté.

Mason gave an exaggerated shrug in return. "Better do something." He reached into his pocket and pulled out a small white envelope. He flipped it contemptuously at Fahrar who caught it with both hands. The Arab opened it and found two passport-sized pictures of Mason, obviously taken that morning.

"If you're as good as I give you credit for," Mason snorted, "you can whip up a false-flag job for me in no time. Right?"

Fahrar fingered the pictures noncommittally. He raised his eyes to look at Mason.

"I like to have a brandy at the Silver Lion pub on Celestra Street," Mason said. "When you've made me ready to travel, find me."

Fahrar put the photographs in his inside jacket pocket. His hand moved slowly.

139

"And Fahrar," Mason noted in closing, "I feel very strongly about my privacy, particularly in the evening. If anyone follows me, I'll shoot him."

For a second or two astonishment registered in Fahrar's eyes. But then the poise was back and he simply nodded.

"I knew that you'd prove to be a reasonable man," Fahrar finally said. "A man who recognized his own interests."

"Old American proverb, Fahrar," said Mason acidly. " 'Screw yourself.' "

17

As Bill Mason sat somewhat anxiously in the British Airways Tri-Star, his mind drifted back to another arrival in Paris, a decade and a half earlier.

He had taken a steamer across from Florida to the Mediterranean, disembarking at Marseilles. It had been a brilliant morning, just past seven A.M. When he stepped off the vessel and began his first tour abroad, all around him was the limitless expanse of azure sky so familiar to the southern coast of France. Though he moved through the sun-drenched port as a stranger might, he felt himself at one with the magic of the adventure before him. It was an inner sense of rectitude perhaps, a sense of purpose. He still possessed his hopes, his idealism, his sense of pride, and the latter years of his youth. He had not yet truly accepted his own mortality. His mission and his life beckoned as the sky above: clear, untroubled, limitless. It was only when he moved northward to Paris, a month or two later, that the weather had changed.

Bill had established himself quickly in Paris and had put together his proper networks. There wasn't an American or British newsman of importance whom he didn't know or know of. The lines were open. The information flowed. Gradually friends became commodities, valued for what they had access to. Mason had congratulated himself on the subtlety with which he worked, the effortless way in which he learned to function, manipulating contacts to betray whatever small trust someone else had placed in them. As an exercise in sabotaging middle-class values of loyalty and integrity, it was an excellent one. But, as they'd insisted back in Langley, it was all for a higher purpose. He was more committed to country and agency than to friends. How could he do the job otherwise? The world was a dangerous place and someone had to do the

141

job in the back alleys. If it was enjoyable, so much the better.

The British Airways flight buffeted jerkily for several seconds. Even the flight personnel glanced around apprehensively. Mason was distracted from his thoughts; then, as the aircraft steadied, he again allowed his mind to follow its own inclinations. Once more he was using the pressurized isolation, the elevation from the earth, as a moment of reflection and meditation. A time to think even farther back now.

With what spirit had he been imbued when he joined the agency in 1964? A disproportionate sense of duty? A bad case of jingoism? He tried to discover what his feelings had been because he no longer recognized what they must have been.

He had known that a CIA career would not occupy his entire life. What then had he been seeking? Odd, he thought as the aircraft began its descent toward Paris. That emotion, whatever it had been at the time, was so foreign now as to be incomprehensible. Now he felt nothing except an instinct for self-preservation. It was as if the world had tightened. There was a sense of unfinished business, Lassiter's death, to be sure. But allegiance? That, like sorrow, was private.

At customs he picked up his bag and strolled toward two sleepy-eyed inspectors. Mason's French had never been fluent but once had been passable. Now it was rusty; his tongue was disobedient. The two customs officers asked him whether he had anything to declare.

He held aloft his passport, shook his head, and moved through the line. For some reason he couldn't shake the memory of another day, thirteen years earlier, when he'd arrived in Paris from Marseilles, twenty-four years old, one canvas suitcase in hand. Every uniform had made him nervous.

The passport today was Canadian, in the name of Michael Tully, provided by Fahrar and dropped in his pocket at the Silver Lion two days before Bill's departure. Later that evening Mason had examined it well. An excellent false-flag cover, a cleansing nationality, the universally welcome red maple leaf. Mason examined the document inside out. Perfection on short order, a masterful document. It had told Bill what he'd known already.

He was dealing with professionals. He was glad he had purchased the weapon. Friendliness toward defectors carried only so far.

He passed by immigration with barely an eyelash flinched, on his side or the other. He took the bus into Paris and installed himself in a moderately priced hotel on the Rue de Rennes. Restlessly he walked around the city and performed various maneuvers to convince himself he wasn't casting a shadow that didn't belong to him. Satisfied, he went to work at seven thirty.

Doesn't surprise me at all, Mason thought. Not at all.

The woman was shaking her finger to indicate no and was rattling onward in rapid French which Mason couldn't possibly understand. Language was failing; but the general point was being made. Monsieur Norden, Monsieur Eric Norden, the journalist whom Mason sought, no longer resided at this address.

Figures, Mason thought.

Her hair was in pink clips and metal rollers. She was, as they say, a real sweetheart.

He stood in the vestibule of the building. The courtyard beyond. This was the last address he had for Eric Norden.

The squat little concierge had picked him up immediately when he passed through the double doors leading from the gate.

"Plus ici," she'd replied. *"Il n'habite plus ici."* She made a rapid and disparaging motion with her thumb. Eric Norden had departed on terms less than friendly and more than speedy.

Mason tried to wrestle with the language of Voltaire. *"Où?"* he inquired. *"Où il est maintenant?"*

"Aucune idée, monsieur," she'd snarled. A dog began barking in her apartment.

She closed the door. Mason placed his foot in it.

She whirled angrily and picked up a broomstick. She was fully prepared to use it to transcend the language barrier.

But as she looked, he was holding aloft a fifty-franc note which captured her attention.

"Où maintenant?" he asked again. *"Monsieur Norden?"*

143

She studied him for a moment, then flung the broom-stick against the wall. She released the door.

"*Suivez. Suivez,*" she said.

He stepped into her apartment. It smelled like a locker room. The dog, a middle-sized black-and-white mongrel, approached within two feet of him, snarling furiously. When Mason stamped his foot at the animal, it retreated and continued to bark from a safer position. The concierge turned and cursed him.

"Just the address, God damn it. Just the address," he said in English.

The dog was still sounding off. She pulled a battered black ledger down from a shelf, leafed through it quickly, said something aloud which sounded like an address, and looked up at him.

It hadn't registered. She pointed to a space in the book. Mason stepped alongside her and looked.

In a semilegible scrawl, he saw a forwarding address. Mason printed it clearly on a scrap of tissue paper from his pocket.

She was saying something again, something which sounded like numbers. When he couldn't grasp it, she wrote it down. It was a year. 1975. Norden had moved out in 1975. He confirmed it by gesturing with his thumb, pointing outward from the building as if to indicate some-one leaving.

She nodded vigorously, and whacked her dirty finger at the year again. She was speaking louder now, evidently convinced that increased volume would overcome his linguistic shortcomings.

He dropped the fifty-franc note on her kitchen table and nodded with obsequious politeness. "Fuck you," he said. She mumbled and snatched the money without any gesture of gratitude. He flirted with the idea of grabbing it back, but preferred to leave without the broomstick across his head.

He found the second address within an hour. It was a small rooming house in the sixteenth, an old plaster-faced building with a peeling front. No Norden. Eric had been moving recently. Mason wondered whether there was any reason behind it and whether the journalist was still in Paris at all.

But a landlady appeared at the second address and

was as amiable as the previous concierge had been hostile. She made an effort to understand his terrible French, dutifully handed him still another address and mentioned the name Darcel. Mason followed on it immediately. He arrived just past nine thirty P.M. at a seedy Parisian tenement in a white section just off from Belleville.

On the residents' listing in the vestibule, past the broken front gate, he saw no Norden. When he scanned the names more closely, he noticed the name *Norden* scrawled in tiny writing next to the larger, printed name, G. DARCEL. Mason grinned. It was a second-floor apartment.

He climbed a flight of rickety stairs, walked through a shabby hallway, and rang a doorbell with the name Darcel beside it.

A girl no more than seventeen came to the door. If Norden had a roommate, she was a young one. She had light blond hair and the cherubic, open face of a little girl. She had freckles, a smile, and wore a blue bathrobe.

"Monsieur Norden?" he asked. *"Là? Il est là?"*

She seemed not to know what to reply so she began shaking her fair head. She looked at Mason as if trying to decide whether or not she recognized him.

Fortunately, Eric Norden answered the inquiry for himself. He stepped from behind a string curtain which led from another room. Mason saw him before she was aware that he was there. Norden said something to her in French and she turned toward him quickly and obediently.

"Ça va," Norden told her. *"Je le connais."* His French carried an unmistakable American accent, yet it was fluent.

He stood in the center of the room, a tall stringy man with dull red hair, an angular face, peculiar jaw, and piercing green eyes. His hands were on his hips. He wore a white shirt, a loosened tie, rumpled suit pants, and looked as if he'd just returned home.

"William Mason," he said. His face, which had a quotient of cruelty to it, warped with a wide smile. He invited Bill in.

The girl moved to Norden and seemed upset at being caught in her robe. She said something softly and secretively to him, which he dismissed brusquely. He patted her bottom and sent her scampering through the beaded curtain.

145

Mason caught a glimpse of the room beyond, a cluttered bedroom tastefully decorated in pink and purple. Then the beaded curtain rattled back into place.

"Sorry about the rude greeting, Bill. My little Giselle doesn't speak English. Easier that way, you know. How about a drink? For old times, huh?"

"I wouldn't mind."

Norden turned and shouted authoritatively at the girl. Moments later she appeared again, this time clad in an inexpensive and wrinkled pink pullover which was tied at the waist and which descended to a point three quarters of the way northward from her knee. She wore a pair of rubber sandals and obediently fetched a pair of cloudy-looking glasses and a bottle of red wine.

"Sorry," said Norden, relaxing in a worn sofa and lighting a cigar. "We're out of the hard stuff. A local rotgut will have to do." He blew his breath into his glass and shined the glass with his necktie.

"It's fine," said Mason.

Giselle leaned over Bill and poured, then poured some wine for Norden. As she finished he grabbed her, pulled her lecherously into his lap and gave her a bearish hug. She giggled. Female emancipation had not arrived in this apartment. She struggled playfully to her feet and Norden tweaked her supple breasts as she escaped.

"She loves it," Norden explained. "And by God," he mused as she disappeared, "this one keeps me feeling young."

"I noticed."

Norden took a long gulp of wine from the glass. "When d'I see you last?"

"Three years ago, maybe?" Mason suggested.

"Washington, wasn't it? February, seventy-four?"

Mason nodded. Norden's mind was clear and sharp as ever, particularly his memory.

"You and another man. Phil Gardner, I think. Economist who used to work in Bonn in the sixties."

Mason nodded. "Who's your friend?" he asked, motioning toward the corridor where the girl had disappeared.

"My latest," said Norden with total sobriety. "I've always figured women are worn out by the time they're twenty. Stretched." He smiled and poured more wine. "So I do the wearing out." He sipped. "I like this one.

146

Nice little tail. Found her in a department store about five months ago. She shrieks like a banshee and she digs her nails into my back. Aside from that. . . ." He paused, as if checking a compulsion to tell more. "What's on your mind, Bill?"

"Is it safe to talk here?"

Norden nodded with disinterest. "No one seems to care much what I say. I'm just your hack correspondent." Norden's mean eyes twinkled. He represented a Chicago newspaper and filed a report from Western Europe twice a week. The column was syndicated and reappeared in six smaller papers from Dubuque to Sacramento.

"Still stringing for the Company?" Mason asked.

"Occasionally." Beneath it all, Mason recalled, Norden was a first-class bastard, willing to help those who someday could help him. "How about you?" he asked with sudden interest. "All those firings. What about—?"

"I'm secure."

"Good," said Norden thoughtfully. "Good."

"How much is happening in France these days?" Bill asked.

"With who?"

"CIA. Russians. The lot."

Norden curled his lip. "I've seen busier times of the year. It's the cowboys who need watching. These wild terrorist groups. The Yids are busy watching the Ay-rabs and CIA is busy helping them. Russkies are watching everyone. As usual. French intelligence stinks to high hell and might just as well be on a direct line to Moscow. The dumb-assed Czechs are still going all out against the English, though God knows why. Business as usual," Norden concluded.

The girl reappeared and seemed to be preparing dinner for herself and her roommate. The kitchen was a small recessed corner of the main living room. The dining table was what Norden had his size-twelve feet on. Norden looked toward her to see how she was doing. Mason studied the journalist. Beneath the man's veneer of hardness and cruelty, he decided, was even more hardness and cruelty.

Norden finally looked back to Mason. "What did you want to know? Specifically."

"What do you know about journalistic covers?"

"Excluding myself?" A cold smile.

147

"Excluding yourself, Eric."

"A bit." He sipped more wine. "Want the whole run-down, right up to the most recent? Don't forget, I've been here off and on since the early 1950s. I can remember when CIA was funneling dollars into magazines like Paris *Match* just to keep pro-West opinion afloat before Moscow money controlled every publication in France. Want a smoke?"

He offered Bill a Gauloise, which Mason declined. Norden proceeded to envelop the room with the stench of his smoke. Giselle wordlessly came over to them, filched a cigarette and returned to her corner.

"More recent matters," Mason said. "Ever heard of Middle Eastern News Service?"

Norden reflected for a moment. "Oh, yeah. Oh, sure," he finally said after a thought. "Shifty bunch."

"Shifty how?"

"Beware of philanthropic Ay-rabs," said Norden. "They've got a wire service and news center in Paris. I could find the address if I had to. I think it's on the Rue—"

"I have it."

"Okay, they transmit news and features and low-key Ay-rab opinion, but I think it's a crock. No Ay-rab outfit in the world ever does anything out of the goodness of their tight black hearts. Mid East News is a front for something. Maybe harmless, maybe no." The eyes narrowed and a bushy red eyebrow levitated. "Why?"

Mason had an innocuous answer planned. As he gave it he had the impression that he wasn't convincing Norden. "Background research, Eric," he said. "They've cropped up twice in a case I'm on."

"When roads cross twice," said Norden, "assume they're leading to the same place." He finished his wine.

"I do."

"Want an opinion?"

"Sure."

"It's probably a Moscow job. Just a guess off the top of my head. The Russians are playing it cute these days. Keeping their own people clean and letting the Ay-rabs go at it in the alleys and do the dirty work. Problem is, the Ay-rabs are consistent: They fuck up all the time. *All* the time."

"Don't care for them, do you?"

148

"Scum," Norden said. "I had a brother, you know. Younger. Emigrated to Israel in 1965."

Mason was genuinely surprised. "I didn't know that."

"Joined the Israeli Air Force in '66. Came through okay in the '67 war." He shook his head without feeling. "Not so good in '73. It happened over Sinai."

There was an uneasy moment. Mason felt the violence within Norden. Then Norden turned with utter calm and addressed the French girl in soft, polite tones. He asked about dinner.

"Dix minutes," she replied. Even Mason understood, both the words and the hint.

"Sorry, Eric. About your brother."

"The world turns," Norden concluded philosophically. "Anything else? That's all I know about Mid-East."

Mason shook his head. He thanked Norden and rose to leave. Norden shuffled to the old front door with his guest. "Going to be playing ball with any Ay-rabs?" Norden inquired coyly.

"Ball?"

"You know what I mean."

Mason rolled his eyes to indicate that he didn't know how things would turn out.

"Do me a favor. . . . If you need any legs broken or skulls stomped, I'll only be too happy. Got it?"

"Got it."

The men shook hands. Norden's shake was one of those crunching pumps which served as an advertisement. Or a warning.

Mason walked down the corridor and approached the stairs. Before Norden had a chance to close the apartment door, Mason stopped dramatically, as if stricken by an important afterthought.

He turned.

"Eric. Oh, Eric?"

The door, halfway shut, opened again and the frame of Norden filled the opening.

"Didn't you work with a man named Lassiter once? Robert Lassiter, I think it was."

Norden's angular face hid any outward reaction. "Yeah. So?"

"Bad experience?"

"The cocksucker had it in his head to trade me off for

149

a pair of Czechoslovaks. Only one reason he didn't, I figure."

"What's that?"

"He knew I'd come back and kill him someday."

"Where was that?" Mason asked.

"Korea. Nineteen fifty-three. I can't prove it, but that was how Lassiter built his reputation. Trading off people who trusted him."

"Someone beat you to it," Mason said.

Norden frowned.

"Came back and killed him," Mason said. "Lassiter's dead."

"I'm not surprised at all. Could have been anyone."

Mason nodded. "Almost anyone."

There was nothing else to say. Mason descended the stairs, buried in thought. He heard the door bang shut as he walked. Two drop bolt locks fell seconds thereafter. Then Mason was out the front gate of the building. He walked a block. Still pondering deeply, his appetite led him to a crêpe stand on the corner. Just what he needed.

As he ate, the image of Norden was before him. Against every emotion, Mason trusted the man. It was one of those instincts he couldn't explain.

Less than forty minutes later, Mason wandered aimlessly toward the Boulevard des Capucines. He found a long brass bar which was loud and active. He stood at the distant end of it, away from the entrance and with his back to the wall. He watched everyone coming in and out the door and nursed several brandies, one after another. By two A.M. Bill Mason was very drunk.

His eyes were heavy. He thought of Eric Norden and realized why he liked the man. Norden was old school. Not typically, and not completely, but he resembled the type of man with whom Mason had entered the service.

Now—these new employees in Langley—the young people were different. They weren't clubby and they seemed to play by no rules at all. The sons of sunbelt oilmen. Californians. Southerners who had been junior officers in the military. And on top of it all was Captain Queeg, who distinctly felt ill at ease with the old order and was ringing in the new one on an unprecedented scale.

Mason was halfway through a final brandy. He studied his own blurred image in the mirror behind the bar, as was his habit. He looked rumpled, dispirited, and somewhat dowdy, hardly what one expected as the product of the best social institutions and academies. He gulped the remainder of the brandy, left no tip on the bar, and lurched back to the hotel. A depression was upon him.

He slept uneasily, knowing that at twenty minutes past one on the following afternoon he would renew contact with Fahrar.

Make contact and accompany.

In the middle of the night, at some indeterminate moment between four and five, he woke and felt a stirring within him. What he was thinking of, he realized, what he'd been reliving, was a buoyant, bright August sun in Delwood, New Jersey and lean, tanned, dark-haired Julie Heasman naked in bed next to him. It was not purely a sexual stirring, but a psychological one as well. A sense of isolation. A sense of loss. A sense of . . .

Sleep overtook him again. And again the sleep was troubled. Lassiter was before him now, Lassiter presiding over terrifying images of betrayal and imprisonment. Lassiter trading off one agent for another, letting a young fieldman like Mason be captured to protect an older agent in place. Or to protect himself.

Mason's head ached. He knew he was drunk. He rolled over and over during the night. The sheets were warm and oppressive. A deeper sleep was upon him as dawn lightened the city beyond his window shades. He drifted off.

Then he bolted up hours later. He was bewildered and his pulse quickened. He'd been dreaming about China again, about Lassiter again, but it was a loud bell that had roused him.

The telephone was ringing.

He looked at it with subdued terror and reached for it for no other reason than to silence it.

No one knew he was there. So who was calling?

18

Mason sleepily listened to the voice ask the same question, three times slowly, in French. At the last repetition he caught the words *petit déjeuner*. But then the exasperated voice asked a final time, this time in cracked English, if Monsieur Tully would care for some breakfast. It was ten A.M., and the management was no longer serving breakfast. Would Monsieur Tully like the final *café complet* sent up?

"Yes," said Mason groggily. "Yes. Thank you. I would."

He looked at the clock. He had failed to set the alarm and had overslept. Worse, he had an unyielding headache.

Breakfast arrived. He consumed it and was soon out of his room, allowing the hotel maid to straighten it. Mason marked time, carried both his passports with him (perhaps foolishly, he felt) and killed an hour or two in stores before meeting Fahrar at the designated spot: on the Porte d'Auteuil side of the Sèvres-Babylone metro stop.

Fahrar offered very little greeting. "I'm glad you decided to come. Finally," he said. The tone conveyed displeasure at having been kept waiting. He had no joy to spread.

"Wouldn't have missed it for anything," Mason answered.

"Follow me," Fahrar instructed blankly.

Fahrar led him back up to the street where they boarded a bus. Mason tried to note the winding route that the bus followed but Fahrar was idly talking in accented English.

They disembarked near the Luxembourg Gardens and walked three blocks until they came to an address on the narrow Rue de Thibaux where it intersected Boulevard Saint-Michel. There Mason confronted an unimposing brick building which had been converted into offices. A modest sign in front announced: *Bureau des Informations du Moyen-Orient*. Below, in English, it also read, *Middle Eastern News Service*. Taking even billing with English were Hebrew and Arabic characters, stating presumably the same.

Fahrer led Mason into the building, through an unguarded door, and into a receiving vestibule. A man at a reception desk glanced at Fahrar and continued to work.

"I don't know what you think of us so far, Mr. Mason," Fahrar said, "but I wish you to see that we are a fully accredited, fully functioning news and information service. As a correspondent, you would be working out of this office. Our Paris office. One of our best."

Mason seemed bored. But in fact he was observing that this was a more elaborate setup than he had expected. For a brief moment he wondered if he'd guessed completely wrong about them. He dismissed the fantasy quickly. He had only one use to these people. It was only a matter of time until they tapped him for it.

"I want you to meet Monsieur Sirtira, our bureau manager," Fahrar said. "He would be your direct superior."

"You mean my case officer?" Mason asked as they walked down a small corridor, past rows of open doors that looked into busy, small offices. The pretense of a news bureau was well preserved.

Fahrar laughed unconvincingly. "Really, Mr. Mason," he said. "I was educated in America, you know. But really. I have never known such a cynical man as you."

"Where were you educated in America?" Mason asked.

"Rice University. Texas."

"Figures."

"What?" Fahrar missed the point and Mason didn't repeat it. They continued to walk and eventually Fahrar pushed open a door without knocking. The sign on it said DIRECTEUR and a small, lean man with a cadaverish face, toothbrush moustache, and ill-fitting serge suit stood up from behind a desk. The directeur offered a wiry, narrow hand.

Fahrar introduced him in English. This was Mohsin Sirtira, the bureau manager. Sirtira spoke in lightly accented English and offered Mason a drink and a box of small Brazilian cigars. Fahrar heavy-handedly folded his tinted glasses and pocketed them.

"It's actually something else I'd like," Mason said.

"And that is?" Sirtira asked agreeably as they sat down.

"To cut through all this nonsense," Mason said angrily. "Come on. Let's be done with it."

Sirtira was unmoved. "Are you nervous, Monsieur Mason?"

"Just impatient."

Sirtira shook his head. "Americans. Always in a rush. Come. You haven't seen all our offices."

The two men rose to lead Mason. They went to the door to show him the way. Intentionally, to register his annoyance, he was lethargic in getting up.

But then he followed, down a flight of stairs now, and, he noted ominously, deeper into the concrete inner sanctum of the building. He felt his wet armpits and his shirt sticking to his ribs. So this is what it's like, he was thinking.

Ominously Sirtira led the way down a final set of steps. In what then seemed a bizarre touch, the final part of the corridor was carpeted in a plush, brown Persian runner upon which one's foot sank comfortably. On the walls were tapestries leading to a final door marked PRIVÉ. Mason thought the decorating touch was, at best, someone's odd sense of humor until another thought came to mind.

Carpets and tapestry have functions other than decorative. They insulate and shield sound. Mason was, in effect, in a concrete vault well under the city of Paris, far from any point to which a human voice would carry. The niceties were finished. Now, Mason knew, business would begin. The two other men held Bill in conversation.

"There is someone else you should meet," Sirtira told him.

The door opened and Bill was led into a small room of concrete walls with thick cloth hangings on each. There were two large chairs flanking a desk, another beside the desk, and a wooden armchair before the desk. There was a very small air vent in the corner of the ceiling and somewhere Bill could hear the white noise of a ventilator.

Sirtira and Fahrar closed the door behind them. There was no knob on the inside of the door. Only a keyhole.

154

Mason had made a major miscalculation; now he would pay for it.

"All right," Mason snapped with obvious anxiety. "What's going on?"

"Nothing," assured Fahrar, taking on a smarmy expression and sitting down behind the desk. "Just a few questions."

Sirtira sat beside the desk and pointed to the wooden chair, indicating that Bill should sit down. There and nowhere else.

Hesistantly, he did.

The door opened again. A barrel-chested man with glasses, a hunched look, and an ill-fitting gray suit came through the door. He looked at Mason, nodded to the other two men, and then sat on the edge of a table directly behind Mason.

"Who's our guest?" Bill asked.

"If you don't mind," Fahrar said, "we'll ask the questions."

"I *do* mind."

"It's you who came to us looking for . . . employment," Fahrar said.

"I don't remember it that way," Mason noted.

But Fahrar continued. A bit of background information, Fahrar said they wanted. Just the type of things they would ask any future employee who would be employed as Mason would be.

"What sort?"

"Everything," said Fahrar.

So that was it, Mason thought. They want to debrief even before they decide to hire. The man behind him, leaning against the table, had a noisy, wheezing manner of breathing. Quickly, it began.

"Your life," insisted Sirtira helpfully, a comment which could have been construed two ways. "We want to know all about you."

"Where you've been," said Fahrar. "What you've been engaged in."

Mason eyed one man, then the other. He felt like attacking each of them with something sharp.

Sirtira methodically pulled a small German tape recorder from one of the desk drawers as they spoke. He set it up and turned on the microphone. Mason knew that they would only be recording if they planned to play it back later and check every word against the truth as it was known.

"Certainly," suggested Fahrar, "if you're planning to come to work for us, you'll have no difficulty in answering a few simple questions. Truthfully."

"It's the iron-handed methods I despise," Mason said obstinately. "The methods and the two of you personally."

They were unmoved. So was the third man, the one behind him.

"Tell us about your schooling," Sirtira suggested. "As a start."

Mason found himself discussing Kenfield, not in glowing terms. He lingered on his education until it visibly bored them. He discussed Yale.

"Was it from Yale that you were enlisted?" Fahrar asked.

"Enlisted?"

"US intelligence. Please don't stall."

"Yes," Mason answered.

"By whom?"

Mason named Lassiter. One of them glanced to the broad man over Mason's shoulder.

"How did you know Robert Lassiter?"

"From Kenfield."

"But this man was much older. Ten years older. No?"

"He was an instructor when I was a student."

They professed surprise. Mason knew they were faking.

"So he was your friend, too?"

"He guided me."

"Guided you how?"

"Into intelligence work. As if you don't know."

"Please. . . ." said Fahrar shaking his head sharply, piqued now. "Please do not waste time. Where did you begin in American intelligence? Please to describe."

Mason went on without hesitation, now. He described the early visits to Langley and the training program following his selection for active service.

"How old are you?" Sirtira asked.

"Thirty-seven."

"You have a wife?"

"No."

"You are homosexual?"

156

"Notorious," Mason replied caustically.

"Parents?"

"I had two."

"They are living?" •

Mason paused. "Divorced."

They seemed interested. "Where are they?"

Mason rushed through it. "My father's a retired banker in Boston, Massachusetts. My mother lives in Colorado with her new husband. They're in their late sixties."

"How charming," Sirtira said.

"Fuck off!" Mason snapped sharply. He was instantly sorry. They'd intruded into his private life to rattle him. He knew the tactic; he had used it himself.

"I have a brother," he volunteered.

"Lassiter guided you how?" Fahrar asked, backtracking.

"Into intelligence work. He encouraged me to study Southeast Asian affairs at the university."

"What university?"

"Yale. I just told you that!"

Fahrar, American educated, nodded. God damned frauds, Mason thought. They knew that. Mason continued with the truth; it could always be corroborated.

"What was your first assignment?" Sirtira asked.

"I went to Langley, Virginia, for ten months of initial training."

"What year?"

"1964."

"Ten months," said Sirtira. "Which months?"

"February through November." Sirtira was making notes. Points he'd wish to check more carefully than others, Mason guessed.

"Then . . . ?"

"I was an assistant on a Division Chief's desk in Langley."

"Which Division?"

"South Asia. Indochina."

"Those first ten months," said Fahrar. "What exactly did you do?"

Mason knew what he was after.

"After four months of initial orientation, a decision was made separating those who'd go into overt intelligence

157

gathering and analysis, from those who'd go into clandestine operations and security."

"Which were you?"

"The latter. Of course."

"Is that what you'd wanted?"

"Yes."

"Had Robert Lassiter encouraged you in that direction?"

"Yes."

"How many recruits were there that year? From the universities?"

Mason had to think. "About seventy. I'm not certain. That's an estimate."

Fahrar nodded. "Which universities?"

"Those in the northeast, mostly."

"Ivy League, as they are called?"

"Frequently. Those were the popular recruiting grounds in the fifties and sixties."

"Aren't they still?" Fahrar asked with disparagement.

"Intelligence work isn't that popular in the Ivy League anymore," said Mason. "The junior officers are recruited more from the southern or midwestern universities now. Or the military."

"Curious," Fahrar noted.

You know that, Mason thought.

"Continue," Sirtira said. "You were separated from the others."

"Those going into covert action went to Camp Peary, Virginia, to the training facility there. That's where they taught tradecraft to new recruits."

"Did you learn well?"

"Very."

"What was next?"

"Pushing meaningless papers around a desk," said Mason, "for two years."

"They couldn't have been meaningless to everyone," Sirtira suggested. "What were they about?"

"They were circumstantial alternative papers," Mason said. "Primarily on Vietnam. Some on China. Contingency planning for developments which would probably never occur but which always could. Intellectual masturbation, it's been called."

Fahrar smirked.

"Were any ever put into effect?" Sirtira asked.

"I don't think so."

"You don't *know?*"

"No."

"Why don't you know?"

"I didn't stay in the department long enough to see what was done. And I never heard of any in particular which were used."

"You must have heard of something," Sirtira suggested.

"I don't know what you're getting at!" Mason retorted angrily. "I can't tell you what I don't know."

Fahrar eased the questioning in a different direction. "What was the course of field training for covert action?"

"What do you mean, 'What was it'? It was basic military and physical conditioning in order to—"

"What was the history of the program? As you knew of it?"

"When I was inducted it was a program which had developed from the Special Operations Executive during the war. That became the OSS program and in turn, with modifications, became CIA Basic Field Training."

"What did that consist of?"

"The works," replied Mason dully.

"Silent killing, perhaps?" Fahrar suggested.

Mason looked him in the eye. "Yes."

"Unarmed combat?" Fahrar prodded.

"Of course."

"You're not very talkative."

"This is all so God-damned basic!" Mason snapped. "You know the answers as well as I do!"

"What weapons did you train with?" Fahrar continued, as if to satisfy his own curiosity. "American?"

"We spent four weeks on US-made weapons, another five weeks on Soviet and Chinese weapons. It was 1964, remember?"

"Did you meet a man named Vincent Torello? An instructor."

It was a test, Mason guessed. "No," he answered.

"What about Colonel Harvey Krietler?"

"Yes."

"Who is he?"

"E and E," Mason answered. "He was the CIA's resident expert on escape and evasion in the late 1960s.

He formulated a plan to get me out of China. It didn't work."

"Have you ever met him?"

"No."

They looked at Mason and held his attention.

"No!" Mason repeated.

"Is he still active?"

"I don't know." They held his gaze again. Mason refused to repeat his answer.

"What about Hsu Tsu-tai?"

"He was a Chinese diplomat who agreed to pass information to the CIA. He was murdered in Holland by Peking intelligence. 1970?"

"Sixty-nine," said Fahrar. "But the rest of your memory is good."

"I'm so glad," answered Mason sarcastically.

"Who was the Division Chief for Langley? When you were recruited."

Mason thought. He gave the answer as he remembered it, naming a silver-haired communications intelligence specialist named Michael Bolland who'd retired with cardiac trouble in 1968 and died two years later. Sirtira was writing it down.

"Then what?" asked Fahrar. "After your training and desk assignments?"

"Two tours of duty in France. Raw-information assessor and liaison officer between CIA and US journalists abroad. In 1968 I was transferred to fieldwork. Covert action. China."

"Did you ask to go there?"

"I was selected."

"Why *you?*"

"I told you," he said. "Lassiter. He wanted me."

"Ah, yes. Yes. Tell us about it."

Mason drew a breath. All right, he thought, if they want meaningless details, they can have them. He began in a sultry August of 1964, reliving the autumn of his twenty-fourth year.

It took five hours, during which Sirtira stopped him nine times to change the tape, Fahrar and Sirtira wrote pages and pages of notes, and Mason took a subtle glee in giving them actual details which would, when they fol-

160

lowed up on them, prove either true, meaningless, un-provable, or all three.

Mason brought them to the present day, up to and including his release from the service.

"Why would they release a young man who'd given so much?" asked Fahrar, now standing beside Mason.

"Ask Captain Queeg. I don't know. I suppose he doesn't like me."

"*Captain Queeg?*" Sirtira jumped all over that one.

Mason was forced to explain.

"How do we know you were not put out to be picked up as a false defection?" demanded Fahrar suddenly.

"Jesus Christ!" Mason said hotly. "You don't! But I didn't ask for you people to come after me. If you don't trust me, open the God-damned door. I'll be gone in a minute and you won't see me again!"

To call their bluff, he rose. Fahrar's hand was firmly on his shoulder and there was an intensely hostile moment between the two of them. Fahrar's gesture indicated that Mason wasn't to move. Bill's eyes glared back, insisting that by this time he would do anything he damned well pleased.

Sirtira defused the moment. "No need for anger," he said coolly. "We're all concerned with our own interests. Are we not? Please . . . ?"

Fahrar removed his hand and stepped back. Mason sat down. "Get me some water," he demanded. "Otherwise I shut up." He suddenly recalled Rudy demanding beer.

Sirtira motioned to Fahrar and water was fetched.

As Bill drank, Sirtira took a different tone, one which suggested that he was moving things toward their conclusion.

"Just a question or two more," he promised.

"Why not?" asked Bill sourly.

"Why did you come to England?"

"A friend of mine asked me to," Mason answered.

Sirtira spoke. "Who? Which friend?"

"Robert Lassiter. He asked me to come and help him."

"Even though you were off the payroll."

"Yes."

"Why would he do that?"

"Why the hell do you think?" snorted Mason. "He trusted me."

161

"Should he have?"

"Should he have what?"

"Trusted you?" Sirtira drank a bottle of Coca-Cola.

"Of course."

"Should *we?*"

"If you want to," said Mason. "It's up to you. I can't convince you." He glowered at them.

"Certainly you can."

"How?" Mason threw out the word as a challenge.

"Be honest with us."

"I have been."

"Yes," said Sirtira thoughtfully. "Yes, we'll see."

He spoke in French again, addressing Fahrar and motioning for something from an adjoining room. Fahrar disappeared. He came back alone in sixty seconds. He carried a small black case which Mason watched apprehensively. Sirtira distracted Mason.

"You've been telling us the truth?" Sirtira asked.

"Of course," snarled Mason. "For God's sake. You think by now I'd admit it if I hadn't?"

"One will see." Sirtira nodded to the broad man who had been sitting, listening, and assessing in the rear of the room. The man rose and walked toward Mason.

The man was heavy, spoke English with astonishing fluency, with only a hint of an Eastern European accent. In the middle of his first sentence the realization gripped Mason as to who he was.

"William Mason. I am very pleased to meet you," the man said. He was working lower key than the others, suggesting that he was even more lethal. "I knew Robert Lassiter very well."

"I'm sure you did."

"I will be assuming the questioning now. We will cover some familiar areas. Some areas we have touched on already. We will repeat other questions you have already answered. We must be certain of your use to us."

Mason looked at him silently, with hostility yet tolerance. Then the thick face slipped into a cobra smile and the man offered his hand.

"Forgive me. I have not introduced myself. Dimitri Vassiliev."

Mason gripped the Russian's hand without conviction or emotion.

162

"All you're going to get is the same answers," said Mason.

"For your sake, I hope so," said the Russian. He turned and glanced at Fahrar who was already approaching them. Held aloft was a syringe and a three-inch hypodermic needle.

Mason's eyes froze upon it.

Oh, Jesus! he thought to himself. They had had it all ready for him, long before they had gotten him here.

"Certainly you wouldn't refuse," said Vassiliev, who was obviously now in charge. "Or become agitated. Or violent."

He looked at the three hard faces.

"Certainly not," Mason said. "Even with a bunch of ugly red bastards like you."

He rolled up his sleeve and offered them a muscular left bicep. But Fahrar grasped Mason's right wrist and wrenched the arm sharply. He messily doused the inside of the arm with alcohol, then jabbed in the needle with a stabbing motion. Mason's whole right arm ached. He grimaced.

Mason looked away, knowing raw, cold fear for the first time in many years. He hoped to God his answers would hold up. This was something for which he wasn't prepared. He felt the sting of the serum—whatever it was—surging through his system.

The needle was out. Mason winced. The drug was sneaking up on his lungs. He was somewhere between giddiness and hysteria.

"—hope that didn't hurt too much, Mr. Mason," Vassiliev was saying. "After all, none of us is a doctor."

Mason turned angrily back toward them and they were laughing. They formed a semicircle around him, waiting for the drug to work.

Mason looked from one face to the next to the next. He wasn't sure whether or not he imagined it, but a certain lightheadedness was already upon him.

"Screw yourselves," he mumbled. He gave a long blink of the eyes.

He was staring at his own shoes, knowing now that this triumvirate took this whole thing very seriously indeed and if the answers that would follow didn't check, they would probably choose to stick him with another needle, one which would induce a deep and very final sleep.

"—hope that didn't hurt too much, Mr. Mason," a seemingly distant Vassiliev was now repeating. "After all, none of us is a doctor."

Mason felt puzzled. These people seemed to be his friends. What were they asking him?

"—hurt too much?" one of them said.

Mason smiled. He rubbed his arm. "No. No problem," he said. "It's fine. Just smarts a little. Thank you." He was dizzy, but felt quite tolerant of everything. "Thanks," he said again.

They laughed. He was helpless now. If they wanted to kill him, they could. And would. No one would even follow up on a missing former Company employee.

19

Mason was on a bumpy, hard cot somewhere. His pants were on and so were his shirt and his socks. His belt had been taken from him and his face, hands, and feet were all very wet. Sweating. His shoes were gone.

He sat up and felt himself in the midst of a feverish torpor which had his head swimming and his eyes refusing to focus.

He was in a closed room, eight feet by eight feet, dimly lit by a single bulb, and he had no idea where in the world he was.

He blinked. He rubbed his blurring eyes.

He sat up on the edge of the bed. It was a mistake. Movement made him even dizzier. He swooned slightly but steadied himself with his hands. With anguished gradualness it came back to him.

He recalled sitting in a hardback chair, talking and talking, answering question upon question from men on three sides of him. Vassiliev, Sirtira, and, most aggressively, Fahrar. They'd worked as a team, probing, pressing, confusing, challenging, repeating. They had sucked information out of him for hours. It was like being drained of blood.

He glanced at his watch. It had stopped at ten minutes past twelve. Ten minutes past which twelve? he wondered. Of what day? Of what night? He thought intensely. He had come to this building past two o'clock on Monday afternoon. How much time had passed? For that matter, was he still in the same building? He looked at the walls through eyes that were clouded. The walls gave no clue.

He looked to the door. It was steel and did not have a knob. For several minutes Bill Mason did not move.

He tried to remember, but it was hopeless. His memory was white. He knew he had been subjected to an inquisition. Yet it was a blur. What had he revealed?

165

His head throbbed. He held it with his hands, leaning slightly forward.

He looked around the room for a camera or a microphone but didn't see one. For some reason, there was one picture on the wall—a desert scene with tan sands and a reddish-blue sky. He hated it. It suggested days of one hundred twenty degrees. He was already hot enough. His mouth was parched.

He wondered idly where his air was coming from and when he didn't know a sudden mad anxiety was on him, a crushing claustrophobic impulse combined with a choking fear.

He tried to stand. He succeeded, but wobbled slightly. For the next several minutes he rediscovered the use of his legs.

It was time. Consciousness was returning to him. Whatever fate he had brought upon himself, it was time to meet it. He steadied himself and moved toward the door.

It was sealed securely from the other side. He smashed it with his fist twice. Hard. Then he hit it several more times, harder still.

"Come on you bastards! *Open it up!*" When he heard movement on the other side, he stepped back into the center of the room. The door opened slowly, casting a brighter light into the cell.

"Mr. Mason," said the large-framed man. "We've been waiting for you." It was Fahrar, tinted glasses, endlessly wide shoulders, and white shirt wet with his own sweat. "Have a good sleep?"

"Fuck you," said Mason.

The Arab smiled. He pursed his lips with a mock kiss. "Where the hell am I?"

Fahrar made a broad smile and revealed teeth that bordered on canine. "You passed your test. Come."

Fahrar lumbered through the corridor in front of Mason, not concerned enough about the American even to turn and watch him. Mason followed silently for twenty seconds of slow walking until Fahrar led him to where the corridor connected with another hallway.

Fahrar turned left. Mason glanced right before following. He saw nothing significant, nothing which appeared to be a potential escape route. He followed Fahrar. A moment later he realized he was now in the corridor which had led to the room where he had been interrogated.

He passed over the Persian runners in the hallway and saw the wall tapestry. He had an odd sense of relief, of seeing the familiar again.

Fahrar opened the door, and led him into the room. "Come in. Sit down and wait."

Mason passed Fahrar and entered the room. He sat in the straight-backed chair.

"You may dress if you desire," Fahrar said, closing the door. Mason didn't know what the Arab had meant until he saw his shoes and belt in a corner.

Mason sat for a moment thinking, then put his shoes and belt back on. He sat down and waited. He wondered if it was day or night. His body clock told him nothing. He was totally disoriented.

Several minutes passed. He was slowly realizing that he was hungry. Very hungry. Were they keeping him waiting on purpose? he wondered. Probably.

After several more minutes the door opened and Vassiliev entered with his lackeys, Sirtira and Fahrar, behind him.

Vassiliev went to the desk and seated himself. Sirtira's gaze was frozen upon Mason. Fahrar was poised sentry-style at the closed door. Vassiliev, whom Mason now studied intently, was bespectacled, bulky, and awkward. His forehead shone and his eyes darted. Despite the fact that he was a man of certain authority, and in this position was able to exert it, there was a rabbit quality to his face. He was like a cornered dog who could snarl and bite, but beneath everything there was clearly fear. It was Mason's first good look at Vassiliev. Far from a master spy, he appeared to be a badgered, pudgy, nervous little man. His life was most certainly a daily struggle. His fingernails were dirty; his glasses smeared. And he would have to be considered lethal, nonetheless.

The Russian made a show of glancing through a few papers on the desk. They were a device, Mason guessed. As Mason watched the Russian, he couldn't help thinking. This was the man Lazz had been trailing, both in Mexico and in England. What would Lazz have thought if he could see Bill sitting here?

Mason grew tired of the silent treatment. "Good morning," he finally said.

167

Vassiliev glanced up without raising his head. He allowed a thin smile. "It's afternoon."

"Really? Which?"

Another moment and Vassiliev set down the papers. "Very good," he said. "Very, very good. You wish to help us."

"You're asking me?"

"You've already told us."

Mason was quiet. "I have, have I?"

"Convincingly." Vassiliev seemed to ruminate. He set down the papers and rubbed his hands together slightly. Ivan, Mason thought back. That's what Lazz called him. Ivan. Ivan the Unbearable. He recalled how much Lazz had hated the man. "Like to take him apart with a chain saw," Lazz had said. "Slowly."

"Very convincingly, indeed," Vassiliev concluded.

"I'm so glad," Mason said with sarcasm.

"On what terms did you leave the Central Intelligence Agency?" Vassiliev asked.

"What?"

The Russian repeated.

"What is this?" Another question-and-answer session?"

"Please answer," requested Vassiliev.

"Good terms but sudden terms. I was terminated from covert work."

"What about other work?"

"What does that mean?"

"Another job with the agency? Were you offered one?"

"Not specifically."

"But you were invited to transfer to another department?" Obviously they knew.

Mason cursed himself. "Yes," he said.

"You told us that under questioning. In your second session, the one you probably do not remember so clearly."

"So?"

"Why did you refuse such a transfer within the agency?"

"I didn't want it," Mason said truthfully. "I don't like shuffling papers and reading reports." The Russian was silent, trying to press Mason into adding more. "Look," he said. "It's not like your Socialist Paradise where if they tell you to take a job you have to take it. I didn't want it."

"You preferred the job on the beach?"

168

"On the . . . ?" Oh, Jesus, he thought. They'd gotten even that out of him. "Yes, I preferred that," he said.

"With the girl?" Vassiliev looked downward to the papers. "Jules Heasman."

"*Julie*, you Bolshevik idiot," he muttered. It was a show of force, of strength, on their part. A good one.

"What will you do with Frank Hargrove?" asked Vassiliev.

Mason thought about it. "I don't know."

"But you wish to apprehend the man?"

"Yes."

"But unless you're working for an intelligence service, what might you do on your own?"

What the hell is he angling at? Mason thought.

"Well . . . ?" Vassiliev pressed.

"Look, Hargrove blew me in China and arranged for part of my youth to be spent in a Nanking prison. Then he shoves a lifelong friend of mine out of a sixth-floor window. What will I do if I find him? Use your imagination. It's personal, not political." Mason paused. "I thought I'd shoot him," he added cheerfully.

"We have him," said Vassiliev. "We will give him to you."

It seemed too easy. "Where?" Mason demanded. "You have him where?"

"London. We never brought him out. He is waiting to be brought out."

"Who was his control?" demanded Mason.

"I was. I am." The Russian smiled.

"And you're going to turn over your own man to me?"

"Under conditions."

"I don't believe you. Nothing personal, but you're a liar. Like most Russians."

Vassiliev grinned. "Falsehoods have their place if they further the worldwide Cause."

"Oh, Jesus," sneered Mason. "Spare me that. Spare me *anyone's* God-damned politics, all right?"

"If you fulfilled the proper conditions, why would we *not* give him to you? His cover is gone. He's told us everything he knows. He is no longer in place. And he knows nothing of *our* organization. Never did."

"He's 'garbage,' in other words?"

169

"Yes," said Vassiliev. "Worth nothing to us. Worth a little something to you. 'Garbage,' as you say."

"Your high regard for human life overwhelms me," said Mason. "Particularly the lives of people who helped you. Your own people."

"Hargrove is not a Communist," said Vassiliev. "He is a paid traitor."

"And if he's dead he doesn't have to be paid anymore," suggested Mason. "Nor do you have to risk other people by bringing him out of England."

Vassiliev played with a pencil and gazed blankly at the American.

"You have a heart the size of the Black Sea," said Mason, gazing back at him. "Sounds like there's something you want in return."

"Yes," allowed Vassiliev, slowly.

Mason waited. The ball was in their court. He'd wait all day if need be, for the response.

Vassiliev was in no mood to delay the news.

"We would like you to act in two ways. We would like you to return to Washington. To Langley. And we would like the chips."

Mason glared at the Russian in mild astonishment. "What chips?" he finally said.

Vassiliev's eyes glowered and the Russian smacked the desk with his thick fist. "Don't play stupid games! You admitted under questioning that you had a set of six silicon chips! You did *not* admit where they are! We want them!"

"Why are *they* so important?"

"They are ours! Stolen from us by Robert Lassiter!" Vassiliev was pig-faced.

Liar, Bill thought.

Vassiliev barged on. "And agents do not ask such questions. You act upon orders and you do not interrogate your superiors!"

Just like Langley, Mason noted silently. He appeared to ponder. "All right," he said. "Suppose I remembered where I put them. What's the other half?"

"You return to the United States," said Vassiliev. "You tell your former employers that you have experienced a change of heart. You tell them that you *would* like employment with them again."

"It won't work."

170

"You will have to try!" The Russian was red-faced and adamant. "You will have to!"

Mason appeared thoughtful again. "Look," he said negatively, "I've been dumped on by one service. How do I know you'll take any better care of me?" He keyed on that point. "Yes. Tell me. What's in all this for me?"

"We will give you Hargrove," said Vassiliev soberly. "You may turn him in or do with him as you wish. I don't pretend to care. Then you will have money. For every week you are on CIA payroll in some clerical department, you will receive money into a bank account. Switzerland would be best. Or maybe Denmark or Finland."

Money and Hargrove, Mason thought. That's what they're offering. In return, six silicon chips and a minor-league spy in place in Langley. One paid traitor off their backs and another one on the books. Good economists, they were. Nor were they bad at planting things. Minor-league spies develop into major leaguers as they gain seniority within their agencies and assume more command and authority. Nothing begins big; everything grows.

"It's attractive," Mason allowed.

"It's *very* attractive!" blurted Vassiliev, coarse and belligerent. Mason pictured the Russian trying to sell vacuum cleaners in Topeka, dirty fingernails and all.

"When would I get Hargrove?" Mason inquired.

"After turning over the chips and before going into work in Langley."

"What if they don't rehire me?"

Vassiliev thought. "We would suggest something else for you then. Also in America. You are useless elsewhere. To us."

You sly bastard, Mason thought. Hargrove for the chips, it broke down to. Then a financial stream into a foreign bank in return for becoming an agent in place. In a place which met their approval. Mason knew how such setups worked. He had seen them. He had helped build them from one side or had destroyed them from the other.

He looked at the three men in the room with him and he wondered how much any of them trusted him. Not that it mattered. He would be called upon to produce for them before they risked anything. The worst they had on their hands was a botched recruitment. The worst Mason

171

faced was, say, a trial for treason in the United States plus life imprisonment. Small stuff.

"So I'm going to become a spy again," he said. "Who am I working for?"

"Us," Vassiliev answered evasively. "Us."

"And who the hell's that, Vassiliev? You don't get anything from me unless I know."

Vassiliev's answer was reluctant and seemed painful, as if the information was being twisted from him. He even lowered his voice. "The Soviet Union."

Mason emerged numbed from the bureau on the Rue de Thibaux. He left Paris immediately. He returned to London where he avoided any place where he had been previously. Any place, that was, saving one.

He traveled to Islington with a package beneath his arm, a small parcel about two thirds the size of a shoe box. When he entered the antique emporium of one Maurice Bobbs, the proprietor was sitting behind a counter reading a *Daily Mirror*. Bobbs set down the paper. A smile crept across his face.

"I came looking for another favor, Maurice."

"*Do* tell me," said Bobbs.

"I have to take a small, unscheduled trip," Mason said. He handed Bobbs the bound package. "I wonder if you could 'hold' this for me."

Bobbs took it in his limber hands. He hefted it. "Feels familiar."

"It should."

Bobbs grinned like a gargoyle. "You'll be needing it again?"

"Probably. Yes," Mason answered. "When I'm back in London."

"Which will be . . . ?"

Mason shrugged.

"I'll keep it warm," pronounced Bobbs agreeably.

Mason was almost out the door when Bobbs spoke again. "Oh, *do* tell!" blurted Bobbs irrepressibly and cheerfully. "Do!"

Mason turned. "Sorry?"

"Well . . . ?" Bobbs opened his arms, beseeching.

"Sorry, Maurice. I'm not following you." Mason frowned.

172

"Did it work?" Bobbs begged, motioning to the package. "Did you get him? Whoever it was?"

"Oh. Sorry. *That*." Mason considered his response. "No, Maurice. Hate to disappoint you. I haven't found him yet."

Bobbs snapped his fingers in disgust. "Damnation," he said.

Mason closed the door behind him, knowing the package and its contents would be safe. On his return to London, he could pick it up again and retrieve the pistol along with the other contents of the parcel: six small computer chips, wrapped in aluminum foil and slipped neatly into the barrel of the weapon.

He followed an evasive path, a textbook lesson in how to move without leaving a trace. He traveled by car and ferry to Ireland where, using his Canadian passport, he flew to Montreal. Then he placed his Canadian passport in a heavy brown envelope and airmailed it to himself, care of American Express, London. A day later, carrying his United States passport, but not needing it, he took a train to New York.

He passed a day in Manhattan and bought new clothes. During the late afternoon, he wandered up and down Fifth, Madison, and Third Avenues, then spent five minutes on the north side of East Fifty-seventh Street admiring the suit of armor in the window of Dunhill Tailors. Then it was evening. He had dinner by himself, then took in a nightclub act in the East Fifties from a seat at the club's bar. He was, as he viewed the act from his barstool, invited to a private party by a very attractive woman to whom he'd not been formally introduced. A very private party. Just for two. But expensive.

He resisted.

He felt himself a foreigner in a city which he knew well. And bearing in mind his recruitment in Paris, the sight of anyone—uniformed or not—who might be police gave him pause. He avoided their paths.

On the next afternoon he took a train to Washington. He checked into the Pilgrim Hotel on Fourteenth Street, a few blocks from the White House. He slept for half the day.

Then, gathering his courage, and once he'd rested enough to remove some of the lines and shadows from his face, he picked up the telephone in his hotel room.

173

It was time to renew old acquaintances. Time to sort out the whole damned mess.

But back in London, Auerbach's teeth were on edge.

The disappearance of Bill Mason—and that's what Auerbach considered it now, a disappearance—had a stinging effect. Within Auerbach, the vanishing set off waves of anger and perplexity, followed by more of the same in increasing proportions. It was not the time to step in front of Auerbach's car as he was driving home.

There was no excuse for Mason being absent this long. None. Men and women, even spies, are creatures of habit and when a habit is strayed from, or in this case shattered, there is significance. Auerbach, however, didn't know what.

Every hired ear that he had available was set to the ground. There was no record of Mason having chucked it all and flown home on any scheduled airliner. A few CIA contacts whom Auerbach trusted in England, with whom he retained a distinctly symbiotic relationship, reported knowing nothing—bloody nothing at all, they said—about Mason or his whereabouts. The London bureau of the Company was in obvious turmoil. Yet, as far as Auerbach could ascertain, no trustworthy fieldman had reported a foreign service having picked up on a straying former Central Intelligence employee.

More somberly, and dark thoughts were never far from Auerbach's psyche, nothing had come floating belly up in the Thames—nothing that resembled Bill Mason, that is, and, in an extensive triple check, no hotels, hospitals, morgues, hostels, or anything else turned up any sign of his guest.

It set Auerbach's teeth to chattering. He put three men full time on the streets of London, just looking for Mason in likely and unlikely haunts. As expected, nothing. Hence the reemergence of Louis and Edgar, Auerbach's favorite baby-sitters.

Auerbach sent the two of them into the Cromwell Road flat where Mason had been lodged. He gave them the key, which wrecked half their fun but did allow extra time within the apartment.

There was little of interest for them to find. Louis kept chomping gum and, as he hulked around, took to whistling American pop tunes between his teeth and singing tunelessly, "Oh, baby" at least once every ten or fifteen minutes until the whole concert drove Edgar to utter distraction. No matter. They efficiently combed the apartment. They found most of Mason's clothing, his unwashed laundry, his half-used toiletry articles, no money, and Auerbach's five functioning microphones, plus the sixth one, the one Mason had smashed in the kitchen air vent. Dutifully, they left it as they found it. Planting wires was someone else's job. They reported back to Auerbach.

"Nothing."

The Briton grimaced. He was faced with either outrageous possibilities for Mason's disappearance—he'd taken up with a lady of tarnished virtue and liked it so much that he'd decided to stay—or some very lugubrious explanation indeed—Mason had been recruited out from under Auerbach's nose and was now playing ball for a foreign team altogether. That one rankled particularly. This wasn't wartime in the traditional sense, but then again Auerbach didn't play by traditional rules. He had trusted Mason; primarily on the endorsement and judgment of Lassiter. He had told him probably too much. He had taken him in. If Mason had gone and jumped to another side, that was a heinous crime, indeed. The concept cut Auerbach deeply. It was the type of thing for which he could kill a man.

Intolerable, Auerbach thought as he sipped brown ale and pressed his belt up against a bar in the east end. Bloody intolerable. But no rational reason surfaced for the disappearance. Auerbach might just as well have consulted a reader of tea leaves.

20

Right on time, Mason thought. As usual. The proper Washingtonian.

Seated at a table toward the rear of the restaurant, Mason saw Philip Gardner coming through the front door. Without moving his head, Mason glanced at his watch. Seven thirty. If punctuality was next to godliness, Gardner would belong in someone's pantheon.

A captain led him past the white tablecloths and the banquettes. The motif of Mario's was subdued Milanese, "dignified Italian," as the Washington wags put it. The saltimbocca and fettucini alfredo were not to be missed. Plan twenty dollars per person and arrive half starved.

Gardner extended his hand. Mason rose and took it. "Well, well," Gardner said, clutching a large envelope and laying it by his feet beneath the table. "Can hardly believe it. How's it been going, Bill?" His voice was subtly elegant.

Mason opened his hands noncommittally, a gesture he accompanied with an indecipherable smile.

"Scotch," said Gardner to the waiter. He named a brand and designated it on the rocks with a bit of water. The same drink he had been ordering for ten years, Mason noted. Gardner ran like clockwork.

"You got me on a good night," Gardner announced, turning his attention back to Bill. "Tuesday. Night out."

"Sorry?"

"A little tradition in the Philip Gardner residence," he explained. "Tuesday night is my night out. Thursday is my wife's. No questions, no explanations necessary." Gardner smiled. "Independence within the institution of marriage," he said. "A rare commodity. It works."

The Scotch arrived. Gardner pushed around the ice cubes with his manicured forefinger. Mason watched him. Gardner had slipped gracefully into middle age. The brown

176

hair, always thin, was thinner now and a few dignified lines had appeared where the skin used to shine with youth. There was an incipient sag beneath his chin.

"How long have you done that?" asked Mason.

Gardner pursed his lips. "As long as we've been married," he said. "Eleven and a half years. Don't get me wrong," he added quickly. "I like Betty. Terrific girl. Good mother to the boys. But, we respect our separate lives." He grinned. "Know what we do on our anniversary? We spend it separately. She goes somewhere, I go somewhere. Next night, we're anxious to see each other. Put the boys to bed early so we can do the same for ourselves."

Mason sipped his drink. Gardner produced a pack of cigarettes. He held the pack toward Mason. Mason declined.

"Don't mind the smoke, do you?" Gardner asked. Before Mason shook his head, Gardner was lighting up.

Gardner wore a yellow shirt. That fact, by itself, hinted something. For years Gardner had been the paradigm of the man in the white shirt. An economist with a lean body, and shrewd, sharp eyes, he was doing graduate work at Yale when Mason was a freshman. They hadn't known each other. After Mason's graduation, they'd met each other at an agency get-together hosted by Robert Lassiter. Mason was being primed for the Orient, even though he didn't recognize it yet. Gardner was into African economics even though he'd eventually do time in Bonn. Back then, Gardner had been the very image of the corporate mentality; dark suits, narrow lapels, thin ties, white shirts. Now he wore pale yellow shirts. Not much else had changed.

"How long have you been with the Company now, Phil?" Mason asked. "Fifteen years?"

"Sixteen and a half."

"Economics still?"

"I love it." He sipped his Scotch and made a face. "Oh, you know what some darn fool did to me? Talked me into moving upstairs."

"Upstairs?"

"Literally, in fact. Third floor to fifth. Took me off economic systems and moved me into intelligence quality control."

"For where?"

"Africa." He paused. "There I was, sifting through

177

this collection stuff that was filtering in from all parts of Central and South Africa. Some resident Arab hands had most of North Africa, thank God. Well, there I was; I was supposed to give my impression whether the intelligence had any validity. Half the time I was guessing. If it's not economic, it's someone else's football. They threw *politics* at me. Politics! Lasted four months. Begged to go back. That's where I am now. Central Africa." He started another cigarette. "I heard about Lassiter."

"Yes." Mason looked down for an instant. "Sad."

"How much do you know about it?"

"Next to nothing." Mason hesitated. "I don't suppose you . . . ?"

"Oh, no. Not at all. Out of my area completely. I even asked around," he said after he exhaled a long breath of smoke. "No one seems to know. Just one of those men who fall silently and inexplicably," Gardner said. "What about you?"

The waiter arrived. They hadn't looked at the menu yet, but did so quickly in the waiter's presence. They ordered and resumed talking.

"I'm looking for work," Mason admitted eventually.

Gardner nodded thoughtfully.

"When they let me go," Mason continued, "they did give me an option. I was out of fieldwork completely, but I could reapply internally to start over in another department. Like analysis and deployment."

"And?"

"I turned it down."

Gardner pursed his lips. He was thinking. "So?" he finally asked.

"I've changed my mind."

"Aah," said Gardner, holding the syllable for a second or two. He understood. "And you want me to see what's around. Before you actually reapply."

Mason nodded. "I'm not broke and I'm not desperate, Phil. But the vacation's over. I had a good clean record and I need a job." He made a gesture with his hand. "Let's face it. Part of it is who you know and who can swing some weight. I'll be frank. You're my best contact."

Gardner was moving his head up and down, the mind in full gear behind the gray eyes. He made a sour face. "I can't promise anything."

"I know."

"It's going to be rough. All these damned layoffs," he said, shaking his head. He ran his hand through his hair. "Everyone's scared in his boots of being put out to graze and you want to sign on again, having passed your first option."

"That's right."

It seemed like a major pronouncement from Gardner. "I'll ask around."

"I'd be grateful."

"Got anything else lined up?"

"No."

Gardner had a way of looking through people. "Know what someone told me?"

"What?"

"Skull and Bones. You. At Yale."

"Son of a bitch," said Mason. "Who told you that?"

Gardner was nodding. "I thought so," he said. "Well, now I can stop wondering. Cheer up, Bill. Aah, the food is coming. This looks like ours."

They were claiming their coats in the vestibule of Mario's. It was almost ten, the restaurant was more active, and their leisurely meal had settled well. When they stepped out onto Fourteenth Street the cold air was refreshing. The restaurant had been stuffy. The wine had lent a certain drowsiness to the final part of the meal, espresso notwithstanding.

"Had a wife, didn't he?" asked Gardner. "Bob Lassiter, I mean."

"Yes."

"The marriage was in trouble once, wasn't it?"

"Ended a long time ago," Mason said. "She divorced him."

"Is *that* right?" Gardner stopped on the sidewalk and looked at Mason in mild astonishment. "I didn't know."

"No patience with a part-time husband." Mason looked up at the starless sky. "Long time back now. During the China fracas."

"Aah." Gardner was thoughtful. "Nice-looking girl, as I remember. What was her name? Funny, I can't recall."

Mason shrugged.

"What was it?" Gardner lit another cigarette as they walked.

179

"I really don't remember."

"You were at the wedding, weren't you?"

"I've been at a lot of weddings, in a supporting role." They laughed. They walked toward Connecticut Avenue. "I remember how much Lazz loved that girl." He was shaking his head.

"God, yes."

"Wanted her and his career both," Mason said. "Just didn't work. Some men can manage it. Some can't."

"Sometimes you wonder," said Gardner. "Which is more important? Career? Independence? Home? Know what, Bill? Tuesday nights, when I can go out and have a rip-roaring time, know what I usually do? Get in some extra work at my desk. You don't know how refreshing it was to get out to dinner with an old friend."

Mason grinned. "How about your wife? On Thursdays?"

"I wish I knew," said Gardner. "I wish I knew." He stopped and took Mason by the arm. "Okay, Bill, what else? Before I spring my car from the garage and have an uneventful drive back to sleepy Silver Spring, I want to know. What else can I do for you? I might fail on request number one, you know."

"I know," said Mason. "You explained." Then he snapped his fingers. "Yes, by God," he said, as if he'd just thought of it. "There *is* something."

"Name it."

"Do you know anyone in the Passport Office?"

Gardner's brow wrinkled. "At State Department?"

"Yes."

Gardner thought again. "Yes. I do know some people at State. Why?"

"Can I get access to passport records?"

"What on earth for?"

"I want to check up on Lassiter," he said. "I want to check the applications and some background. Nothing too enormous."

"I can arrange something," said Gardner reflectively. The hint of a wan smile crept across his face and then was gone. "I guess we can trust you, Mase."

A CIA pass, issued above Gardner's signature, was ready the next evening. Mason went by Gardner's house in Silver Spring to pick it up. Gardner invited him in to meet Betty, who was busily preparing dinner, and their two children, Chris and Samuel, who attended an Episcopal school down the road.

It was almost eight in the evening when Mason arrived. Gardner inquired whether he had eaten yet.

He hadn't.

"We'll set an extra place," said Betty Gardner. "If you're interested." Mason was.

Gardner carved a roast chicken and his wife served. After dessert and coffee the boys disappeared to their homework. Mason followed Gardner into the den where four files were wide open on his desk. Economic analyses of Angola and Zaire. Four thick files, amended with pages and pages of notes, all in Gardner's intense, spidery handwriting. Gardner had been working up until the moment Mason arrived. Later, Mason guessed, he would work till two in the morning, analyzing and writing theories, postulating and analyzing again.

"Jesus, Phil," Mason said, looking at the files and notes. "You leave this stuff sitting out?"

"Who's going to take it from here?" Gardner scoffed. "Who knows?"

Gardner dismissed it with a slight wave of the hand. "Who cares?"

US GOVERNMENT PROPERTY was emblazoned on the folders.

"Hell, I don't know. How interesting is it?"

Gardner's academic face illuminated. "Actually, *very* interesting. Zaire has a centrist pro-West government. Their agriculture depends on the crops of bananas, coffee, and rice. Their hard resources come up out of the ground. Copper, cobalt, zinc, and gold. Now, picture what happens economically if the crops fail and the unions stay home from the mines."

"The economy fails."

"And the government. . . ." He made a downward gesture with his thumb.

"So?" Mason said.

"Well, so nothing. Except Zaire is sitting between Uganda and Angola. And we think the borders are being crossed by, shall we say, third parties who would like to fuck up the economy and agitate the mine workers." He

181

raised his eyebrows. "Our restless Russian friends again. Along with their even more restless friends, the Cubans."

"But what angle are you working on?"

"Can't tell you." He gazed at Mason soberly. "Oh, what the heck? Just ways to help them steady their economy. Spread the structure of the economy around. Textbook stuff."

Gardner frowned and opened his desk drawer. Mason recognized a half-truth but didn't challenge it. If Gardner wanted to issue a disclaimer, it was none of Mason's business. But there were those hot files, just sitting there. . . .

"For you," Gardner said.

He had produced an envelope from the top drawer of his desk.

"Open it," Gardner said.

It contained a pass to the Passport Office, virtual carte blanche within nonclassified records. It was on agency stationery, stamped, issued above two signatures including Gardner's, and was good for one day only. The next day.

"You still haven't told me why you wanted it."

"Sure, I did."

"Okay," said Gardner. "Be secretive. Just don't get into any trouble. Okay? How about a cigar?"

Betty arrived with more coffee. Mason declined. Phil Gardner selected a Canary Island cigar from a rosewood humidor, clipped the end of it, and lit it. The room quickly filled with its odor.

"You know, Bill," he pronounced, placing his hand around Betty's waist, "a woman is only a woman, but a good cigar is a smoke."

Gardner's hand slipped southward and he gripped his wife's left buttock, halfway between a tweak and an outright grab. Mason found an excuse to make an early evening of it.

A headache, he explained. It wasn't a lie. And he had what he wanted, anyway.

The Passport Office was on K Street, a long wide boulevard which, running east to west, bisects the capital. The building was a fine example of bland bureaucratic architecture. In the lobby, passports could be applied for and obtained with relative ease and speed. It had earned a certain distinction within the federal government: It was the only federal agency which cleared an annual profit.

In a nearby annex, closed to the public, were records on microfilm and in computer memory banks. The records included all valid or once-valid United States passports issued in the last fifty-two years. It was in the annex that Bill Mason spent two and a half hours, courtesy of the pass provided him by Gardner.

When he emerged, he wore the perplexed and troubled expression of a man who had met his problems face to face, challenged them, and then seen them multiply. He spent the evening in a Georgetown jazz bar, quietly thinking, listening to the music, and brooding.

Mason looked out of his hotel window the next morning and watched the sidewalk below. A tour bus with Georgia license plates had pulled to the curb. From it rushed at least two dozen eager-eyed middle-aged tourists who had come up north from red-clay country to visit the capital city, a town described by one recent President as having northern charm and southern efficiency. Mason closed the sun-screen and called for his breakfast. Then he took out a road map he had purchased in the lobby, spread it on the unmade bed and studied it.

An hour later he had checked out, taken his rented car from the hotel garage, and left a message with Phil Gardner that he'd be back in touch. Mason drove through the city limits. The traffic eased just before the Maryland line.

It wasn't a bad drive. There was not yet snow on the ground and for some reason the freewheeling trip on the turnpike reminded him of late autumn days at Yale when, if a car was handy, an enterprising student might miss a class or two on a bright day and head for the more glamorous enclaves of New York, Boston, Wellesley, or Northampton. A mild euphoria filled him, and it stayed with him until he turned off and headed across the state on a rural artery for another hour.

A sign announced the Town of Wixton. He pulled off the road long enough to check an old address. With the help of a ruddy-cheeked attendant in an Exxon station, he located Bleeker Road.

He found the number easily and parked in front of

a rambling white house with a sagging front porch. There was no name on the mailbox.

For some reason Mason was mildly anxious. He paused and drew a breath, then locked the car and went cautiously to the door.

21

She looked at him blankly for a second. Then her face lit up in great pleasure.

"Bill! Bill Mason! I can't believe it."

"Hello, Sarah," he said warmly.

She shook her head joyfully, as if in disbelief, and opened her arms and hugged him. She kissed him on the cheek. "Bill, Bill," she said, releasing him and stepping back to look. "I mean, of all the . . . I mean, what a surprise. I just can't believe it."

"I can't either," he said. "Can we talk?"

"Oh, I'm sorry. Of course. Come on in. My God, how well you look. It's incredible."

He was, in a way, as off balance as she. He also didn't know what to do.

"Coffee," she said, leading him to the living room. "You always liked coffee, fresh coffee."

"I wouldn't turn down an offer like that," he said. "Not from you, Sarah."

She allowed him to sit and yet she still stood dumbly in front of him, not staring exactly yet not taking her eyes from him either. It was as if a vision had appeared, a pleasant one, and even a moment's distraction would allow it to vanish again.

"Incredible," she then said a final time. "By all odds, incredible." She leaned down, kissed him again on the face, and fled to the kitchen. "You and I," she called across the house. "We have some catching up to do, Bill Mason."

"That's why I'm here," he said. "Just thought I'd stop by to talk." Just thought I'd come two hundred miles out of my way to snoop for some answers, he thought to himself. How long had he known her? Twenty years?

She appeared in the kitchen doorway again. The rectangle framed her and he noted how little her shape

185

had changed over two decades. In a dark red sweater and light blue jeans, she looked as she had when they'd first met. The unavoidable question came hesitantly from her lips.

"You know about Brian, I suppose?" It was a tentative question.

"Yes," he answered. "I was sorry to hear."

She was relieved. "There's no explanation, Bill," she said. "I don't understand it any better than anyone else." She shrugged helplessly but unemotionally now.

"We'll talk about it later," he suggested. "If at all. Okay?"

She smiled. "Thanks."

Minutes later she reappeared with a small blue tray with two cups of coffee.

"Black, right?" she asked.

He smiled and nodded.

"This girl never forgets. Course, I brought cream and sugar anyway. A man can change his habits."

"I'll let you in on a secret," he announced, with an air of confession. He shook his head. "Men don't change. Creatures of habit. All of us."

He lifted his stoneware cup as she lifted hers. "Cheers."

"Cheers, Bill." She looked wistful. "And welcome back."

They sipped and looked at one another for a long moment, each a trifle uneasy. She set down her cup.

"Want a laugh?" she asked. "I nearly said welcome home."

"I wouldn't have minded, Sarah."

She leaned back. "I hardly know where to begin. The last time I saw you was . . . what? Before China, I guess."

He nodded. "Dear old China. I always wanted to see the world. Well, I saw it. Hey? Priscilla?"

A broad, proud grin crossed Sarah's face. "She's fine. Just fine and lovely," Sarah answered. "*And* in the seventh grade—"

"Already?"

"Already. God. I know. Seems just yesterday I was packing her lunch for first grade. Now the boys are starting to notice her and she wants to wear lipstick. She's twelve years old."

186

Her smile was gone and Mason knew distinctly what it was.

"I changed Priscilla's name," she said. "Her family name, I mean. Didn't seem right not to. Brian was the father she knew. So she's Priscilla Woodson."

"I don't blame you," he said. "Given the circumstances."

"I think she's still very shocked by Brian being gone. You know kids." She saw him open his hands plaintively and shrug. "Well, okay, you don't know children firsthand, but you can imagine. They feel things, but they don't say things. It's inside her."

He nodded.

"I should ask, I guess," she said. "Ever hear from her father?"

"Not for a while."

"Honestly, Bill?"

"Honestly." Mason lied, artfully.

"I don't want to know about him," she said. "I just wondered. You can't have a child with a man without wondering about him sometimes. Even after all this time." Her eyes drifted away, then shot back to him. "You're sure?"

"Sarah," he said. "I got furloughed from the Agency earlier this year. I'm a pariah. No one who's employed by CIA wants any contact with me. They're afraid they'll catch whatever I had. Or have."

"You're out of work?" she frowned.

" 'Fraid so."

"And Bob . . . ?"

"Last I heard he was in London. But that was 1974, I think. He had a Treasury Department cover but was still working for the Company."

"Mase," she said with formality and sourness, "Robert Lassiter will *always* work for them. Up until the day he dies. I mean, I'm sure it sounds like resentment coming from me. . . . My marriage to Robert Lassiter was awful. You *know* that." She was shaking her head and continuing, "I'd rather any man of mine to have a mistress than work for that outfit. The whole way of thinking. It gets inside a person. Not just his head, but his soul, too. It destroys the human part of him. You're lucky you were dismissed." She drew a long breath as if unnerved by her own mini-sermon. "Sorry," she said. She sipped some more coffee. "I took one wonderful thing from that rotten marriage. My daughter. I suppose I should look at it that way." She considered it for a moment. "Priscilla Woodson has a better ring than Priscilla Lassiter."

"If you say so."

"Oh, come on, Bill. Don't defend him."

"I didn't come here to debate you, Sarah, but I think you're hard on the man."

"You weren't married to him."

"Yes. But I knew him better than anyone beside you."

"Maybe." She was thoughtful, then the bitterness crept back. "Sometime explain to me what I saw in him, please. *Not* today."

"Sometime," he agreed. "Someday we'll put the accounts straight."

"He was petty and jealous," she said. "Went off to the damned Orient for two years, right after Priscilla was born. Expected me to just sit tight, think about him in my free moments, and raise a child by myself."

As if fixed on a point, she wouldn't allow it to drop. The marriage had ended in a Nevada divorce court in 1968. She still seemed to need to flush it out by talking about it.

"Sometimes a man tries to do too much," Mason offered.

"I'm familiar with the old sob story."

"Sarah, he loved you a lot. Whether you knew it or not. The man *should* have spent more time with you. He—"

"Do you know what that petty, petulant, and jealous ex-husband of mine did after I was remarried?" She didn't wait for him to ask. "He used CIA facilities and methods to spy on us. *Us!* Can you believe it? He was always snooping on Brian's work—"

"With ITW?"

"Right. Wouldn't leave my husband, my *new* husband, alone. Always finding out what he was doing, what he was working on. Jesus, Bill, he was driving us *silly* for about three years. Seemed obsessed by the man who'd replaced him. It was as if he was still trying to *own* me," she intoned bitterly.

"The divorce was traumatic for him," he said weakly. "All I'm saying is—"

"Did you come here on his behalf?" she suddenly asked.

"Not at all. You brought his name up. Remember?" And he was still wearing your wedding ring when he hit the sidewalk, he thought.

"I'm sorry," she said. "I didn't mean to accuse you."

"Someday you might remember Lazz without all the bitterness," he said. "That's all." He considered it for a moment, then began to smile. "Do you remember the time, just after you two were married, when you couldn't get a taxi one rainy Friday? You were down on Wall Street, I think, and Lazz was at FBI headquarters on East Sixty-ninth Street. You called him and he sent a Treasury Department car—flashing red beacon and all—to pick you up and—"

"Let's drop the subject," she said, completely unmoved. "There are more pleasant topics." She paused, then announced, "I do have another gentleman friend. It's all very platonic, damn it. Are you ready for this? He's a minister."

"That's a new one for you, isn't it?"

She laughed. "Just me and the preacher man. Imagine that. I think he's about ten years younger, too. Just friends, Bill. Just friends."

"How'd this come about?"

"Not long after Brian—you know. Local church. He sought me out. Guess the parish likes to aid recent widows."

"I see." He paused. "That's nice."

"He's new in the area."

"Oh, really? How new?"

She pushed a lock of brown hair back behind her ear. She reached for the pack of cigarettes, and took one.

"I don't know. It was about the time I lost Brian. Why?"

"No reason."

"You'd like Paul. Maybe he's not exactly your type. Rather bookish, maybe a trifle dull. But sincere. He cares and he's gentle."

"If I'm around long enough perhaps I should meet him."

"Where are you staying?"

"A motel in Keyston."

"Oh, for Heaven's sakes," she said. "If you're going to be around, don't stay in a dive. I've got a guest room."

He immediately protested, saying he couldn't possibly. Propriety in a small town. Neighbors.

"To coin a phrase," she said, "screw the neighbors. They wouldn't know, and I don't care now if they did. My God, fate isn't throwing too many long-term lovers into my life, Bill. The least I can have is a few platonic gentlemen friends. Like my parish preacher man and now my old bosom pal, my retired spy." She held her breath. "That's not a dirty word these days now, it it? Spy?"

He grinned and shook his head. "Maybe in some other quarters, but not here with you, Sarah."

She laughed merrily. Her eyes danced and he was aware of what an enormously attractive woman she had remained. She had endured. Sarah must have been doing something right.

"Hey now, Mase. No way I'm sending you back to a sleaze-o motel. No telling what kind of loose-moraled women might be hanging about there. I'm setting you up in the guest room, and each night you can give me a very chaste kiss on the cheek to tell me that we're still old friends. No more, no less."

He fumbled for words.

"Hey, Bill. I'd really appreciate it. I could use the company."

He opened his hands as if to give up. "How can I say no?"

"Marvelous." Then her mood turned darker. "Hey?" she said, almost as an afterthought. "What did they use to call it in spy talk—'tradecraft'?"

"The word exists. Why?"

"Got a little mystery here, Bill. The police don't believe me but I had a burglar a few night ago. He didn't take anything. Left no signs at all."

"Then what—?"

"He rustled through some things Brian was working on before he . . . before he died. Hey," she said, blinking ever so slightly above her coffee cup. "Want to know a dark secret?"

"Go ahead."

"This brave little woman you see before you, she is scared to death. Something's happening, Bill. Brian was involved in it. I know."

So do I, he thought.

"Sarah," he said. "Tell me something. Brian wasn't by chance an expert on silicon computer chips, was he?"

"Why, Bill," she answered with surprise. "How did you know? That's exactly what he was. He designed them."

22

"Yes," she said. She shuffled her feet and one hand played with a strand of brown hair. She cocked her head. "Those silly little chips. Smaller than a contact lens. Brian designed them for ITW. Why? Does that mean something?"

"Well, maybe. Maybe not," he said haltingly. "You know how it is. I hear rumors. And your late husband *was* involved in Defense Department work. It's—"

"He was?"

"ITW definitely was," Mason said. "I assume Brian was, also."

"He never told me," she said in a strange tone, sounding hurt.

"Might not have known it himself," Mason said. Her eyes were disbelieving. "And it was his work area that someone was picking through?" he asked.

She nodded. She took the cigarette pack but tossed it aside again in disgust. "Want to see where Brian worked?"

"Sure."

She led him downstairs to the basement. Her mood perceptibly changed. She folded her arms in front of her as she talked. It was as if her presence in this section of the house forced her to relive some aspect of her marriage which would be best left forgotten.

"Not long before he died," she said slowly, "Brian was obsessed by his work. ITW has what they term 'open problems.' Brian was working every night on one of them."

"What's an 'open problem'?"

She explained.

"Any idea what the problem was?" he asked.

She shook her head. They arrived at the small niche where her late husband's desk had been. She flicked on a light. A small window high up on the cellar wall gave a trifle more brightness to the area.

"No idea at all," she said. She sighed. "There were so many of them." She pursed her lips and looked pensively at the cluttered desk.

Mason sensed the other man's identity permeating the surroundings. It was as if Brian Woodson would be back at any moment to resume what he had left unfinished.

"Want my own opinion?" she asked. "I don't think the 'open problem' was more special than any other. But you see, the company gives bonuses."

"Money, you mean?"

She nodded. "Up to fifteen hundred dollars, often, if an employee can find a solution that's escaped everyone else. I think Brian wanted the money. I think he wanted it very much."

The question *Why?* occurred to Bill and he was still thinking of a tactful way to pose it when she spoke again.

"We were planning a child," she said steadily. "One of our own."

He looked at her and nodded with understanding. "Sarah," he said softly. "I'm really sorry."

She hunched her shoulders ever so slightly. "Guess we won't be having it," she said flatly. There was a very awkward pause. She gave a slight shiver. "It's damp down here," she said. "Do you want to look around?" Something caught her eye. "I'm going back upstairs."

He said he'd like to browse through the papers left by her husband. There'd probably be nothing, but all the same. . . .

"More coffee?" she asked. She crossed the small room behind him, still attracted to whatever she'd seen.

"No, thank you. I'm fine," he said. He watched her. Even here, in these circumstances, he couldn't help realizing what kept drifting through his mind: Sarah Woodson, delicate, dark-haired, dark-eyed, was a sexy woman. Just something about the way she spoke, the way she carried herself. The way she was. She had always been attractive and always would be.

And Lazz gave her up for China? Mason wondered.

"I'd forgotten all about this," she said absently.

"What?"

From a pile of forgotten items she pulled a United

193

States Army duffel bag. It was dark green, old, and wore a layer of dust. She shook it.

"Recognize it?" she asked.

She shook it again. A name was stenciled on the side of it, faded somewhat, but visible beneath the US Army logo. Mason saw one of the middle S's and the T-E-R at the end. In smaller letters, across the bottom, Mason could see U.S. ARMED FORCES, KOREA.

"Indeed I do," he said. It had belonged to her first husband.

"The crazy thing is that Brian wouldn't let me throw it away," she said. "He thought it was campy. 'Perfectly good bag,' he said, 'so why throw it out?'" She folded it contemptuously. "I'm getting rid of it. It bothers me."

Bill offered no argument. He was looking at a paper on Woodson's desk.

As she walked toward the stairs, he spoke again. "Who is Stanley Lerner?" He glanced up and saw her stop.

"He was Brian's former collaborator at ITW," she explained slowly. "All the physicists and technicians work in teams. Why? Is there a significance?" She waited.

"Probably not," Mason said. "I just saw the name and wondered."

"I'm anxious for you to see Priscilla," she said. "You'll like her."

"If she looks like her mother, I'm sure I will." He was almost sorry he'd said it, afraid of how it might have sounded. But she smiled and didn't seem to mind. "There's one other thing," he said quickly. "The minister. I'd like to meet him."

"Easy," she said. "I'll invite him for dinner tonight. How's that sound?"

"You don't have to. Not that soon, I mean."

"No trouble at all," she said with enthusiasm. "None. I'll give him a call now, while you look around. Okay? It's set."

He watched her leave. His eyes followed her as she paced away, dangling the duffel bag from one hand, the other hand in a sweater pocket. She was graceful even as she climbed the stairs.

He rubbed some sleepiness from his eyes and sat down in the deceased's chair.

Looking through Woodson's notes, prowling through the technology which had occupied the final days of an-

194

other man's life, Mason had the sensation of trying to enter the dead man's mind. Somewhere within the disorder of papers, notes, print-outs, and technical brochures, there had been something monumental for Brian Woodson, something obsessing. Mason examined the notations, tidily scrawled, line by line, in a methodical Palmerian handwriting. Mason tried to see with Woodson's eyes. He couldn't. The technician eluded him. An hour passed. Then two.

Sarah reappeared and asked Bill how he was doing. She would be going out in a few minutes and today she would be picking up Priscilla after school.

"I also talked to Paul," she said.

"Who?"

"Paul Frost," she reminded him.

"Oh. The minister?"

She smiled. "He can't come tonight," she said. "But tomorrow's good. Tomorrow night at eight."

"Fine," Mason smiled.

He returned to the disorder in front of him. He had come to only one conclusion about Brian Woodson. The man had been tired—exhausted emotionally and physically. Despite the disciplined manner in which Woodson approached his work, he had been in the habit of doodling, of drawing pictures—concentric circles, boxes, and rectangles mostly, all penciled in heavy, repetitive lines—and enclosing neatly printed key words at the centers of his absentminded sketches.

One word was repeated, until its repetition was almost tragic in itself.

Fatigue.

Over and over a disturbed man had written the same word, then boxed in or circled the word each time. Riveted to his desk, he must have been strained to the breaking point.

Had it been an intrinsic flaw in the man's character? Or had there been something else, some *external* pressure?

The day faded into evening, evening into night. Midnight passed, as did the hours of one and two. The sofa in the ground-floor guest room, made into a bed for Mason, still waited as she had left it.

He was tired, but he was also unnerved. Unable to sleep, he sat in the living room of her house, a dim reading-light near him. He had nothing to read. His eyes were heavy and yet his mind churned.

Something external, he thought. Pressure. He thought of Gardner, oblivious to Mason's real motives, trying to get him reassigned within the Central Intelligence Agency. Trying to make a technocrat out of him. His smile was slightly pained. He glanced at his watch. It was ten past three.

He heard footsteps. A slight shuffling, like an unseen person moving over aging floorboards.

He was suddenly alert in his chair.

The steps were clearer. He was looking for something hard or sharp to clutch when he realized the precise location of the sounds. Someone was walking downstairs.

"Bill?" she called softly and tentatively.

"Yes. Here," he answered, relaxing.

"Are you all right?" she asked.

She looked sleepy. Her dark hair was messed and she wore no makeup. A pink housecoat was wrapped snugly around her, tied with a sash at the waist.

"Yes. Of course," he answered. "Couldn't sleep, that's all."

"I saw the light," she said. "I didn't know whether you'd fallen asleep with the light on or what."

"Sleep? No. Not yet."

She sat down on the arm of his chair.

"What about you?" he asked.

"Me?"

"What gets you up at an hour like this?"

She brushed a phantom piece of dust off her robe, just at the top of her right leg. "Don't know," she said, her eyes not meeting his. "Vaguely uneasy tonight, I guess." She looked back at him. "Not unusual," she said. "I wake up in the middle of the night a lot. Sometimes I lie there, waiting to fall asleep again. Other times I read. Or listen to the radio." She was pensive for a moment. "Find anything?"

"Downstairs, you mean?"

She nodded.

"No."

She played with the sash on her lap. She slid off the arm of the chair and slowly crossed the room to the fireplace. "I didn't think you would."

He made no reply. He only watched. She was look-

196

ing at something on the edge of the mantel. When he moved his eyes from her he realized that it was a silver-framed portrait that had caught her attention.

"See that?" she inquired. "My wedding picture."

"I noticed it earlier."

She seemed not to have heard him. Not completely. "October 26, 1968," she said. She paused. "Incredible. You know, Bill, it's frightening." She turned back to him. "I looked at that picture yesterday and I looked in the mirror immediately afterward. You don't see yourself change day by day. But you do. To me, that's a young girl of twenty-six in the picture. There's a middle-aged woman of thirty-six in the mirror. When did one become the other? On what day?" She came back to him and sat down on an ottoman by his feet. "Answers?"

" 'Fraid not," he said.

"Thoughts?" There was a hint of a sly, melancholy smile.

The words, unwise as they perhaps were, probably slipped out because he was so tired.

"What are you afraid of?" he asked.

She looked at him with mild astonishment, as if he had spoken the unmentionable. "Growing older. Being alone. Maybe both."

There was a long silence.

"Know what one of the worst parts is?" she added. "Know what I can't get used to most of all? Sleeping alone."

"Is that why you came down?"

"For almost ten years Brian and I . . . every night we were together. I don't think we slept apart once." Her eyes, which had been examining her sash as she fidgeted with the end of it, rose and met his. "A woman gets used to certain things," she said delicately. "I'm sure a man does, too."

"That's a generous assumption," he said. "About men. Very kind of you."

She smiled teasingly. "I was thinking of sleeping with Paul Frost," she said.

"Your holy man?"

"I don't think he would," she said. "I don't think *that* would do. Know what I mean? Locally? Little minds, big mouths." She paused very thoughtfully.

He sensed her mood, the reawakening within a woman

197

who had lost her mate. But she was not just the widow of a man he had never met. She was Lazz's widow, too, and the reassertion of that fact sabotaged his own mood, the feeling that had been building quietly within him since long before she had descended the creaking, wooden staircase.

Lazz's widow, he repeated in his mind. She would have left the room had she known what he was thinking.

"Priscilla's a sound sleeper," Sarah said. "She never wakes up." For the first time, his hand moved and came to rest on hers. "Hey, Bill," she said. For a moment it looked as if her lower lip had given to slight trembling. "Oh, God," she said. "It's all right, isn't it? I mean, a woman can only stay in mourning so long. I mean, I loved Brian. I loved him dearly, but—"

He raised his finger to her lips to silence her. "You don't owe any explanations," he said. "Not to yourself. Not to anyone."

"Bill?" she asked. "Here. Not upstairs. Okay?"

"Do you expect me to complain?"

She began to laugh, then silenced herself with a girlish smirk so as not to wake her daughter. He took her in his arms and brought her close to him. At first she seemed tense and uncomfortable, as if an uncertainty had to be overcome. Then her own arms embraced him.

He was in the guest room on the converted bed, waiting for her, as she neatly folded her robe and nightgown and draped them over a chair.

He watched her in the dim light. Naked, she was at once shy and vulnerable, tantalizing and exciting. In the presence of a new lover and old friend, she acted uncertain, as if taking a major step, and unsure how wise it was.

She let him pull her down to him and she kissed him as passionately as he kissed her. For both of them it was a moment of isolated magic, a small expanse of time when the rest of their lives could be closed out of the room, and the present could be given over to passion.

Mason could see the face of his watch on a nearby table. Four twenty. He had to nudge her bare shoulder to rouse her from a light sleep. In response she nestled closer to him.

"Sarah," he said gently. She came awake slowly. "Getting late," he said.

Her eyes opened. "I don't want to go upstairs," she said affectionately. "Nicer here with you."

"It's nicer that way for me too," he said. "But. . . ."

"*I* wake *her* up each morning," Sarah said. "Priscilla won't know. I get up fifteen minutes before she does." She considered it. "I'm too comfortable to move."

It was not his house, his daughter, or his decision. And Mason was not inclined to argue. Sarah drifted off to sleep again within minutes, nestled snugly on his shoulder. He was enormously tired, and began to drift off. And then it happened. Just this side of sleep, in the odd, dreamlike void, he saw geometric designs. Concentric circles and squares. Rectangles, boldly lined. The unconscious meanderings of a dead man's hand.

Fatigue. The word came back and wouldn't leave. The long, narrow rectangles weren't rectangles at all. Now suddenly he saw it.

Priscilla had long since been packed off to school. Sarah had errands in town and had gone to do them. There was coffee on the stove, breakfast within the refrigerator. She would be back sometime toward early afternoon. If he wanted a key, there was one beneath the telephone in the kitchen. On the bottom of the note, she had drawn a small heart and written beneath it, "You are a very sweet friend."

He went down to the basement, to Brian Woodson's desk. He prowled through the papers again and looked at the doodlings. Sure enough, subconsciously Woodson had drawn several sketches in conical shape of fat pencils, or missiles. Two or three were crude but very distinctly rockets.

Mason put all the papers in the top drawer of the desk. Then, taking the key she had left for him, he left the house, and drove until he found a telephone booth.

He dialed Washington. It took a few minutes, and several dimes and quarters, but eventually the voice he wanted came on the line.

"Bill?" Gardner said. "Where are you?" I tried to reach you at—"

"I checked out," Mason explained. He was visiting, seeing old friends, and staying here or there a day or two at a time.

"Well," huffed Gardner. "I tried to get you."

"What's new?"

"Not a lot. But a little. Your name passed the first hurdle."

"Tell me all about it."

Gardner explained. Gardner had suggested him for an interim appointment within an analysis unit at Langley. There was nothing available. Every desk was filled at the moment and with the new austerity that had come to Washington from southern Georgia, no one could expect to be adding new bodies to his department.

"But your application is a strong one," said Gardner. "You're on the top of some lists. Might take a few months, but there should be something. Eventually, at least. Anything else?"

Bill pondered for a moment, then began slowly. "There *is* something else. Do you have records of government contracts? What plants are working on what?"

"Can you be more precise?"

"Computer microcircuits. I want to know who's making what." Mason elaborated for a few moments.

"I'll see what I can do," said Gardner.

"That's always more than enough," Bill said. "Thanks, Phil."

"Can I call you back?"

"I'll phone *you*. I don't have a permanent address yet."

The two men signed off. Bill Mason stood in the booth for a minute, thinking. When another driver pulled off the road to use the telephone, Mason left and drove back to Sarah's house.

She was home. Priscilla wasn't. Sarah, unless he was imagining it, seemed radiant that afternoon. She kissed him and was all smiles. She made them lunch and coffee and afterward, sitting in the comfort of the living room, conversing amiably and relaxing, the same thought was suddenly upon both of them.

They returned to the guest room. There was a joyful, irresponsible abandon to their lovemaking, as if the mere act of being together in bed, totally new to each other as lovers, in the middle of a November afternoon, was in itself an act of unparalleled sensuality. In the daylight, completely unclad, she was as beautiful to him as she'd been the night before. For her part, seeing his trim body, still with the suggestion of a summer's tan, he excited her even more than he had the night before.

Whatever inhibitions they had had were gone. They enjoyed themselves for so long that Priscilla, returning home twenty minutes early, almost caught them unaware. Mason took a long shower and shaved for the second time that day.

Paul Frost arrived at seven thirty.

The predinner conversation was casual and amiable. Toward eight thirty, just before they were to sit down and eat, Mason helped Sarah lift the roast out of the oven. Then he walked back into the dining room. Frost was gone. The door to the basement was open.

Frost struck a particularly unclerical pose leaning over Woodson's desk. Mason stood at the far end of the corridor leading to the work space. He watched the younger man. Frost was casually browsing through papers. He had probably been there for several minutes.

"Looking for anything in particular?"

Frost looked up abruptly, taken by surprise. "No, no. Not at all. Just curious."

"Very curious, I'd say," Mason walked toward him, looking him up and down. He looked at the man's face, hands, clothing.

"Just trying to help," said Frost.

"Help what?"

"Help us," Frost sneered. "What the fuck do you think I'm talking about, Mason? The fucking chips that your incompetent friend Lassiter was screwing around with."

"You know," said Mason slowly, "Captain Queeg is going to go through the roof when he finds out you people are doing domestic bag jobs again."

"Captain Queeg is an asshole," said the holy man. "He won't know."

"*Won't* he?" said Mason.

"No," said Frost authoritatively. "He won't. Besides, this is strictly personal initiative."

"What did you get the night you broke in?"

Frost hesitated. "I don't see why I should tell you."

"Don't you?"

Frost considered it. "Look, Mason. She says that you spent a day and a half going through Woodson's notes.

If you did, you know as much as I do. I've already filed a report to Langley. There's probably nothing here but I want to get these things out of here for one fucking night so that I can copy them." He paused. "Want to help?"

"No."

"I can see why they let you go. You're an asshole."

"Maybe."

Frost went back to work, opening drawers and trying to assemble Woodson's notes in some order so that they could be removed and returned easily. "Don't screw me up, Mason," he snapped. "Once I've got these things finished, there's just one more order of business for me here."

"Really?" asked Bill, watching the younger man. "What's that, Reverend? Pray, tell."

Frost looked up. "I've had a hard-on for that broad upstairs for weeks now. I'm planning to bang the daylights out of her before I get transferred to another case."

"Is that a fact?" Mason asked.

Frost was about to say that, yes, it was a fact, and was just raising his head to speak. But as he turned, something resembling a freight train smashed him squarely in the center of the face. It was a sucker punch, of sorts, but that was Frost's problem. When the fist landed, breaking his nose, the Reverend's lights started going out. He hit the floor and didn't know where he was for several seconds. It took Mason to revive him, but then there was the problem of all the blood running from his nose and mouth. Somehow Mason knew the roast would have to wait.

Looking back on it, later that evening, Mason realized how stupid his mistake had been. Why couldn't he have sensed the error he was making before he had gone ahead and made it? Why is the most obvious conclusion to circumstantial evidence always wrong?

Sarah had thrown him out, of course, and he'd gathered his belongings while she drove Frost to a nearby doctor. The friendly dinner for the four of them, including her daughter, was, to phrase it kindly, postponed indefinitely.

Frost's nose could be repaired. The other damage Bill had done could not be.

Irate as she was, Sarah had demanded an explana-

202

tion. He had told her just enough for her to know. His interest in IC chips and Woodson's death was more than personal. It was professional.

"All you people do—you CIA people—is destroy," she retorted viciously. "It gets into you. It corrupts your kindness and humanity until you don't have any. Then you turn on others close to you. You sacrifice them like pieces on a chessboard. You lead them into trusting you, even *loving* you, and then the truth comes out. It's simple manipulation. A ruse to get something you wanted. Some useless tidbit. Every one of you is the same." The sermon continued.

Mason hadn't followed everything she said. He had only known that she spoke from experience. First Lazz, he supposed, and now—much more briefly—himself. Her eyes were wet, her voice frenzied and the only visible compassion she had was for Frost, who denied every allegation Mason made. Yet Frost's cover was totally blown.

The worst part about it, Mason recognized, as he lay on the bed in a motel room with a black-and-white television on in front of him, was that there was truth in each accusation.

"Damn it," he said aloud.

23

Lerner wasn't a mechanic. He was a different sort of technician.

Nonetheless, he leaned over the open hood of his new station wagon. The tidy lawn of his home was behind him. Beyond was a modern split-level brown ranch house. The station wagon was by the sidewalk, in front of the house.

It was noon on Saturday. The street was lined with comfortable, modern homes on one-acre lots, the type of Maryland suburb where there were no Democrats. There was a smattering of trees, thoughtfully provided by the developers after the original forest had been knocked down. Lerner, tinkering with the car's engine, was aware of a second car stopping behind his station wagon. The inquisitive driver stepped out as Lerner looked up.

"Help you?" he asked Mason.

Mason looked at the house and looked at the man. Lerner had thin, squarish glasses, pale brown hair, a narrow face, and taut lips. Fortyish. He wore a green car coat, an open plaid shirt, and looked like a high-school basketball coach. "You wouldn't be Stanley Lerner, would you?"

"Would be. And am," said Lerner. He wiped his left hand on a rag and looked to Mason expectantly.

"I was a friend of Brian Woodson. My name's Bill Mason." He offered a hand.

For a moment Lerner hesitated, then offered the wrong hand. "Left hand," he said. "Hope you don't mind."

Lerner moved his wrist slightly to indicate the reason. He had no right hand. It was instead a prosthesis, a mechanical hook as an artificial limb.

"Don't mind at all," said Mason, recovering quickly. Bill guessed that Lerner liked to get the psychological drop on people by flashing his hardware.

"A friend of Brian's," Lerner mumbled thoughtfully. "What was the name again?"

"Mason. I wondered if we could talk for a few minutes."

"Only a few. Your timing's not so hot today."

Lerner looked back toward the house. His daughter's eighth birthday party, he explained. Ten kids in the house. In another fifteen minutes he'd be ferrying the whole crew over to the local movie theatre.

"My wife's going to be taking the other car. Six kids in one car, four in the other. Think we can do it?"

"Don't see why not," Mason said.

"What did you want to ask me?"

"You were Brian's closest collaborator at ITW. I wondered if you might be able to tell me one or two things."

Lerner was obviously wary. "I made a statement to the police, you know."

"I'm sure you did. That's not exactly what I had in mind."

There was an uneasy silence. Lerner looked as if he'd just as soon be in a dentist's chair.

"I don't mind answering a question or two as long as they're fairly general," Lerner said. "But I'd like to give Sarah a call, make sure she doesn't mind my talking to you. Maybe you could stop back in an hour or two. Or tomorrow."

"I'd rather not."

"Excuse me?"

"I'd prefer that you didn't mention to Sarah that I came to see you."

Lerner looked at Mason as if seeing him in a new light, enshrouded by new doubts. He picked up the rag with his hook and wiped his good hand on it again.

"Just a few questions," Mason repeated. "I was a personal friend. And I'm also investigating the case for Connecticut National Insurance Corporation. Life insurance."

Mason could see, by Lerner's expression, the sour taste engendered by the word "insurance." He had guessed wrong.

"You're a claims investigator. Is that it?"

"No," said Mason. He took on an expression of sincerity. "I'm in risk analysis. To tell the truth, I hate the damn company. I'm leaving it myself next May, just as soon as I can get my ten-year severance. What I'm doing is for Brian, not the company."

Lerner obviously didn't believe him. "And what's that, Mr. . . . ?"

"Mason. I'm trying to build a case on Sarah's behalf. Trying to establish that Brian was under mental stress when he . . . did what he did."

Lerner thought for a moment and Mason sensed he had struck something. "How would that change anything?" Lerner asked.

"Maybe not at all. *Maybe* it will help. See, if a man kills himself, and apparently did it just to leave a premium to a beneficiary, the company is under no obligation to pay. Mental stress, however, is another matter. The claim could be reopened. Sarah could challenge the settlement in the courts. The company would probably agree to compromise. That would help her. She's having a rough go of it financially, you know."

"I know," said Lerner blandly. He closed the hood of the car and looked at it. He clicked something with his mechanical arm and then brushed some dirt off the hood with the rag. "I dislike insurance companies," he announced.

"Don't we all?"

"But you *work for* an insurance company," Lerner countered.

"That doesn't mean they own me. Does ITW own you?"

"What did you say your name was?" Lerner asked.

"Mason. Bill Mason. I'm sure Brian must have mentioned me from time to time."

"No. Never."

I'll never get anything out of him, Mason thought, and looked offended. "I'm surprised," he said. Then, thinking, he added, "Well, you knew Brian. He was a private person."

"That he was," Lerner conceded.

"Look. Something was troubling Brian before he died. That's obvious. There's not an awful lot of time. I *know* you can help me. If you will."

Lerner looked sullen now, as if looking for a convenient escape.

"It seemed to me to be work-related," Mason suggested. He shook his head. "Other people are saying other things. Vicious things."

He had grasped Lerner's attention. "What things?" Lerner snapped.

"Skirts," Mason said softly, as if he feared being overheard.

"*That* is a filthy, rotten—!"

"Of course it is!" Mason interrupted. "And do you think it's not getting back to Sarah?"

Lerner's anger searched for a direction.

"I want to disprove it," Mason said. "Brian's problem was work-related. Brian was home every night. Downstairs. In his basement. 'Woodson's Warren.'"

Lerner gazed at him blankly.

"Mr. Lerner," Mason begged. "You owe it to Brian. You owe it to yourself. Want me to tell the story to you? And you can give me corrections?"

"Tell you what?"

"How Brian's work had gone wrong," Mason said. "I know Brian was trying to repair what he thought was a major error. A major error of his." Lerner flinched. "And maybe of yours, too. You were Brian's partner at work. Right?"

"What is it you're angling at, Mr. Mason?"

"I'm not angling. Brian told me enough. I need confirmation. *Fatigue*," said Mason throwing his only trump card. "Fatigue and those missiles."

Lerner looked like a man who had just seen a traffic accident. Shock, bewilderment, fear, and utter fascination. "You *know?*"

Mason nodded. "I'm not out to make trouble. Just want to help a friend." He turned the knife gently. "I don't want to drag your testimony into court."

Lerner had the appearance of a man whose Saturday had just been ruined. "How the hell did you—?"

"I'm telling you," Mason insisted. "Brian and I were friends. He told me almost everything."

"He said he didn't tell a soul about the fatigue problem."

"He told *me*," Mason intoned sharply. "Didn't even tell his wife. But he told me. That's what the poor guy was doing down in his basement all those nights. All the nights when he's being accused of carousing. Home, working on an open ITW problem. The damned fatigue," Mason pressed. "That damned fatigue. Those missiles."

Lerner shook his head sadly, angrily, in utter disgust. At first Mason feared that he had missed completely, that Lerner was going to evade the whole subject. But then Lerner spoke, and suddenly it was all rolling out.

"The fatigue wasn't in the aluminum," Lerner said softly. "*Or* the silicon. That's what Brian and I couldn't understand. Why was the aluminum showing metal fatigue when it hadn't even been used? It just sat. Just remained idle and suffered what looked like metal fatigue. Looked like. But wasn't."

"How long did Brian know about the fatigue?" Mason asked. "About two months, I'd guess."

Lerner began to open up. Slowly. Uncertainly. "Yes. That's about right. It was thrown to us first. Our team. We couldn't crack it. Then it became an open problem. It went around to everyone. I guess that's when Brian started taking it home with him." Lerner shook his head. "You knew Brian. Perfectionist. He figured he had created the problem so he had to solve it. Point of personal honor, point of professional honor. It eluded him."

It was a moment to press. "But that wasn't all," Mason suggested firmly. "Not by a long shot."

Lerner looked at Mason as if with a sudden revelation. "You don't work for any insurance company. I've seen enough insurance companies to know what they hire. You're not it."

Lerner was nervously rubbing his hook against his good palm now. Each knew who was on the defensive.

"I'm coming clean with you," Lerner said. "How about you coming clean with me?"

Mason drew a breath. "A man in a sensitive research position committed suicide. Brian was enough of a professional to handle his work. He could live with mistakes. And he could correct mistakes. But scandal? That might be the type of thing a man would commit suicide to avoid. To spare his family. I'm not wrong, am I?"

"Who do you work for?"

"Central Intelligence Agency," said Mason. He watched Lerner's fearful reaction. "All I want is answers. Quiet answers."

Lerner puffed. "The men who work in microtechnology at ITW aren't stupid," he began. "Officially we don't know what we're working on. We're not told. But we know what microtechnology makes possible. We know what the Department of Defense pays for. And we know what IC chips can do."

Mason listened obediently.

"Don't get me wrong," Lerner said. "We don't talk; we don't run off at the mouth; no one outside the plant is getting classified technical data. But it's impossible not to know sometimes what you're working on, even if it's the small part of a whole."

"A very small part," Mason said.

Lerner nodded, sensing that Mason was sympathetic and pursuing answers, not guilt. "We had guessed years ago what we were designing components for. One of those chips can be used for anything from microwave ovens to MIRV missiles. Well, the Defense Department isn't making ovens. Not when they quietly sent in sixteen guided-missile specialists—a bunch of geniuses—to oversee what we were doing. That clinched it. We all knew."

Lerner looked absently at his home. Children's delighted voices were squealing within.

Mason nodded. Lerner could run with it now. No use to interrupt him while he was talking.

"Somewhere there had to be a whole class of multi-warhead missiles sitting in silos around the country—billions of dollars' worth of tax-financed hardware—and the smallest components in them were defective. I ought to know. Brian Woodson and I designed them."

"The smallest components," repeated Mason, picturing the microcircuits he'd retrieved from Lassiter's watch. "The chips."

Lerner nodded. "Fatigue," he said. "Not exactly metal fatigue because it wasn't exclusively the metal. And not silicon either. Silicon is a crystalline substance and won't react that way. But it was the combination of the two together. Sitting in the silos."

"How do you know your chips were ever implemented?" Mason asked.

Lerner frowned. "What?"

"How do you know your chips really went into the missiles? How do you know for certain?"

"I know what we designed," Lerner said sadly. "Brian and I figured out exactly what our chips had to have been used for. No way around that."

"And so the missiles with the defective chips . . ." Mason began.

"Would never have worked. If anyone had pressed a button the entire missile's system would have jammed and shorted out. It would have refused to launch."

"So billions of dollars' worth of nuclear hardware would have been sitting around useless," Mason said.

"Not a dime's worth of firepower. No nuclear deterrent, no defense system at all." Lerner's eyes met Mason's.

"How could it have happened?" asked Mason. "The fatigue malfunction."

Lerner shook his head again, almost in disbelief. "We still don't know," he said. "The chips are made like wafers, a layer at a time. An initial layer is silicon dioxide. It insulates the rest of the chips from stray electrical charges. All I can suggest," he said slowly, "is that the silicon dioxide we used at the time was reacting for some reason. Hence, the whole circuit jammed."

Lerner shrugged helplessly. "I'll tell you," he said. "I've lost a fair bit of sleep about it myself. Hell, we haven't gotten any official feedback on the problem, but I'm no damned fool. Each side is afraid to hit first because the other guy will get off his counterattack. Now, imagine if the other side knows, or even *thinks*, that ours don't work. No more balance of terror." Lerner shook his head fearfully. "Imagine."

"Imagine," agreed Mason. He thought of Vassiliev. The chips sealed in the book, waiting to go to Moscow until Lassiter, in a final action, had burglarized them away. A doomed man's final small triumph.

"It was all too much for poor Brian," said Lerner. "He was convinced of a scandal. He sensed ruin as a computer physicist. And he figured the whole mess would descend on his family. I don't know. He wasn't solely responsible, we *all* were. But he got so depressed. It really got to him."

"So. . . ." said Mason with exhaustion. And he pictured Woodson quietly going to a strange hotel one day. To the very end, he had been a loving husband. He had done it in a hotel and called the police beforehand. He didn't want Sarah to see him that way. In a strange and ironic fashion, Mason felt he finally knew the man. Woodson had wrapped his head in a hotel towel to cut down on the inevitable blood and mess. Then he'd fired a bullet through the left eye and into the brain.

"I just can't get it straightened out," said Lerner. "I mean, there wasn't a scandal. There doesn't seem to be any urgency about the chips. A study is continuing, that's all. We all face mistakes and correct them. Keep them secret while we work." He paused. "I mean, what Brian feared was imminent never happened. What else could he have been afraid of?"

"I have no idea," Mason said. "None at all."

Lerner looked up, sensing a bond now that the full confession was before them. "Will you find out?" Lerner asked.

"Probably not."

Lerner grimaced painfully. Then he winced when six children, none any more than ten years old, burst from the front door of his house and ran joyfully toward the station wagon.

"Shit," muttered Lerner angrily. "Poor Brian. It all stinks. And here come six of the most obnoxious little brats you've ever encountered."

So there it was. Half an explanation, distilled from lies which had been strewn everywhere. As Mason drove aggressively toward New York City from Maryland, it began to make partial sense. He turned it over and over. It was like searching a corpse, finding something new each few seconds.

The sun was going down and the traffic was heavier. He was only in central New Jersey. It was a cold, gray day now. Evening crept in soon after four o'clock. Something made him think of sunny warm days in Delwood. He hit the accelerator, sensing insecurities and jealousies of his own. He arrived at Kennedy Airport in New York by eight that evening.

There was only one item of business. At nine fifty that evening, Mason contacted Philip Gardner by telephone. Gardner, steady as ever, had unearthed a list of American firms manufacturing microcircuits for the Department of Defense. Whenever there were questions, Gardner had the answers.

Mason stretched out like a derelict on an airport bench, woke again at four thirty and spent the next hours

211

in a coffee shop, leafing through newspapers and magazines. Sitting, thinking, reflecting.

At seven thirty his flight to London was paged. He boarded.

When the flight attendants looked at the red-eyed man in the rumpled clothing, they took him for a chronic boozer and tried to remember to avoid his aisle whenever possible. They had seen the type before and prepared themselves for the worst. Aggressive passengers were rarely fun and were preferable only to tires blowing out during landings.

But they were pleasantly surprised when Mr. Mason dozed soundly and offered no trouble or disturbance at all. He seemed, in fact, in those moments when he was awake, greatly preoccupied.

24

A very unsettling incident transpired as Mason was passing through British immigration. It reminded him that it was always the little unattended details which give birth to trouble.

It was past ten in the evening, London time, and Mason stood in line to pass through Heathrow immigration. The line progressed arduously. Dragging a small suitcase by his side across the concrete floor, inches at a time, Mason made the inspector's desk by ten thirty.

All the questions were routine. *Citizen of the United States, sir? How long will you be staying, sir? Nature of your visit, sir?*

Yes. A week or two. Vacation, strictly.

The inspector reached for his metal stamp, gripped it in his fist, then set it down without using it. Something in Mason's passport had caught his attention. He leafed from one page to another. Mason watched, his concern growing.

"Something wrong?" Mason asked finally.

There was no immediate answer. The line of people behind him grew restless. The passport was open to the photograph. The inspector glanced up, looking Mason squarely in the eyes. "When did you enter the United Kingdom last, sir?"

"Approximately three weeks ago."

"According to your passport, you never left."

And suddenly Mason realized how careless he had been. The inspector's brow was wrinkled and there was curiosity in his heavy brown eyes.

"I went to France from England," Mason said. "I don't know whether they stamped my passport or not."

The inspector studied it again. "It shows no reentry into the United States. Yet you just flew here from New York."

213

"I flew from France to Montreal. Then I crossed the border in New York state. One is merely waved through."

Again the eyes were lowered briefly and disbelievingly onto the passport. Pages were flipped. "But no entry is shown into Canada, either," the inspector said. He pursed his lips thoughtfully, closed the passport without stamping it, and looked at Mason quizzically. His thumb flicked the passport pages, his other hand under the desk.

"Sometimes they're careless," Mason offered lamely.

"Of course." The man was thoughtful. "You have luggage?"

"Only what I'm carrying," Mason answered. The man looked. It was getting worse.

"Traveling very light for a vacation, aren't you, sir?"

"That's how I like it." Mason already knew. The conversation, the low key statements, were a stall. Under the desk, a button had been pushed. Now he could only stand and wait, while he privately cursed the Canadian passport.

A heavyset man with a moustache and shiny bald head appeared beside Mason. He thanked the inspector and asked Mason to kindly accompany him.

"Of course," Mason said placidly. "But I don't see what this is about."

"Luggage? Other luggage on your flight?" the man asked.

"None," answered Mason again.

"I see," deadpanned the man.

Mason was led to a private room in a special area. The man, who answered to the name of Mr. Dennis, asked for his passport. Mason gave it to him. Then the passport was handed to someone in a uniform, who disappeared with it.

"Routine check," Dennis explained. "Sorry for the inconvenience."

"You *are* delaying me," Mason suggested.

"I'm afraid your passport wasn't in order. Not our fault entirely, sir."

Mason explained about France and Montreal, the *je-m'en-fous* attitude indigenous to both places.

"Yes. Of course," Dennis agreed with a false smile. "Should be more careful, they should. They're causing you a terrible inconvenience, I know." The man scratched his ear. "Would you mind opening your bag, sir?"

Mason opened it and slid it to Dennis who prowled

214

through it carefully, removing all the contents. Dennis honed in on a toiletry case and opened it. He found a small flask of brandy, opened it, sniffed, smiled, and sealed it again.

"Tsk, tsk," he said with his tongue against his teeth. "Hennessy, I'd say."

"Asbach Uralt," Mason said. "Magnificent stuff."

Dennis set it aside, hardly concerned. "Do you have friends in the United Kingdom?"

Mason thought of Auerbach. And, for that matter, of Fahrar, and Vassiliev. "No," he answered.

"Where are you going?"

"London."

"Reservations anywhere?"

"No."

"You travel light," Dennis noted suggestively. "Just two dirty shirts, some sleepwear, a book, and some toiletries." Dennis ran his hand along the inside lining of the suitcase.

"I'm eccentric." Mason answered.

Dennis looked at him peevishly. "Evidently. Who is your employer?"

"To tell you the truth, I'm out of work."

"*Are* you? I'm so sorry. What did you do last?"

Mason hesitated much too long. "I worked for a tobacco company."

"Which one?"

"Du Mar."

"In Virginia?"

"New York. I was in marketing."

Dennis knew it was a lie. Mason knew he knew.

"Would you mind emptying your pockets?"

Mason glared. Then, rudely, he humored him, pouring out everything onto the table, wallet first. He broke open a pack of chewing gum and laid out the seven sticks side by side on the desk. "Want me to strip, too?"

The uniformed assistant reappeared and wordlessly set the passport in front of Dennis. Mason didn't have to ask. Its authenticity had been verified in triplicate. Without doubt the bindings, printing, paper, ink, and photograph had also been checked. Mason had obviously passed.

"No. No need," Dennis answered. He picked up the passport, took a final gaze at the American, compared him with his picture, and set the passport on the table, open

215

to the center. From a drawer he pulled out an immigration stamp, punched it against an ink pad and stamped Bill's entry into the U.K.

Mason studied every motion and every facial expression made by the man. He searched for ulterior purpose. Had CIA put a tail on him? Was this a charade? Had Immigration been looking for him specifically?

Or was this a random incident with no meaning at all?

"Sorry, sir," Dennis said simply. "You may go."

Mason gathered his belongings on the table. As he turned and left the room, he felt Dennis's glare upon his back.

Mason went by bus from the airport to Hounslow. He stayed overnight in a small rooming house. He would enter London and rendezvous with Fahrar the next day.

But the lesson had been learned. Small mistakes cause large problems and larger inconveniences. How could he ever have made such a rudimentary mistake? It was the type of error which, under wartime circumstances, cost men dearly. Sometimes, sadly, their lives.

On the following afternoon, Mason stood across from Victoria Station. He resisted the temptation to glance at his watch. He was all too aware what the hour was. He passed through a ritual which had been prearranged.

Holding beneath his left arm a copy of that morning's *Daily Mirror*, he stood on the corner expectantly, not glancing one way or another.

A quarter hour passed. Then more. Mason turned and walked toward the Underground. He studied the faces and the formations of people around him. He traveled a zigzagging route underneath London, emerging eventually at Tottenham Court Road.

He walked four blocks. It was two thirteen. He found a pub and strolled in for a brandy before the two thirty closing. Then he wandered again for half an hour before reemerging at a corner of Soho Square at three o'clock exactly.

He switched the newspaper from one arm to the other, indicating to his pickup that he was certain that he was alone.

Five minutes passed. He expected a private car. Instead a London taxi spewing diesel fumes clanked to the

216

curb in front of him. When the rear door opened on the curb side, he saw Fahrar.

"Get in, get in," Fahrar invited him with surprising civility.

Mason dropped the newspaper into a receptable and stepped into the rear of the cab.

"Well . . . ?" Fahrar asked.

"Success," said Mason. "Langley's taking me back."

Fahrar said nothing. But he seemed pleased.

The taxi crawled through afternoon traffic. Mason attempted to follow the route, but it was impossible. He was led through unfamiliar neighborhoods and tried to gather, from the position of the sun, in what direction he was going. But the sky had become overcast. He saw one large sign pointing toward a turnoff for CRYSTAL PALACE. He guessed he was somewhere vaguely in the southern portion of the city.

They arrived at a wooden Victorian house in the center of a long grimy block of similar houses, each indistinguishable from the one next to it. Mason couldn't find a street sign as he was hustled inside. The Arab, interestingly, had not paid the taxi driver. No one had.

Fahrar led his guest up a flight of stairs. The house was functional and depressing: no maintenance, few furnishings. Mason was taken into a room on the second floor. Fahrar gave him a chair. Vassiliev was waiting.

The Russian, as usual, was not one to delay moving to the heart of the matter. "Have you been successful?" he asked.

"Yes."

Vassiliev betrayed emotion for the first time. His hands clenched together; the palms rubbed slightly. Mason noted anew the stubby, bitten fingernails and the layer of grime on the man's spectacles.

"Tell us," Vassiliev said. *"How* have you been successful?"

"When can I see Hargrove?"

"You will see him in due time."

"I don't trust you."

"You have no choice but to trust us!" the Russian snapped. His small brown eyes glared. "You must trust us and obey! Otherwise you are nothing. *Nothing!*"

Mason wondered what that meant.

217

"I see Hargrove before you get a single chip," Mason asserted. He was about to continue, but Fahrar's hand was suddenly under Mason's left arm, the other hand just below his left ear, the large thumb and fingers wrapping halfway around Mason's neck. The thumb was placed, suggestively, flush against his Adam's apple.

"Will you now answer our questions?" the Russian inquired. "Or will we break your neck?"

What they lacked in subtlety they regained in effectiveness. Mason answered, yes, that answering was the pleasanter alternative. He knew they weren't prepared to kill him. Not there, not yet. More likely they would break something. Like a finger or one of the small bones in the foot.

"I contacted a man in Washington," Mason said. "A man named Philip Gardner."

"Where does he work?" The Russian began writing while still watching Mason.

"Langley. He's an economic-development specialist. Central Africa."

"He is a former associate of yours?"

"I've known him for fifteen years." Mason twisted in discomfort. "Get your creature off my throat, would you, Vassiliev?"

The Russian gave a slight, affirmative eye movement to Fahrar. Reluctantly the hands released, but not before a thumb jabbed harder into the throat.

Mason rubbed his neck. Fahrar took up a sentry's position at the door.

"Tell us about Gardner," Vassiliev instructed.

Bill told everything he knew. And more.

"He's arranging a position for me. I would return to the United States and take it, if I want it, at the—"

"You want it," insisted the Russian.

"—at the end of the year. The agency is not hiring anyone new. Internal politics. This would be treated as a transfer assignment from within." Vassiliev studied him. "That's why I don't have to reapply. If Gardner weren't sponsoring me there'd be no chance at all."

There was silence in the room.

"I will have to undergo a new FBI check," Mason warned. Vassiliev smiled. "I'll have to account for all my time between last March and now."

218

"What are you suggesting by that?" Vassiliev asked with apprehension. "You will not pass?"

"One never knows."

"You will pass," the Russian said gruffly, as if there were no question about it. "What will you be doing? In Langley?"

"I don't know. They don't give details in advance." Mason appeared pensive. "Accumulation and analysis of intelligence, probably. I'd be retained as an analyst. A God-damned technocrat."

"What locations?"

"Probably the Orient. It's what I know. It's what they need. Probably it would be combining new field reports with satellite photographs. That's about all I know. A C-7 Department, Far East Analysis."

"C-7. That's on the seventh floor in Langley?" Vassiliev tested casually.

"Fifth floor," said Mason. "There are only six floors."

The Russian nodded.

"I'd be working with an older officer at first." Mason watched the Russian playing with a pencil, sliding it from one end to the other in his hand. "Which officer, I don't know."

"No names at all?"

A real fox, this one, Bill thought. "I don't know names yet," he said again. "Give me time, will you?"

Vassiliev didn't speak immediately; the silence seemed to accuse. He pursed his lips and seemed to consider Mason profoundly.

"That's all I was told," Mason repeated. "If you've got any plans about sticking me with a needle again, forget it. You'll get the same answers. And I'll never do another God-damned thing for you."

"Don't anger," replied Vassiliev. He was still brooding. "Now," he announced. "The chips."

"Now Hargrove," Mason countered.

Vassiliev seethed quietly. "We will have to trust each other sometime." He blinked from moment to moment.

"I don't trust you at all. Come on, Vassiliev. The only thing Russians are worse at than table manners is keeping a promise. You want silicon chips? You deliver Hargrove. Alive. That's all there is to it."

"Simultaneous," muttered the Russian. "We will let you see Hargrove. Then you will turn over the computer cells to us. He is in a private flat in London. Guarded. He is waiting for us to take him out of England. But his own people are looking for him."

"Who? CIA?"

Vassiliev didn't answer. Silly question.

"You will do with him as you wish," said Vassiliev. "Where are the chips? Your willpower is excellent. Under medication that was the only answer you would not give. In the barrel, in the barrel, you kept saying. Where are the chips?"

"When do you want them?"

"I want them now."

Mason thought. "It will take a day to recover them. Maybe two days to do it without suspicion. Will you have Hargrove ready for me in two days?"

"Evening," answered Vassiliev. "It must be evening."

"Why?"

Vassiliev rankled a bit. "The chips will be taken out of England immediately. There is an Aeroflot flight to Luxembourg that evening at ten. I will be on it with the chips. Comrade Fahrar will be on it. Hargrove will be expecting a man to take him to the airport. The man will be you. He will not go to the airport."

"You expect me to shoot him, don't you?"

"As you wish. We are finished with him."

"You're too kind."

"There is only one more item," Vassiliev said. "The chips. You are not a stupid man. Difficult to predict, perhaps. No doubt one idea has occurred to you."

Mason turned toward Fahrar abruptly, but the nose of a small automatic pistol was pressed against Bill's ear. Fahrar made a show of releasing the safety catch and twitching the finger that was upon the trigger.

As Mason looked frontwards again, Fahrar nuzzled the snout of the pistol to Mason's ear lobe.

"You would not substitute chips, would you?" Vassiliev asked. "And give us the wrong ones?"

"What the hell for?" snapped Mason, angry yet apprehensive.

"Where did you *really* go in Washington?"

"I told you."

"And this section that you would be added to?" Vassiliev asked. "Why have I never heard of such a department?"

"I have no idea."

"Where did you hide the chips? The ones obtained from Lassiter?" There was a long silence. Fahrar pressed the pistol harder, steel to flesh, against Mason's head. The barrel was pointed slightly upward now, implying a trajectory that would carry a .38 caliber bullet into the brain.

The Russian's eyes moved slightly to the left. He gave a nod to his enthusiastic assistant.

The gun was pulled away. As the Arab pushed the pistol into a holster beneath his belt, Fahrar turned quickly and slapped the back of his hand viciously across the side of Mason's head, jarring him soundly. Reverberations rang through Mason's brain. He was shaken. Fahrar, with a quick movement of his foot, kicked the chair out from under Mason, who landed on the floor, hard.

Bill thought it was over, the message delivered, until Fahrar cracked a knee against his left shoulder and sent Mason sprawling. The Russian watched nervously from the desk. It was as if Vassiliev were watching a movie.

Mason looked up, dazed slightly.

"An unfortunate lesson," Vassiliev said, "Don't betray us. And in the future, you will address Mr. Fahrar with a great deal more respect. He will be your case officer after I return to the Soviet Union. Mr. Fahrar will visit Washington from time to time."

I can't wait, Mason thought.

"Have you anything further to tell us?" Vassiliev asked.

"Nothing of interest," Mason answered.

"Anything at all?"

"Only that interpersonal relations seem lacking in this organization," Mason wheezed.

Fahrar let go with a brutal kick with the side of the foot which Mason blocked with both arms. He glowered upward at the Arab and the two of them might have continued. But the Russian interceded.

"What about the needle?" Fahrar asked Vassiliev.

Vassiliev assessed Mason carefully, scrutinizing him as he lay on the floor.

"Not necessary," Vassiliev decided. "We haven't the time. I'm sure our employee no longer doubts our sincerity. Or our purpose. How do you say it, Mr. Mason—'Welcome aboard'?"

They returned Mason to the street. Fahrar had a car,

221

and drove him a dozen or more blocks in one direction before the car halted at an Underground stop.

Fahrar looked at his passenger and motioned with his head. "Out," he said.

"It's just a thought, Fahrar," he said, "but I'll bet you're a talented man with your hands."

The Arab looked at Mason blankly.

"Bicycle chains," Mason added, envisioning Lucille Davis' battered head and throat. "Bet you know all about them."

Fahrar couldn't resist a sadistic smile. "All about them," he affirmed.

Mason stepped from the car and watched it disappear through traffic before descending into the Underground. Mason had a headache that throbbed every time he moved his eyes. Vassiliev and company were much too anxious to turn over Hargrove. And much too interested in having Mason shoot him.

Something, as Mason knew, was wrong.

25

Mason mopped his forehead. He had arrived hot and disheveled at Bobb's small shop, having made a wild dash from the Highbury Underground station. Mason had feared that the antiquer would shutter his doors early.

"Santa Claus is com-ing *to* town," Bobbs began singing absently as he opened his stamp case. "Hey, Billy boy, guess who they're looking for."

"Who's 'they'?"

"The local Langley brigade. Your London office."

"Okay. Who are they looking for?"

"They're looking for *you*," Bobbs chirped. He grinned. "In some sort of trouble, Billy boy?"

"No."

"They can't figure out," Bobbs said, with marked sarcasm, "what you're doing in England. Something about passport trouble at the airport?" An innocent grin. "They wanted to know if I'd seen you. Of course . . . I haven't. Not for *years*."

Mason looked at Bobbs with relief. "Thank you, Maurice."

"A friend is a friend is a friend," pronounced Bobbs. "Here's your toy."

He removed the package from the stamp case. He handed it to Mason.

"Get in good and close with it," Bobbs advised puck-ishly. "Blow a hole the size of a balloon from ten meters. More than fifteen, we discuss watermelons." Bobb's teeth shone. His nostrils flared as he laughed. His voice was melodic: "Un-til we meet a-gain." It sounded like Gene Autry.

Bobbs slapped him on the back. Mason caught a whiff of his breath and basic suspicions were confirmed.

"You ought to control that stuff," Mason said dourly. "In your line of work, Maurice."

"If anyone lights a match near me," he intoned with forced sobriety, "I go up like a Buddhist monk." And he convulsed with laughter again. He was singing when Mason went out the front door.

A block down the road Mason found a pub and made his way to the men's room. He went into a stall and carefully unwrapped the handgun. He checked the magazine, and found it empty, as he had left it. He held the Walther downward and let the silicon chips, still bound in foil, slide from the barrel.

Wrapping them in a handkerchief, he stuffed them deeply into his pants pocket. He loaded the pistol and left the pub.

His hands felt clammy, his clothes rumpled. He found a taxi and studied the rear view as he directed the driver around the man's native city. At a corner in Chelsea he handed the driver one pound above the three-and-a-half pound fare and got out.

Mason began walking. He studied the urban terrain in all directions. Idly he wondered if the lock to the flat— Auerbach's flat—might have been changed. He guessed it wouldn't have been. They would be concerned with shutting him in, not out.

When he arrived, there was no surveillance on the block. He turned toward the building, saw from the street that his flat was dark, and walked to the door. He climbed the stairs. There was a slight tremor to his knee, a quirk he had never noticed before.

He unlocked his door, turning the key slowly. He gripped his weapon firmly in his right hand and reached inside, sideways to the door. He illuminated the room without stepping into it.

He stood listening. Everything was exactly where he had left it, yet he knew that the flat had been torn apart and carefully put back together again. Auerbach was predictable.

Mason carefully closed the door behind him and holstered his weapon. He held his hand on it and noted the dampness of his palms. Hands never used to sweat. Age, he thought. He moved to the bedroom. Nothing. The flat was empty.

Mason checked for details. Everything was perfectly in place, as if the flat had been tidied by a curator. He

224

checked the electronic ear he had bashed in the kitchen vent. That, too, was as he'd left it.

He pulled every shade and sat in the living room, his automatic across his lap.

"Okay, Auerbach," he said. "I'm back. We've got lots to talk about. I'm waiting for you."

It took the walls the better part of an hour to respond.

"Don't even bother to sit down," Mason said. "I assume you have a car." He appeared almost relaxed: his hands folded behind his head, the weapon across his lap, his feet propped comfortably on a small footstool.

"What the bloody hell are you talking about?" Auerbach snarled. The Englishman was a portrait of controlled temper.

"What I'm talking about is you and me," Mason said. "Don't let this make you nervous." He indicated the pistol in his lap. He picked it up and slid it into the small holster under his arm. "Yes, it works, yes it's loaded and no, I'm not planning to use it."

Auerbach eyed him warily. "Where have you been?"

"Out conducting your search for you."

"You've got no bloody right to—"

"You and me, Auerbach," Mason said, "we've been grabbing at the wrong end of the right stick. Where's your defector? Still in Bath?"

"We moved him. He's closer."

"Where are your baby-sitters?"

"Closer still."

"I don't budge until you tell me."

A wary, sneaky grin came from somewhere else and crept across Auerbach's face. Edgar and Louis appeared in the doorway, their own arsenals in their hands.

"As I suspected," Mason said. "I knew you wouldn't travel alone. Car?"

"Of course. Two, in fact."

"Go with me on this, Auerbach, and I'll dump Hargrove in your lap within two days."

"Dead or alive?"

"No guarantees, Auerbach. Your Prussian is a liar."

Nervously, Auerbach frowned.

"It was a setup. We both fell for it." Bill Mason rose anxiously from his chair. "Auerbach, old man, it finally dawned on me. It's another false flag job. We're not dealing with Russians."

They traveled in Auerbach's car, just the two of them, with Louis and Edgar following. Auerbach's foot turned to concrete again, and Mason was convinced they would arrive at their destination a few seconds before the beams from their headlights. It was a dark, fast journey along the motorway, then over some twisting back roads. There was a mist.

Auerbach didn't like what he was hearing.

Rudy had spun a damned fine yarn, Mason suggested pointedly. A fine one indeed for a not-so-bright soldier. The tale had been ninety-nine and forty-four one-hundredths percent pure, but it was the other miniscule portion which refused to settle. Or, as Mason said, "it wouldn't wash."

The clouds and thick mist on the roadway didn't slow Auerbach in the slightest. Before them Mason could see the yellow triangular reaches of the headlights as Auerbach switched from high beam to low beam and back to high again. Mason prayed there would be nothing sudden in their path.

"How much farther?" Mason inquired.

They flew through a traffic rotary. Heaven apparently was with the driver who had the right-of-way on the other side of the white dotted line. Mason's foot was pressed to the floorboards.

"Ten minutes," Auerbach answered. "Less. We're on the periphery of Salisbury."

"Where'd you find Rudy?" Mason asked.

Auerbach didn't answer.

"Well."

"I bought him," Auerbach said.

"You told me that. Now tell me the rest!"

"*What* rest of it?"

They took a curve. The tires sang. The vehicle shuddered.

"I'm warning you. . . ."

"What do you want to know? What part?"

They were on a side road, passing several two-family brick houses and Mason was convinced that the locals who hadn't taken in their pets for the night wouldn't have them in the morning. Mason turned and was amazed at

226

Edgar and Louis, obviously experts, close behind them. *Too* close at that speed, but it hardly mattered anymore.

"Who found who?" Mason insisted.

"*I* found *him*."

"You're lying!"

"What's it matter?"

Mason was incensed. "*Tell me!*" he howled.

Auerbach screamed in return, snapping off each word as if it hurt. "Your own damned bloody US intelligence picked up on him in Geneva! Rudy went to them. Kept putting microfilmed copies of vault material in a mailbox of a CIA connection. Gave out reams and reams of papers. Copies. Everything. Then he stopped. He wanted them to take him in. CIA wouldn't."

"Didn't trust him, did they?"

Ignoring the speed, Auerbach glanced at him and turned back to the wheel. "No."

"But *you* did."

"I still do."

Mason uttered a sour laugh.

"You're a fool, Mason," Auerbach snorted. "Rudy's clean. Everything, I repeat, *everything* he's ever told us has checked, double-checked and triple-checked. Every last syllable."

"Almost everything."

"You tell me. What's wrong?"

Auerbach decreased speed as they came up to a red light, then took off again with squealing tires. A final mile.

"Purpose," Mason said. "Motivation."

"We're here."

The car pulled into a driveway and came to a halt. Auerbach stepped out slowly. There was a small, modern house beyond a brick walkway. They were by the carport. Mason looked at Auerbach's face; he saw terror, the terror a man feels when events have broken out of control.

The second car arrived. Auerbach and the American were still standing there. Louis and Edgar came up behind them and looked to their leader. Auerbach gave two short taps to his horn, then followed with two more. He looked at the dimly lit interior of the house with growing alarm.

"There's something not right," Auerbach said softly. "I always keep a man on the outside doorstep."

The four men watched the quiet house.

"The horn was a signal," Auerbach said to Mason.

"Two plus two. They should know I'm here safely with a visitor. They should have put on the outside light and opened the door."

There was no movement at all. It was eerie, the four men looking at a spectral vision. It was like the silence before a scream.

"I don't understand it," Auerbach muttered twice.

"I do," said Mason. "We're late. We blew it."

Mason cursed violently and Auerbach was gawking at him.

"We?" Auerbach asked. "Now we're to share the blame, are we? Thought it was all mine."

"There's enough for all of us." Mason ran his hand through his wet hair, matted from sweat, as a chilling breeze swept them. "There's especially enough blame for idiots like you and me, Auerbach, men who are employed to analyze. To make decisions. To think." Mason seethed. "Come on. You'll see."

The front door lock had been jammed. That in itself suggested much.

Auerbach led the others around back. Mason joined them. Louis used a tire iron to pry open a recalcitrant cellar door. Edgar remained behind, rear sentry, while the other three men assaulted the cellar and a creaky set of stairs which led upward through the house.

They ascended to the foyer and then heard, faintly in the distance, the tinny sound of a small radio.

Auerbach opened the door. In awe, he walked through. Louis followed. Mason was third. It was, partially at least, what he had expected. They had come upon a small battlefield. But the firefight had been over for several hours. Only the casualties were left.

Mason saw blood at his feet. He reached down and touched it. It was hardened but smudged when he pressed it firmly. It was, he guessed, four to six hours old.

The sentry, the star-crossed Englishman who'd been assigned to cover the door, was lying not too far from his post. He was in the inside hallway, spreadeagle on the wooden floor. He lay in the position in which he'd fallen, like a soldier in combat, or a doll that had been discarded.

Auerbach stood above the body, looking down helplessly. He was wordless, perhaps making a silent apology. Mason looked at him and looked at the body. The sentry had been cut down by a heavy impact and had probably

228

been dead before hitting the floor. There were several ugly bullet holes and stains in the wall behind him.

Edgar was checking the other room, main floor first.

"So they came for Rudy," said Auerbach, after a long lapse of time. He gnawed painfully at his lower lip. "But how? No one knew. Only Rudy and I."

"Did *you* tell them where Rudy was?"

Auerbach glowered at Mason.

"All right then," Mason said *"Rudy* told them. He was theirs all along. He got a message back to them."

"Poor bastards," muttered Auerbach. "I told them to resist if anyone came near."

"Rudy issued their death warrant," Mason said. "You signed it."

The other baby-sitter was only a few feet away, around the spiral staircase and lying face down in the dining area. His blood had left dragging stains across a wooden floor. Mason read the signs.

He had been machine-gunned, then he had crawled until life had escaped him. Pathetically, his tin-voiced radio still lay on the second step of the staircase. It played. Presumably he'd been listening to it when he heard the commotion downstairs. He had come downstairs with the radio and an automatic weapon.

Once shot, he had staggered, dropped his own weapon, and then had probably crawled mindlessly toward a side door. He had managed three yards.

"It's never happened this way," a shaken Auerbach complained. "They'll pay for it."

He knelt and felt the second man's wrist, then dropped the slack hand. It thudded against the floor.

"They wanted their Rudy back that badly, ay?" asked Auerbach. "They had to come and take him back."

"Take him back?" Mason said. "No. I doubt it. A big dumb lug like that?" He shook his head.

Auerbach considered it for a second. Then Louis reappeared, having searched the entire house. Auerbach and Mason were still in the dining area.

"See him?" asked Louis.

"Who? See who?" Auerbach answered.

"Your Rudy, sir." With his large curly head, Louis nodded toward the kitchen.

Auerbach strode crisply to the small kitchen. He

stopped short, Mason behind him. Rudy's death pose was the most telling of all.

The German had been backed into the narrow kitchen and had obviously been cornered at the far end of the room. Right in front of the oven. He had raised his hands, either in supplication or in a meaningless gesture of protection. But neither words nor gestures were a match for bullets. He had been cut down viciously: chopped across the middle by a series of shots. Thrown over backwards by the fire-power, he had landed in a sitting position, the lower part of his back against the base of the wall. His body, slumped slightly to the right, leaned against the cabinet beneath the sink. The eyes were at half mast. So was Auerbach, who felt sick.

"I've never. . . . I've never. . . ." Auerbach was muttering.

Mason couldn't understand what he might be trying to say.

"Why?" Auerbach asked. *"Why?"* He angrily threw a chair across the dining room, shattering a mirror.

"Why what?"

"They came to shut him up, right?" said Auerbach. "He'd told too much."

"No," Mason said. "He told just enough. Rudy was a tape recording. They'd given him just what they wanted you to hear. No more. No less. They had to include some good new material for you to accept the bogus information, too. Rudy thought that when the time was right, they'd come and take him out. That's what he expected when he signaled them in some way. That's what he thought they'd come for."

Auerbach was still silent. Louis was looking around nervously yet, examining small details.

"But they had to cover their bets with Rudy," said Mason. "Couldn't take the chance that he might *really* defect. After all, now he'd seen much too much of the West. He also had information of genuine value. He'd taken part in a good false game and you'd bitten for it, Auerbach. You bought the act."

Auerbach glared at Mason. "That's not your usual KGB game, and you know it. They take their people back. They might terminate them later, but they bloody well bring them back."

"That's right," Mason answered.

"So if not KGB, who?" Auerbach snapped angrily. "Tell me that! Who?"

"Chinese."

Auerbach blinked twice. "What?"

"Someone's running a Pro-Chinese network which isn't actually within the Chinese intelligence apparatus. The network runs by itself with its own rules." Mason paused. He thought of the two Arabs ostensibly being run by the Russian, Vassiliev. "It has all the traditional trappings of an old-line North African network; the Ruskies and their little brown brothers. Too much so, Auerbach. It's a false flag job. Vassiliev works for someone else." Mason turned away from the corpse.

Auerbach stared at the dead German. "Know how many times I debriefed him? Eight. Eight times!"

"Could have done it eight hundred," Mason said. "Wouldn't have made any difference. Rudy told you the truth as he knew it. They encouraged him to defect. They let him get into the vault. They knew just what they were feeding you."

"But Rudy's story stood up. Completely. The China incident involving you, Lassiter, and Hargrove."

"Maybe not."

Auerbach held his gaze on Mason.

"Work it in reverse, Auerbach. Suppose it's a Chinese game. That means Rudy tells a pinpoint story that's only one nuance off: It discredits the wrong person at the end. We started with the assumption that Lassiter would never have blown me, so it had to have been Hargrove. Rudy's story served to reaffirm that belief to us so firmly that we'd never suspect that our initial assumption had been wrong."

Auerbach considered it, then scoffed sullenly. "You're theorizing, Mason. Nothing more."

"I don't think so."

"Why?"

"If Hargrove was really their man, they'd never give him back to us. They're ready to trade him for a set of computer chips. I think they've grabbed Hargrove off the streets. I think they're setting him up to look like a turncoat and a defector. Damned good way to throw into total turmoil all of US and British intelligence in western Europe. Marvelous way."

Auerbach looked like a man in total defeat.

"You, of course," Mason concluded, "were in a rush to make a name for yourself. So you picked up whatever defector you could. You bought Rudy and you bought his story with him."

"And how the hell did they find him, genius?" snapped Auerbach angrily.

"Simple. Screwdriver?"

"What?"

"I need a screwdriver."

Edgar found one. Bill picked up the radio from the floor of the foyer. He pressed the blade of the screwdriver into the plastic case and broke the case open.

With the steel blade again, he pried upward a small disc-shaped object which was hardly a part of the original radio. Mason held it in his palm.

"A directional transmitter," he said. "Cute, huh?"

A long moment passed. "So what the hell's next?" asked Auerbach.

"Same as before. We try to steal back Hargrove. Fact is, he might know everything."

26

One long, disturbing day had come and gone. Mason left the flat toward ten in the evening. He stepped from the front door and stopped upon placing his foot on the sidewalk. Bill didn't own an umbrella—an irksome inconvenience as it was raining hard enough to prompt the construction of an ark.

He pulled his trenchcoat close to him, darted across the street and was soaked as he moved in a fast jog through the park.

The rain was making a strong, pounding, splashing noise in the rippling puddles which had already gathered on the concrete and gravel pathways where the children normally played, and through the section where the old people sat.

His left foot splashed hard into a large puddle, sinking ankle-deep and spraying water in every direction including upward.

There. That makes it complete, he thought. Some night for a dead drop. Some occasion for short messages. Thanks, Fahrar, you bastard. Fuck you, Vassiliev. He wondered if Hargrove was alive.

The rain was cold, the water everywhere.

He took the Underground. It was the usual routine, looking for faces which repeated, seeing none. He boarded, departed, walked a block, reversed himself, boarded again, and rode again.

At Covent Garden he waited until the train's doors were about to close. Then he stepped out. He rode the long escalator to the street. It was raining even harder. He watched behind him, as always. Nothing.

He walked through a dark area of reconstruction around the old Covent Garden flower market. And then— abruptly—he stepped into a recessed doorway.

He waited for half an hour. The rain persisted. Nervously he felt the weapon beneath his coat. His other hand was firmly in his coat pocket, holding a small aspirin bottle which he had purchased at a pharmacy that afternoon. Half the aspirins had been emptied from it. A small, short message had been added, written in pencil on a scrap of paper folded six times so it would fit within the vial.

With the sleeve of his coat Mason vainly mopped his matted hair. Then he looked at his watch. Eleven thirty-eight. He left the doorway and walked directly toward the river. At quarter to midnight he walked along the park at the Victoria Embankment behind the Savoy.

He passed the benches by the riverside. He finally saw one that had been marked with a streak of red paint —the apparent work of vandals. He passed the bench and stopped at the next one. It was ten to twelve.

He paused for a moment, then leaned on the bench, as if slightly drunk or sick. In the same motion he dropped the aspirin bottle behind the bench.

He kept walking. Despite the rain he watched the Thames and the metropolis beyond. His gaze was toward the Royal Festival Hall on the opposite bank. This would be a marvelous time and place, Mason thought, to get shot. At five of midnight he turned.

A figure he didn't recognize was retrieving the bottle. Mason breathed a deep sigh of relief. The connection had been made. The message had been delivered and received: TRANSFER NOW POSSIBLE. The strange figure vanished in the other direction.

Transfer. Six silicon chips for Frank Hargrove.

Mason could go home now. It took, due to the path he followed, another ninety minutes, most of them in the rain. He shivered. Nothing would be finer than a good stiff belt of brandy when he got back.

On the next night the procedure repeated itself. This time in reverse and without the rain. Mason had a head cold from the night before. His throat was raw, his nose ran, and thanks to strong antihistamines purchased in Chelsea, his forehead suffered a dull, incessant throb.

The timing was exactly one hour later. Same place. This time someone else dropped and he received. It was even the same bottle, back again. He could use the extra aspirins.

He returned to his flat, convinced that he had sanitized his trail, before opening the small jar.

He read. HAVE CHIPS IN YOUR POSSESSION TOMORROW NOON. GO DIRECTLY TO PREVIOUSLY USED CORNER OF SLOANE SQUARE BY FIVE O'CLOCK. GO DIRECTLY. DANGER. PREPARE FOR TRIP TO PARIS AGAIN.

His forehead creased with a frown. Directly? Danger? What in hell? What were they trying to do?

He sat in the armchair, sniffling, the scrap of paper on his lap. He popped two aspirins into his mouth and chewed them with distaste until he could swallow them. Something was very wrong. It wasn't just the matter of defection or loyalties. It was their logistics.

He sat and thought for a long time, knowing that he was now committed.

Mason moved quietly around the flat. He was going through a short mental list. Things to take with him: small things. Only one small attaché case would accompany him. It had to appear that he would not be returning. He wore the Walther in his belt.

The bag was complete. Only one item remaining, Mason thought. The six chips.

They rested in his palm. He assessed them as a jeweler might weigh raw uncut diamonds. A minute passed in utter silence and concentration as he considered every conceivable notion concerning them. Lethal, he thought. He closed his hand on the tiny components, picked up a thin, hollow steel cylinder which he had obtained for the occasion, slid the chips into the tubing, and sealed both ends.

Pleased with its neatness, he hefted it in his hand. He stuffed it into his sock.

Hope you like the packaging job, Vassiliev, he thought. It's just for you. He nearly spoke the words aloud, but remembered the electronic ears, wherever they were.

Minutes later, he was out the door. It took only a step to realize exactly what he had walked into.

There was a man behind him, obstructing his retreat into his own building. Two others, including Fahrar, climbed out of a panel truck, wearing laborers' clothing. A fourth man was in front of him, squat and bull-necked. He grabbed Mason by the sleeve.

235

"Come along," the man suggested rudely. Mason was having none of it. The man pulled. Mason yanked his arm back. Suddenly all four had a piece of him as he was thrown toward the panel truck and slammed hard into the side of it. A door opened and they tried to force him in. One of them was clutching Mason by the throat, fingers digging toward his windpipe. Someone else cuffed him hard across the back of the skull.

But he was *not* getting into the truck.

He used any parts of his body to resist or obstruct. He flailed with his elbows and knees. They cursed at him in accented English and what sounded like Arabic.

"The chips! Where are your chips?" Fahrar snarled.

Somehow Mason got an elbow free and swung it in Fahrar's direction. It caught the larger man in the cheekbone. Mason hoped he had broken Fahrar's nose. But he hadn't.

One or two curious passersby witnessed the scene with mild amusement. In cities like New York or London, one saw everything.

Mason continued to fight wildly. One of them grabbed his hair and battered his head four or five times onto the side of the truck. He felt himself losing badly.

"They're in my sock, damn it, Fahrar, you bastard! They're in my right sock!" he snarled.

He slackened for a moment, went slightly limp and they tried to guide him into the truck a final time. Just as the doors were about to receive him he flailed desperately a final time, slipping to his left.

He broke one grip, then a second. One man wrestled him to the sidewalk, falling on top of him and almost cracking Mason's ribs from the jolt. Mason crawled, dragging the man along, just far enough. He got to the iron fence, a railing which ran the length of the building front. Grabbing an iron rail first with one hand, then with the other, he arduously pulled himself to it. The man on top of him didn't sense the strategy until it was too late.

Mason's arms reached through the rails and he pulled himself flush against the fence, stomach first. He lay his head down to his shoulder. They couldn't reach the front of his body but they kicked at him and yanked at his hair. They tried to pry his arms loose. He hung on for his life.

Someone, probably Fahrar, was grabbing at his feet.

His shoes were ripped off, as were his socks. Out rolled the container.

Mason started to yell. He yelled at the top of his lungs for help. One eye was aching from a blow delivered to the temple, but out of the same eye he could see. A small crowd had gathered. There must have been a dozen witnesses.

Mason shouted murder.

The assailants backed off. They had what they wanted. Fahrar's hands were the last upon him.

"One sixteen Old Kent Road," Fahrar said. "Second floor. That's where you'll find your Hargrove. We were going to take you."

Dazed, Mason looked at the Arab. He swore violently. Fahrar was grinning.

For good luck apparently, Fahrar delivered a shattering instep kick to Mason's side. But Bill managed to block it with a lowered elbow. The blow was deflected, but pain riveted his arm and side.

He knew they were giving up on apprehending him right now. But parting shots? They'd have some. He heard their panel truck roar to life. Someone gunned the engine.

Mason held tight to the iron fence, keeping himself flush. They could only do small things. Rupture his spleen. Break his backbone. Split his skull.

Shoot him as they departed.

He heard the vehicle's doors slam. The engine raced. Mason looked over his shoulder and saw three men in the van. Fahrar was on the sidewalk, an open van door behind him. Fahrar reached beneath his jacket.

Mason let go of the iron workings and slid to the sidewalk. He staggered to his feet, his hand lunging for his belt. Fahrar fired the first of two shots, but Mason stunned the larger man when Mason's hand came up firing.

Fahrar's second shot was no better than the first. It struck the bricks behind Mason's head. But at the same moment, Mason, firing almost blindly, put two bullets into Fahrar's lower abdomen.

A perplexed look twisted Fahrar's face. His knees buckled, but he remained standing. He lowered his own weapon and groped for the vehicle door behind him. Mason wasn't watching, he was fleeing back into the building, but one of the other assailants pulled Fahrar into the van as the driver noisily hit the accelerator.

The small horrified crowd had dispersed with screams as soon as the shots had rung out. Mason, now in the entrance foyer of his building, knew there would be police.

Something wet was on his face. Blood. He lurched and staggered up the stairs to his flat. His hand was unsteady and the key jammed.

He fell into the living room, then regained his balance.

He shuddered at his own appearance in the mirror. He mopped himself with a reddening towel and tried to dress the bruises and wounds. It was survival training from years back returning to usefulness. A man never forgets self-preservation.

His whole body throbbed. He felt something in his mouth and spit it into his palm. It was part of a tooth. His entire mouth ached. He would have liked to have been a lifeguard again.

Then he spoke, addressing the unseen ears in the room, the ones he'd tried to destroy, grateful that he hadn't.

Old Kent Road, he said. That's where they may or may not find Hargrove. Alive, dead, or somewhere in between.

"One thing's for sure, Auerbach," he said. "I'm not going in there alone. It's either a trap or an insult."

His lower jaw spasmed and at first Mason thought it was out of joint. He couldn't understand how no bones had been broken.

Putting on his remaining pair of shoes, he straightened himself as best he could. Then he heard another commotion outside his window. He pushed back the shade slightly and saw the excited witnesses describing to the police exactly what had happened.

Mason's socks and shoes littered the sidewalk, along with the attaché case which had been smashed open.

"Oh, Jesus," he muttered. "Already."

He was down the stairs in seconds. He went through the building's basement and found a window which, when he pulled himself up to it, allowed him access to a dirty alleyway. But the alley led in the proper direction, away from the front of the building.

27

Alone on Old Kent Road, Mason was overcome by a sense of impending disaster. Why would they turn over a live Hargrove to him? Were he and Auerbach being lured? Mason watched the building at one sixteen. His mind, eyes, and body were bruised and exhausted. "Come on, Auerbach," he muttered. "Hurry up, damn you!"

Mason thought of Vassiliev and Fahrar. He thought of the chips but didn't worry about them. He was glad he was alive. Vassiliev and Fahrar had a surprise coming.

Mason realized he was looking far down the street, seeing a figure more than two blocks away. He recognized the hurried walk. Quite careless of Auerbach, he noted, approaching in a straight line like that. But then Mason, too, had made a target of himself, standing alone for twenty-two minutes. He wondered how many times in his life he'd done the wrong thing and survived. When it boiled down to basics, survival was a matter of luck.

He watched Auerbach approach, a little man in a big hurry. The Briton crossed the street with his normal bellicosity, striding boldly in front of a cab which had failed to halt as he stepped off the curb. Mason heard the vehicle's tires screech and saw Auerbach exchange curses with the driver.

As Auerbach drew nearer, he and Mason seemed to assess each other for a final time. Distrustful still, cautious, assessing, but allied nonetheless. From armies of different nations. United in purpose, yet, beneath it all, unable to trust completely.

Auerbach. A conniving little twerp if ever there was one, Mason thought. Looking out for himself and that's all. Mason waited until Auerbach was before him. There

239

was no greeting or handshake. Auerbach saw Mason's condition.

"What happened to you?"

"Something of a firefight." Mason paused and Auerbach waited. "I shot their head gorilla."

Auerbach winced. "You better get yourself out of the country as soon as this is over. If the police find you they'll have us all by the short hair."

"I know," Mason answered.

Auerbach seemed either not to know what to say next or to be unclined to say anything.

"Come on, then," Mason finally mumbled. "No use to wait any longer."

"Did you go up?"

"Now how the hell can I go up alone? And what good would it do if I did?" They walked toward the front of the building.

"What good will *I* do?" Auerbach asked rhetorically. "I don't expect that Hargrove's there, anyway."

They entered the building and climbed a carpeted staircase. The steps squeaked. Auerbach seemed particularly on edge. On the second floor he reached beneath his jacket, pulled out his handgun, and inspected it, checking to make sure that it was loaded. He released the safety catch.

"You have anything with you?" he asked Mason.

Mason nodded.

"You want to check it?"

"I did. No need to do it twice."

He moved toward the door. Auerbach knocked. The two men stood away to the sides, not knowing what to expect. They allowed several seconds to pass and knocked again. Again, no reply.

"Something's bloody wrong," Auerbach said.

Mason knew immediately that something was. It was too late to be playing games. There had always been an intended swindle.

Auerbach knocked again.

"I don't like surprises, Mason," he growled.

"You think I do?"

"Sometimes I wonder."

Auerbach tried to stuff a burglar's splint into the keyhole of the door. But just as he fitted it in place, he felt

240

a weight on the other end of the doorknob. He removed his hand and looked at Mason.

The two of them stepped away from the doorway for a moment. Auerbach and Mason held their weapons. The door opened.

Hargrove stood before them, as expected, but the look on his face was not one of relief or surprise. Instead it was a glazed expression, with no comprehension behind it. Mason recognized it, having seen it twice before in his life. It was the look of imminent death. The brain was gone. The body struggled instinctively.

Hargrove staggered, then swayed. It was Auerbach who caught him as he began to fall forward. As Auerbach moved his own arm there was fresh blood on his sleeve.

"Oh, Jesus," Auerbach muttered. He looked to Hargrove's back. A long stream of blood cascaded down the back of Hargrove's head and neck. "Bloody Jesus," Auerbach snapped. "They must have just left."

They set Hargrove back on a chair. The eyelids drooped. Auerbach shook the man to revive him. With some strange burst of strength Hargrove had been able to walk. But he was a dead man. All that remained was for the heart to stop. It did.

Auerbach celebrated his bereavement by stepping back and unleashing a torrent of livid obscenities.

"Ruined the whole blasted thing," he was saying. "The whole wanking thing. I wanted this man *alive!*"

Unthinking and furious, he shook the body, as if that would help. Hargrove's head drooped to the right, much as Lassiter's had in death.

"Alive, God blast it. Alive!"

Disrespectfully he shoved the body back into the chair, and stood with defeat etched in the lines of his face, looking like he might scream or cry or both. He was breathing heavily. He looked at the dead man's face and the mask it wore.

"It's him," Mason said simply. "Furman, late of the China station. Hargrove. One and the same. Not that it matters. Poor bastard."

Auerbach was silent. "I wanted to save him," he said finally. "I wanted that much at least."

Mason looked at the wet, red wound in the back of the dead man's skull, brushed away the blood with his hand, then wiped his fingers on the arm of the chair.

"Not a bullet, you can see that," said Auerbach. "They used something else."

"Does it matter?" Mason asked, though he already knew.

Auerbach shrugged. "Their network's shot. But that's all. A fucking execution," he said, looking at a second hole below the ear. "Something long and sharp which stabbed upward into the brain." He paused and added suggestively, "Like a stiletto."

Auerbach waved his hand in a helpless gesture. "One fast, hard thrust and Hargrove is gone. Must have been a strong man to shove it in like that." Auerbach looked hopefully to Mason. "Any ideas?"

"None."

Auerbach wistfully studied the body. "What do you think, Mason. Was he theirs or yours?"

They don't kill off their own like that, Mason thought. They just don't work that way. "Ours," he answered.

Auerbach's eyes jumped back and forth from the dead American to the live one. "What about Lassiter?" he demanded urgently. "Think Hargrove had him pushed? Maybe Hargrove pushed him himself."

"Doubtful," Bill said.

"Well, then . . . ?"

Mason raised his eyes to Auerbach. "When you've been in business long enough, Auerbach, you'll learn something: Sometimes you never know, sometimes you never find the answers. It's a stinking game and in real life that's how it often ends."

Auerbach swallowed, seeming to be back at square one. "Better call your pederast friend Lasko," he mumbled sourly. "More work for the pansy mortician."

"You can call," Mason replied. "I'm finished here."

"What about the chips?"

"Don't worry. You'll read about it."

"But—?"

"They're not even important."

As Bill departed, he caught a view of Auerbach in a most uncharacteristic pose: seated on the edge of a sofa, inclined slightly toward the dead man. His face, or at least the lower half of it, was in his hands. Mason didn't know whether it was a pose of thought or resignation, perplexity or resolution.

Defeat perhaps? Bill Mason wondered.

He closed the door behind him, but the image followed. The Vassiliev case was only a skirmish in a larger war that went from trench to trench. Nowhere in sight was there a decisive victor or loser.

EPILOGUE

The service began at twenty-four minutes past two on a Wednesday afternoon. Bill Mason, if asked, wouldn't have known the date exactly; he'd stopped counting such things. He only knew that it was a late November day and it was very cold. Pneumatic drills had been needed to open the frozen earth. Mason was in Arlington; so was Lazz. Bill could see the Capitol and the Washington monument. Lazz couldn't. When the funeral began, Bill was the only one in attendance. An airplane bound for Dulles rumbled overhead.

A young military chaplain began speaking softly and, due to a sweeping cold wind, Mason could hardly hear him. No matter. Lazz had wanted a Christian burial and he was getting one. It was religious mumbo-jumbo to Mason; he didn't care if he heard it or not. His mind was elsewhere: back at Kenfield Academy, where Mr. Lassiter used to tell the students about the Korean War. Firsthand.

Mason had Kenfield on his mind as he stood before the coffin balanced above the grave, with an honor guard of four soldiers. He was aware of a movement behind. At first he thought it was her.

It wasn't and he was disappointed. It was Gardner. Solemnity upon his face.

"I heard the service was this afternoon," Gardner said in a whisper. "I thought I'd come by."

"Decent of you," returned Bill.

"His widow?"

Bill shrugged. He gave a gesture with his eyes, meaning look around. It was just the seven of them. Gardner, Mason, four soldiers, and a chaplain. With a forgotten man named Lassiter.

"I called her," Bill said. "She knew."

Gardner was sorry he'd asked and refrained from asking about the deceased's daughter. "Damned shame,"

Gardner muttered with genuine regret. "It's really not right."

"I honestly thought she'd be here," Mason said. Then he shrugged. They listened to the cleric for the next few minutes.

"I thought the agency might send someone," Gardner said finally. "I'm surprised they didn't."

"They never admitted he worked for them," Bill whispered in return. "You know clandestine services. Never an official confirmation. Liars from womb to tomb."

"Mmmm," agreed Gardner thoughtfully. His gloved hands were folded respectfully in front of him.

The memorial service was short; the eulogy brief and impersonal. The minister hadn't known the man he was now dispatching to the Almighty, but the proper words were said. In that respect, it was all God's humble servant, Robert Gates Lassiter, 1930–1977, might have asked for. No more, no less. There were no tears.

After it was over the chaplain removed the flag from the coffin. He folded it appropriately and held it under his arm, close to his Bible. The coffin was lowered. Gardner and Mason stood by.

The coffin was in place. Presumably it would stay where it now rested for the next few millennia.

The chaplain, an eager and earnest man who was surprisingly youthful (Mason guessed maybe twenty-five), approached Mason when the service was complete.

"Normally the flag goes to next of kin," he said tactfully. "A wife. A parent. A brother or sister."

"I'll see that it goes where it should," Mason answered.

The chaplain seemed appropriately hesitant. Then he handed it to Bill, a triangle of folded cloth, white and red stripes, no white stars or blue field showing. "Thanks," said the minister. A burden had been lifted.

He asked Bill if he minded terribly if the gravediggers began immediately. "Filling in the hole, that is. No disrespect, of course. It's cold. Freezing."

Bill said he didn't mind.

Mason moved away from the gravesite with Gardner. But not too far. They walked down a path slowly, speaking. The chaplain had already hurried ahead. The man hadn't even worn an overcoat. Bill understood.

"I know it's not the time to bring up something like this," Gardner said, "but as long as I have you here. . . ."

Bill asked.

"The job you were inquiring about," Gardner explained. "I think something's opened up, after all. I can give you a telephone number. You could make an appointment for an interview, but I'll tell you now. You want it, you have it." Gardner smiled lamely. "I'll warn you now. They're going to put you behind a desk."

Bill nodded. A few seconds later he stopped on the path. Gardner kept talking. Government pay on the GS-13 level and Bill's seniority returned, Gardner said, though he didn't know exactly what Bill would be doing. "They don't tell me everything, you know. In fact, they don't tell me much at all."

"Thanks," Mason said. "But I'll punt."

"What?" Gardner frowned.

"I don't want it. Tell them I'm not interested."

"But I thought you said—?"

"I was just toeing the water that day, Phil. Just testing the ocean temperature."

Gardner made a slight face, as if annoyed; then, as he watched Mason, he started to grin slightly. "What shall I really tell them?" Gardner asked as they walked.

"Tell them. . . ." Bill began slowly. "Tell them there's not another damned thing in the world that I know how to do. Tell them that they can screw themselves. And that I'll start at the first of the year. Dust off the God damned swivel chair for me. I'll buy some neckties."

Gardner nodded as if it were a matter of course. Perhaps it was. "You're making the right decision," he said.

Mason didn't answer. The men walked together for several paces, then Bill slowed, explaining that he wanted to remain there for a few more minutes, despite the cold.

Gardner nodded. He excused himself and went on ahead.

Mason held the flag under his arm, his hands buried deeply into his pockets. He went to a nearby bench and sat down, his breath making small cone-shaped clouds in front of him.

To his right, in the near distance, the gravediggers were finishing. To his left, a huddled figure approached. Mason waited.

He considered the events in London, looking at them with some perspective, though they were fresh in his mind. Several careers had ended. Several lives.

Over what?

There had been no top-placed spy sabotaging London operations, no technological secret that had to be protected, no life that had to be saved and no operational confidences which had to be prevented from entering enemy hands.

There had been, in the end, only people. Players in a larger game, to be sure, but men and women involved in duplicities, lies, ruses, and betrayals as petty and unimportant as they themselves were. There had been, sadly, no significance to what had happened, other than to those immediately involved.

Why, Mason wondered, had anyone bothered?

He waited until the approaching figure was within a few steps. He was freezing.

"Where's Priscilla?" he asked.

Sarah stood near him. "School."

"Just as well." He looked at her, squinting slightly. "Want to sit down?"

"It's much too cold."

"No argument there." He nodded his head once, toward the folded cloth beneath his arm. "The flag is yours, you know. If you want it."

"I don't."

Then there was a unique moment as they looked each other squarely in the eye. For the first time, each fully understood the other.

"You liked your Brian, didn't you?" he asked. "You really liked him."

She nodded. "Not at first. But later. Much later. It was difficult for me."

"Must have been," he said. "How did Brian figure it out?"

"I'm freezing, Mase."

"How did Woodson figure it out?" he asked again.

She drew a long uncomfortable breath. She understood perfectly the question and its implications.

"I don't know exactly," she said. "I suppose he was downstairs one night and it came to him. Like magic. Like one of his solutions."

Mason nodded and waited. He demanded that she continue.

"Brian knew I'd been married previously to a Langley man. Then one day some security people came to see him. He learned that some of the IC chips he'd designed had a basic structural flaw. Worse, it was suspected that a man named Colbourne had given them to a Russian named Vassiliev in Mexico."

"And you'd given them to Colbourne," Mason added. "With the intention that they be passed on. But not to Moscow."

She shook her head slightly. "You're insightful, Bill. Too bad you're on the other side. Don't you believe in the course of world socialism?"

"Maoism has never appealed to me," he answered. "I've got more respect for the rights of the individual than all the ideology you can throw at me."

"A shame," she said. "A shame. Maybe someday—"

"So all the circumstances closed in on your second husband," he said, interrupting as he pictured the beleaguered ITW employee in his basement warren. "Woodson feared two scandals: He feared that his work would be publicly exposed as faulty, creating a national defense breakdown. And he feared an even worse exposure: that he'd married a very clever woman who always married men in sensitive security positions."

She opened her purse slowly and removed a pack of cigarettes. "You don't mind if I smoke, do you?"

"You know, of course, that these particular chips were never implemented."

She turned toward him quickly. "What?"

"The design flaw was discovered in a routine check before implementation," he said. "The contract remained with ITW, but it was also sent to another microcircuit firm in Santa Clara, California. While ITW doubled back to find their own mistake, Silicon Valley, California, came to the rescue. *They* made the chips which were actually implemented in our missiles."

Sarah Woodson, deep in thought, blew out some smoke.

"You'll read about it in the newspapers," he said. "Within a week, I'd say."

Cautiously, she asked, "And how do you know all that?"

"Gardner told me. Before I went back to London."

She made no response.

"And that reminds me," he began. "Lazz. Your first husband. That's where you went wrong. When the chips were taken out of Vassiliev's apartment and when he traced them back to the manufacturer, he began to suspect something about you. Strange coincidence. He looked for ways in which Woodson's work could have gotten to Vassiliev. You were the logical guess. Couldn't prove it, of course. And he still carried this insane flame for you."

She snuffed out the cigarette. "That wasn't my fault," she insisted softly.

"No. It wasn't." He paused as the Arlington wind ripped through them. "Just before I came to visit you in Maryland I found something interesting. At the passport office in Washington."

Her eyes never wavered.

"Seems you took a little trip back in September. Four days in London. About the time Lazz had an accident."

He fingered the flag. She waited.

"Lazz wouldn't have been lured to that window by Lucille Davis. Auerbach wasn't up there and Hargrove was shuttling back and forth to Madrid. But *you*. That would have been different. Despite his growing distrust, Lazz would have gone anywhere with you."

"I suppose he would have."

He mused. "A loose network of western women, like you and Dr. Davis, stationed at various points accessible to intelligence sources. A brilliantly oriental idea. Plays on sexism and racism. No one suspects women because everyone's looking for male agents. No one suspects Chinese because all anyone sees is western faces." Mason shivered.

"Lassiter blew you in China, you know," she offered. "Had to let you be captured to protect another agent. Tossed you to the wolves."

The wind was turning his face to ice, but he managed a pained smile. "I realized that a long time ago," Mason said. "I was aware of it when Lazz came to find me in New Jersey. Then I had it reconfirmed in Paris by a man named Norden." He shivered. "That's the way the lousy game is played. I was naïve to have ever expected anything else."

His tone of voice changed. "There's just one final

249

point." He assessed her carefully as he asked, "Who are you? Where are you from? Back before I knew you."

"Sorry," she answered impassively. "Not that."

He grimaced and then hunched against the cold. He started toward an exit.

"What are you going to do?" she asked. "Freeze me to death?" She followed him.

"You might begin," he said, "by putting your house up for sale. A move would be in order. Maybe to Canada to start with. Then farther. You could enroll Priscilla in a Swiss school for a year or two. Your life's bound to be a trifle unsettled."

He stood slowly, the flag still tucked under his arm. "Come with me."

"Where are we going?"

"I'm walking you to your car," he said. "Prisons are rotten. So are interrogations. I'm doing someone a favor, and it's not you."

He took her arm and led her. "I'll expect a card each Christmas, Sarah. Maybe from a farther point each time. Just keep moving. Don't come back to the United States."

She was less hesitant. She was willing to go with him. "What about Priscilla?"

"Her? Her I care about," Mason said. "She's as much Lazz's daughter as yours, remember? I want to hear all about her. Everything. I'm doing this for her."

They arrived at her car. He closed her into the front seat and she looked at him a final time. No further words were spoken. As she drove off Mason was aware that he was still holding the widow's flag.

No matter. For some strange sentimental reason, he'd been planning to keep it.

ABOUT THE AUTHOR

NOEL HYND was born in New York City and grew up in Connecticut. He graduated from the University of Pennsylvania and began his writing career at the age of twenty, covering true crime stories for magazines in the United States and Europe. His first two espionage novels, *Revenge* (1976) and *The Sandler Inquiry* (1977), were published to widespread critical acclaim. He has recently completed the screenplay *Agency* and is presently working on a fourth novel and an original screenplay.

RELAX!
SIT DOWN
and Catch Up On Your Reading!